THE
OUTSIDER

Jane Casey has written fourteen crime novels for adults and three for teenagers. A former editor, she is married to a criminal barrister who ensures her writing is realistic and as accurate as possible.

This authenticity has made her novels international best-sellers and critical successes. The Maeve Kerrigan series has been nominated for many awards: in 2015 Jane won the Mary Higgins Clark Award for *The Stranger You Know* and Irish Crime Novel of the Year for *After the Fire*. In 2019, *Cruel Acts* was chosen as Irish Crime Novel of the Year at the Irish Book Awards. It was a *Sunday Times* bestseller. Jane's standalone thriller *The Killing Kind* has been adapted for television.

Born in Dublin, Jane now lives in southwest London with her husband and two children.

𝕏 @JaneCaseyAuthor

📷 @janecaseyauthor

Also by Jane Casey

THE MAEVE KERRIGAN SERIES

The Burning

The Reckoning

The Last Girl

The Stranger You Know

The Kill

After the Fire

Let the Dead Speak

Cruel Acts

The Cutting Place

The Close

A Stranger in the Family

STANDALONE NOVELS

The Missing

The Killing Kind

JANE CASEY
THE
OUTSIDER

HEMLOCK
PRESS

Hemlock Press
An imprint of HarperCollins*Publishers* Ltd
1 London Bridge Street
London SE1 9GF

www.harpercollins.co.uk

HarperCollins*Publishers*
Macken House, 39/40 Mayor Street Upper,
Dublin 1, D01 C9W8, Ireland

This paperback edition 2024
3

First published in ebook format by HarperCollins*Publishers* Ltd 2023

A catalogue record for this book is available from the British Library

ISBN: 978-0-00-867139-6 (PB b-format)

Typeset in Sabon LT Std by Palimpsest Book Production Ltd, Falkirk, Stirlingshire

Printed and Bound in the UK using
100% Renewable Electricity at CPI Group (UK) Ltd

MIX
Paper | Supporting
responsible forestry
FSC™ C007454

This book contains FSC™ certified paper and other controlled sources
to ensure responsible forest management.

For more information visit: www.harpercollins.co.uk/green

1

Trouble was the last thing on my mind as I drove down a leafy country lane on a sunny autumn morning, but trouble found me anyway. Strictly speaking, I found it as I rounded a bend to discover a low-slung Mercedes skewed across the carriageway, its bonnet crumpled against the broad trunk of an oak. I'd been deep in thought and about half of my attention was on driving; I'd expected to see the Mercedes in front of me, a safe distance ahead, as it had been for the last ten miles. Instinct took over. I slammed to a stop inches from the black, shining bodywork of the other car even as I was still realising what had happened.

I switched off my engine and listened, and the silence was too loud. No one stirred in the Mercedes. One occupant, I thought. The driver had been heavy on the accelerator and the brakes, but he hadn't been speeding. A new car, less than six months old. The road was narrow, but the bend wasn't sharp.

Why did you crash?

Why aren't you getting out of the car to check the damage?

Why aren't you on the phone, calling for help?

One thing at a time. Swearing under my breath, I started my engine again and reversed my car around the corner so it could sit in the carriageway and stop any other cars from crashing into the Mercedes, its driver and me. That was frankly all that my car was fit for: it was an ancient Golf on its sixth and final owner. I was going to take great pleasure in scrapping it one of these days. I left its hazard lights flashing and ran back with a warning triangle to block the road in the other direction. I was hoping to find the driver upright and shaken but all right, fundamentally. The Mercedes had an exemplary safety record. You couldn't pick a better vehicle to drive into a tree. He would be fine, I assured myself, in spite of the feeling of dread that was tightening my jaw.

Nothing had changed in the minute or so since I'd come upon the crash. No one moved. Now that I was out of the car I noticed the hot stink of petrol and engine oil that hung in the air. A slick of liquid had started to pool under the car. Not a problem, I told myself, and hoped I was right about that. Cars didn't just explode when they crashed, unless you were very unlucky. As long as no one lit a cigarette, we should be fine. I didn't smoke, and the driver presumably had other things on his mind. Fear knotted my stomach anyway as I jogged fifty metres ahead of the crashed car to set up the triangle in the roadway. I had no reason to be afraid, and I had every reason. I approached the Mercedes as if it contained a fully-grown tiger and not a fellow motorist in need of urgent assistance.

The driver's door was still closed, which worried me; either he'd made no attempt to get out or he was stuck in there. The white cloud of the deflated airbag hid him from view but it was another bad sign that he hadn't moved it away from his face. I tried the door and it came open easily despite the damage the car had sustained: German engineering at its best.

'Hello? Are you all right? Can you hear me?'

No response.

Fuck.

2

I shoved the airbag out of the way so I could see him: late fifties, grey hair, slumped forward over the wheel. I slid a hand between his jaw and his collar, looking for a pulse, finding nothing. My internal swearing went up a notch. Move him and I'd risk damaging his spine. Leave him where he was and he had no chance whatsoever.

No choice, really.

I reached across him to undo his seatbelt and pushed him back in his seat gently, supporting his head as best I could. Maybe I'd just missed his pulse . . .

His flesh was clammy under my fingers. I was still talking to him, babbling cheery nonsense, but not so much as a flicker of awareness crossed his features.

'All right, mate. Think we need to get you out of the car. I'm on my own so this might be a bit rough, but bear with me.'

I emptied his pockets quickly, shoving his phone and wallet into my jeans so they didn't fall onto the road when I lifted him. I slid his seat back as far as it would go, away from the twisted dashboard, then swung his legs out of the car with a silent prayer that I wasn't doing irreparable harm. I tipped his arms over one of my shoulders and leaned into his torso before hoisting him up.

Dead weight. The words had never been more appropriate.

At least he wasn't very tall, I told myself, my knees buckling as I stepped away from the car and along the roadside towards a flattish bit of grass on the verge. How long since I'd come across the crash? A couple of minutes, no more than that. Time was stretching, as it tended to in a crisis.

I lowered him to the grass as gently as I could and tipped his head back so I could look into his mouth. No obvious blockage to his airway. Nothing was stopping him from breathing, except that he wasn't. I undid the buttons on his

3

shirt and put my ear to his chest, which was completely still. Long-ago first-aid training came back to me: the instructor barking instructions. *You can't make 'em more dead, whatever you do.*

I put the heel of one hand in the middle of his chest and leaned my other hand on top of that, and began chest compressions, counting under my breath, horribly aware that I was on my own and that I wouldn't be able to keep it up indefinitely. Proper CPR breaks ribs, I'd been taught. I did my best.

The sound of a car engine broke my concentration after a couple more endless minutes. I looked up to see a small Peugeot humming to a stop just in front of the warning triangle. The driver – a slight young woman with long brown hair – got out.

'Is everything OK?'

Not really, I thought, and didn't waste my time saying it. 'Can you call 999? We need police and an ambulance. Tell them one casualty, not breathing, no pulse.' It took me ten breaths to get the words out.

Her hands were shaking as she dialled. I listened to her end of the conversation, well aware of what the operator would want to know.

'Where are we? I – I don't know.'

'Sarsden Road, off the B4450,' I said. 'About a mile from the turn-off, heading west.'

She repeated what I'd said, word for word. 'Yes. One casualty. He's not breathing. Yes, there's a man here doing that. No, he's on his own. No! No, I couldn't. I'm not strong enough.'

My shirt was sticking to my back. I wasn't far off being exhausted. I stopped and put my fingers to his throat. Nothing.

Get on with it.

I heard another engine, this one throaty and deep. I glanced over my shoulder to see a large man getting out of a van behind the Peugeot. He jogged across to me.

'Need a hand?'

I nodded and moved out of his way, sitting back on my heels. My arms felt like lead. The large man was maybe twenty-five, with colourful tattoos crawling up his arms and a full bushy beard. He was muscular rather than fat, and competent enough that I could watch him while I got my breath back and stretched out my limbs. When I noticed him starting to struggle, I took over again, and we went on like that for another three or four minutes, checking for a pulse with diminishing hope.

What a mess, I thought. What a complete and total disaster.

'Try again?' The big man leaned away and I pressed my fingertips against the driver's throat.

'Anything?'

I hesitated. Was it just that I wanted to feel a pulse? But no, there was a definite flutter under my fingers, regular and steady. I put the back of my hand over his mouth and felt warm air on my skin.

'You *beauty*.'

'Is he breathing?' the big man asked anxiously.

'Yeah.' I shook my head. 'I didn't think that was going to work.'

'Me neither.'

'Is he OK?' The young woman had come closer, her face white. She was still holding her phone to her ear.

'No, but you can tell them we've got a pulse and he's breathing on his own.'

She repeated it and listened, then relayed, 'They're five minutes away.'

Five minutes. He could stay alive for five minutes, I thought, until the proper professionals turned up.

It was the longest five minutes of my life.

*

'You did a decent job marking the accident.' Grudging praise from a traffic officer who was sternly inspecting the scene, but it was still praise.

'I just wanted to make sure no one else crashed.'

'Got any training?'

'My driving instructor was a retired police officer.'

The officer grunted. 'He did a good job on you.'

'She was a good teacher.' I couldn't resist correcting him but I'd have been better to say nothing, as the officer took himself off for a tight-lipped tour of my car. They had ways of punishing smart-arse members of the public; I'd be lucky if I was allowed to drive it away.

The road was still covered in oil and broken glass, but a recovery vehicle was preparing to remove the crippled Mercedes. An ambulance had taken the driver away twenty minutes earlier, driving off at a respectable speed, though he was stable, and breathing, and semi-conscious. The girl had got into her Peugeot and left, still trembling, followed by the bearded man. He had continued his Good-Samaritan routine by promising to make sure she got home OK, which prompted her to stare up at him with adoring eyes. He had at least got her number out of the accident, I thought. What a way to meet. A story for the wedding reception, maybe, one day.

I had hung back so I could speak to the police officers. Judging that the one who was inspecting my car wasn't likely to be forthcoming, I wandered over to where the other was photographing the road.

'Any idea what caused the accident?'

'Best guess is that he had a heart attack and crashed.' The officer squinted at the road surface. 'You can see he wasn't going fast. And we have your statement that he was driving all right up to this point. Would you have seen if anyone else was involved?'

'Yeah. I came round the bend just after it happened – a few seconds, not more than that. I wouldn't have missed another vehicle or a bike or a pedestrian.'

'And he was on his own in the car?'

'As far as I could see.'

'Single-car collision, and he wasn't breathing when you found him.' The officer shrugged. 'The crash could have finished him off if he'd been going faster. If you hadn't happened to come along, he'd have died anyway. He was lucky.'

He'd had a heart attack and written off his very expensive car, but he was still lucky. It was all a matter of perspective.

'Do you know where the ambulance took him?'

'The JR. It's the closest hospital.'

The JR was the John Radcliffe Hospital on the outskirts of Oxford, and it was the best facility in the region. Lucky again.

'I want to check up on him. See if he makes it.'

The officer nodded, not particularly curious about it. 'You'll need his name.'

'I'll find him.'

'Fair enough.' He'd lost interest in me, and the conversation, already.

I went back to my car, which had been judged to be just about roadworthy, and made my escape while I could.

I didn't need his name.

I'd known who he was long before the car crashed.

2

At the hospital I didn't quite tell the receptionist that I was a close relation of Geraint Carter, but I didn't tell her I wasn't either. Geraint was in A&E, where they were stabilising him and assessing him to see if he needed surgery. I could wait, she told me with a sympathetic head-tilt, with the rest of the family in the private waiting room.

I knew they kept the private waiting room for the families of patients who could go either way; Geraint wasn't out of the woods yet. I walked along the corridor in a thoughtful frame of mind, and tapped on the waiting-room door before I stepped into the lion's den.

At first glance the room was full of faces, all turned to me with that mingled fear and suspicion that I recognised from long nights of waiting for news from doctors myself. I raised a hand in an apologetic salute.

'Sorry to bother you.'

'Are you a doctor?' The question came from a small, dark-haired man with heavy eyebrows and a handsome, sulky face who had been pacing up and down in the small room. Bruno Carter, straight from the pages of my files: Geraint's first-born son.

'No, I—'

'A nurse?'

I shook my head.

'Then what the fuck are you doing here?'

'If you gave him a chance, maybe he could tell us.' The rebuke was a mild one but Bruno bristled all the same, glowering at the man who'd said it. He was thirty-two but losing his hair fast, and he was a good six inches taller than Bruno. I knew his name was Den Blackwood, and that he was married to Geraint's older daughter, Cassie. He peeled himself away from the wall where he'd been leaning and came towards me, putting himself between me and Bruno with what I guessed was habitual caution. 'Are you in the right place?'

'I'm looking for Geraint Carter's family.' I hesitated a little over the name, making sure it sounded as if I was unfamiliar with it.

'That's us.' There were two women in the room, sitting down in the corner, their arms around each other. One was pale and pretty with frightened eyes: Naomi, Bruno's wife. The other was the one who had spoken: Juliet Carter, Geraint's younger daughter. She gazed at me with frank interest, her eyelashes spiky and far too long to be real. Her tan was deep and unnaturally even and her nails were elaborate fakes too, but there were recent tear tracks on her face: she was there because she was worried about her dad. She had won the genetic lottery with her looks, taking after her mother in having regular, neat features, but she was built on her father's scale. I guessed Bruno really minded about his height and Juliet didn't need to; there were definite advantages to being on the female side of the Carter family.

'Who are you?' She asked it confidently, but without her brother's belligerence.

'I'm Mark. Mark Howell.' It came out naturally, because that

9

was how I'd been taught to say it – drilled in my second identity until I'd almost forgotten my first. Rob Langton didn't exist as far as these people were concerned, and I wanted to keep it that way. I looked around the room, as if I was trying to work out who everyone was. There were two other men in addition to Bruno and Den. One, bald and bull-necked, was Harry Dillon, also known as Geraint Carter's muscle. The other was a thin, gangling twenty-year-old with acne and hair that badly needed a cut: Carl Carter, the youngest of the children, who looked as if he would rather be just about anywhere else. He was sprawling on a chair, away from everyone else.

'Should that mean something to us?' Bruno again.

'I wanted to see how Mr Carter was doing. I was driving the car behind him when he crashed.'

Den's interest in me sharpened. 'Did you see what happened?'

'No. I came round a bend and found him. I didn't see the crash. He was driving fine up to then.'

'Was anyone else there?' Harry Dillon asked. 'Any other car?'

'That's what the police asked me.' I hoped I was looking confused enough. 'No. No one.'

'Sure?'

'No one went past me and the road was straight after the bend – I'd have seen them. I'd have heard an engine.'

'The police told us he wasn't breathing after the crash,' Den Blackwood said.

'Not breathing, no pulse.' I winced as Juliet gave a little wail. 'Sorry – I didn't mean to upset you.'

'Were you the one who did CPR?' Den, pursuing the issue to understand exactly what had happened. He liked the details, I thought.

'Me and another bloke who came along a bit later. I didn't think we'd get him back, to be honest with you.'

'Thanks.' Den came forward with his hand out and shook

mine, clapping me on the shoulder for good measure. 'You saved his life.'

'I hope so,' I said honestly. 'I hope he's going to be OK. I didn't want to intrude on the family, but the receptionist sent me in here. How's he doing?'

'He's got a chance.' It was Harry Dillon's turn to shake my hand. He squeezed hard enough to crush the bones together and I just about managed not to wince.

Bruno was still looking at me with a thoroughly unnerving hot-eyed glare, and Carl seemed to be lost in his own world. Juliet jumped up and sashayed across the room. She walked as if she was in high heels though she was wearing baggy tracksuit bottoms and trainers.

'I don't know how we can thank you, Mark.' She threw her arms around me and I was enveloped in a cloud of very sweet perfume. A kiss on the cheek left me blinking and slightly sticky.

'Give it a rest, Juliet.' Bruno looked even less impressed. 'What do you want, pal? A reward?'

'No. Nothing of the sort.' I reached into my back pocket for the wallet and phone I'd taken out of Geraint's jacket. 'I thought he might need these back though.'

Harry gave a low hum of relief and took them out of my hands, turning them over to examine them.

'We thought they'd been nicked.' Bruno's voice was cold.

'I meant to give them to the paramedics but I didn't get a chance.' I had quite deliberately let the paramedics go without them. Before I went to the hospital I'd taken the opportunity to download the phone's memory to a handy little data stick which was already on its way to my boss. Then I'd gone through the wallet and photographed everything in it, from receipts to the photographs Geraint carried around with him: his wife, his grand-daughter, Juliet and her sister Cassie, Carl as a boy. Bruno was conspicuous by his absence and I wondered if he knew that. I'd

11

got full value out of the phone and wallet before I gave them back, and if I'd done my job properly, Geraint would never know.

Harry handed the wallet to Bruno, who weighed it in his hand. 'Did you help yourself to any money?'

'No,' I said calmly, as if it was a reasonable thing to ask. 'It's all there.'

'For God's sake, Bruno,' Den said. 'Don't be so fucking rude.'

Bruno whipped around to glower at him. 'Dad carries a lot of cash. It would tempt anyone, let alone someone like him.'

Someone like me. I kept my expression absolutely neutral, amused if anything. Bruno clearly didn't appreciate my worn jeans and faded T-shirt, or the cheap watch on my wrist, or the battered trainers that were well past their best. Bruno was wearing the kind of watch that will get you mugged in the wrong postcode in London. Everything he was wearing had the buffed perfection and discreet logos that spoke of wealth.

'I'm sorry about my brother,' Juliet said, her voice edged with contempt. 'He has no manners.'

'It's fine.' I shrugged. 'If I wanted to steal the money I probably wouldn't have brought the wallet back, though.'

'He's got you there, Bruno.' Harry gave an actual chuckle and Bruno looked crosser than ever.

'Well, thanks for taking the time out of your day to return it.' Den was smooth, I thought, and obviously used to being courteous with strangers when Bruno was not.

'I didn't have anywhere better to be. I was on my way to a job interview when Mr Carter crashed his car. Once I'd missed that I had nothing to do today.'

'Are you unemployed?' Bruno, giving the question roughly the same sort of horrified intonation as if he'd asked me, *are you diseased?*

'At the moment. The last few months have been a bit rough since I lost my last job.' I shook my head as if I didn't want to talk about it and allowed myself to look faintly troubled. 'There'll be other interviews.'

'Where were you working before?' Den's face was open and friendly; this was polite conversation rather than an interrogation. His curiosity suited me down to the ground.

'I was driving for a company in Swindon. Luxury cars, like Mr Carter's Mercedes. Weddings and funerals and special occasions.'

'How did you lose your job?' Bruno again, presumably hoping for some disgrace that I wouldn't want to talk about: theft, dishonesty, a brawl, sleeping with the boss's wife . . .

'Usual thing. It was a family business and they had a cousin come over from Pakistan who needed a job.' The back story was so familiar to me that I hardly had to think about it; we had worked on it for weeks, adding in details that might hook Geraint Carter's attention. Just because he was out of action, that didn't mean I couldn't use it, since I'd been handed the chance. 'My boss needed to get rid of one of the drivers and I . . . didn't fit in the way the others did.' I tried to laugh. 'He did give me a good reference, so I should be grateful.'

'Sounds rough,' Den said with real sympathy.

'I should have known. They look after their own.' It wasn't quite overt racism but you couldn't mistake my meaning. If I'd heard someone say that, I'd have felt jarred at the least, but there was no shock on the faces around the room, just nodding. Even Bruno looked marginally less hostile. He flipped open the wallet and pinched a wad of cash. He held it out towards me without counting it.

'Here. Take this.'

'No, thank you.' I took a step back, as if I needed to physically distance myself from the temptation to take it.

'You earned it.' Juliet put her arm around her brother. 'You saved Dad's life.'

13

'That wasn't why I helped him. I don't want anything in return.'

'But you missed your job interview,' Den said. 'And you're unemployed. Won't that leave you short?'

'I'll manage.' I shoved my hands in my pockets, awkward. 'If you heard of a job going somewhere you could put in a good word for me. Otherwise . . .'

Bruno snorted. 'Do we look like a job centre?'

'Sorry,' I said quickly. 'I shouldn't have asked.'

'Don't be silly.' Juliet took a step away from Bruno, her face troubled. 'It's no problem. We can ask around – or Dad might know someone, if he—'

She broke off and bit her lip, remembering that her dad was currently halfway between life and death. I bowed my head.

'You're very kind but please, don't worry. I'll be off. Give him my best when you see him.' I turned and got as far as putting my hand on the door when the cloud of perfume swirled around me again.

'No. Wait. Daddy would want to thank you.' She blinked the heavy lashes a few times as she started tapping on her phone. 'Daddy *will* want to thank you. Give me your number.'

'There's no need—'

'Just do it.' Harry's gravelly voice cut me off. 'She's right. Her dad will want to get hold of you when he's back on his feet.'

I took the phone and keyed in the number and my name, then gave it back to her with a smile. She stared into my eyes for a beat and then let her gaze slide down to my mouth.

'See you round sometime, Mark.'

'Hope so.' I said it with just the right amount of feeling in my voice, which was considerably less than I was actually experiencing.

Provided that Geraint didn't actually die, it had turned out to be a good day after all.

3

When I got back to the flat, I couldn't help imagining what Bruno would make of it. The best you could say was that it was suitable for someone who had been sacked from a dead-end job, which was how it was supposed to look. It didn't bother me much to live a bleak life, even though my family had money and I'd grown up in a privileged world. I was uneasy with inherited wealth and had always sheared away from taking advantage of it. I had walked out of my old life to take on this job, leaving without warning, and the few things I'd kept were now in storage. The flat, horrible though it was, counted as my only home at the moment. I told myself that I preferred things to be simple, though I still missed some things: a comfortable sofa, my old colleagues, the king-sized bed I'd shared with my girlfriend, and most of all the girlfriend herself – Maeve.

I only allowed myself to think about her now and then. DC Kerrigan was just another colleague on the same murder investigation squad until I'd fallen for her, hard. I hadn't thought she would ever feel the same way, and I'd been right about that, because even though she'd been my girlfriend I never felt she was truly mine. She had become the centre of my world.

I'd loved her, and wanted to marry her, but every time I'd hinted at it she had backed away. Not ready. Not sure. All I'd succeeded in doing was pushing her away.

I shifted uneasily on the battered sofa, replaying it all in my mind against my better judgement: how I'd loved her to distraction, how I'd thought we would be together forever. And then the gradual realisation that she was holding something back, and I knew she wasn't even aware of it, but it broke my heart. And I hadn't given it time, or talked it through with her. I had too much pride. Instead I lost my patience and my temper, and walked away, taking on this new, solitary life, where I had already had two different identities and disrupted two major criminal conspiracies. Most of the time it felt like a good and satisfying substitute for what I'd had.

Most of the time.

You can't keep what you never had. It was what I thought whenever I wanted to kick myself for what I'd done.

This was my third major investigation, and the toughest, even though the biggest danger so far was dying of boredom. The last few months had tested not my courage but my ability to withstand loneliness and a spartan existence. My boss, Opal, took the view that bank records could give you away, just like phone records, so I lived the part of Mark, unemployed failure. As Mark, I had started off with a small float and got the jobseeker's allowance I'd have been entitled to had I really lost my job. I had made very little of the unpromising space I'd rented. The flat was in a purpose-built block that dated from the period in the eighties when builders didn't bother with decent proportions or access to daylight. The narrow living room ended in a cheap kitchen, and both were dingy. The bedroom was just big enough for the bed and a rail for my few clothes. The bathroom was windowless and smelled even though I kept it spotless. The stained couch looked more than

16

usually depressing that evening and the fridge was empty apart from a single bottle of beer.

If I'd taken the money Bruno offered me, I could have had a takeaway.

At least the beer was cold. I sat on the couch and stared at the wall while I drank it, gathering the energy to go out and buy some bread or noodles. I'd eaten more toast in the last few months than ever before in my life. I did make soup or a stew now and then, just to get some vegetables, but it wasn't healthy, long-term. I was ready for a change. All in all, today's adventures were looking as if they'd be to my advantage.

Ringing interrupted my thoughts: my phone. Not the one I'd been carrying around all day – the *other* phone. I grabbed it from its hiding place on top of the kitchen cupboards and answered it without looking to see who was calling. Only one person called me on that phone.

'You have a lot of explaining to do, young man.'

Opal Gilroy was ten years older than me, if that, but she talked to me as if she was my mum, and fed up with me, and that was at the best of times. This was not the best of times.

'Boss.'

'Well?'

'It wasn't planned.'

'I know that. You were doing surveillance to familiarise yourself with the target, not trying to winkle your way into his life. It's too soon. You're not ready.'

'I didn't have a choice. The man died in front of me. What could I do?'

'Say a prayer?'

'Come off it. I had to try to help.'

'That's what the training says but I train you to think beyond your training.' Her voice sharpened. 'What if they realised who you were?'

'They didn't.'

'You don't know that.'

'It was a good opportunity to meet the family. I'll never get a better one.'

'But that wasn't the plan.'

'I had to change the plan.' I let myself sound amused. 'Thinking beyond the training, ma'am.'

'Don't use my own words against me.' She sounded marginally less irritated though. 'All right. I'll forgive you. Tell me what happened from the start. Where did you pick him up today?'

I described how I'd been following him as he drove across country, hanging well back. I hadn't been doing much close surveillance in case he started to recognise me. This had been a one-off, motivated more by curiosity than anything concrete.

'And then he crashed into a tree,' I finished.

'What caused it?'

'If I had to guess, I'd say he had a heart attack, then crashed. There was nothing coming in the other direction and no sign of any interference. I think he passed out and drove off the road.'

'And you brought him back from the dead.'

'Yeah.'

'Did you give him the kiss of life?'

'I did not.'

She chuckled. 'Never mind. I've been on to the hospital and he's out of surgery. They're happy with him.'

'That's helpful.'

'Isn't it? It would have been a lot of work down the drain if he'd died. Who was at the hospital?'

I listed the various members of his family and hangers-on.

'Must have been strange to meet them.'

'It was, a bit. There's a weird family dynamic.'

'Go on.' She listened as I told her about Bruno and Den butting heads. 'Could be useful to us.'

'Could be.'

'So what happens now?'

'I told them I was looking for work.'

'Did you use the back story we'd agreed?'

'Yes, and I think it went down well. Hard to tell. No one said anything but after I told them what had happened Bruno tried to give me some money.'

'Did he? Nice of him.'

'Well, it was his dad's.'

'Everything is his dad's.' Opal didn't have a lot of time for Bruno. 'What happens now?'

'Juliet has my number.'

'And do you think she'll get in touch?'

'She will if her dad doesn't.'

'Fell for you, did she?' Opal sounded smug. 'That's why I wanted you on this. You've got the looks and the charm and the brains to back it up.'

'It's not like you to be so nice.'

'This might be the last time we talk. I need to leave it on a high.'

'Thanks a lot.'

'Listen to me.' Her voice became more serious. 'You did all right today but this has started something that you can't control. You have to let it play out at their pace now. I wanted us to choose our moment, but the moment chose us.'

'That's probably better though. More natural.'

'It's rushed. I don't like rushing.' She sighed. 'From now on you're on your own, kid. Get in touch when you need to but if I don't hear from you, I'm going to assume you're OK. Until the body turns up, that is.'

'Cheerful,' I observed.

'That's how this works. You have to be careful around these people. Don't underestimate them. Don't let your guard drop. If it goes wrong, I probably won't be able to save you.'

'I understand.'

'Do you?' She hesitated. 'They've killed before, you know. Not one of us, but that wouldn't stop them.'

'OK.'

'So be careful.'

'I will be.'

I ended the call and sat back on the sofa. There was a half-inch of beer left in the bottle but I didn't want it. Nor did I feel like going out for food anymore.

Something about what Opal had said – and the way she said it – had made me lose my appetite.

For the first few days I told myself not to expect Geraint to phone me, because he was in hospital recovering from major surgery and a life-threatening accident. For a few days after that, I sat and stared at my phone, willing it to ring, from six in the morning until midnight. I took it with me when I went running, when I went to the shops, when I had a bath. I kept it on the table in cafes and balanced it on my knee in the car so I could feel it vibrating, on the off-chance that I'd switched the ringer off by accident.

It didn't ring, and it didn't ring, and after nine days, I gave up. He wasn't going to call. Juliet had forgotten to pass on my number, or she had tried and got nowhere. Geraint was the kind of man who expected people to do things for him. Saving his life was one step up from washing his car. Why had I expected him to thank me?

I sat on the sofa for endless hours and felt wretched. Now that they knew who I was, I had to wait for them to contact me. I couldn't think how to engineer another meeting without making them suspicious. I'd had my opportunity in the hospital and I'd blown it. This would be someone else's job soon, and Opal would find something else for me to do. Paperwork, probably.

Eleven days and five hours after I dragged Geraint Carter out of his car and saved his life, my phone rang. I almost knocked it off the coffee table in my hurry to answer it.

'Hello?'

'Is that Mark?' A deep voice, confident, scrubbed so clean of class signifiers that it was impossible to tell where he had come from or how hard that might have been. I should have felt triumphant, or just relieved, but what I felt was cold, all the way down to the pit of my stomach.

'Speaking.'

'This is Geraint Carter. You saved my life a couple of weeks ago.'

Forget everything you know about him. Treat him like a stranger.

'I remember, believe it or not.'

'I don't.'

I was surprised into sincere amusement. 'You weren't in the best shape to take notice of what was going on.'

'One minute I was driving along, the next I woke up with a nurse leaning over me telling me I'd had an operation. At least she was pretty.'

I actually laughed at that. 'How are you feeling now, sir?'

'Better. Much better. They cleaned out the pipes and gave me some pills to take and I feel fine now.'

'Good to hear.'

'Yes. Well, they tell me that if you hadn't come along I wouldn't have made it.'

'I just did what anyone would have done.'

'Most people would have waited for an ambulance to come and I'd have been dead.'

'I had to make a decision and I guessed right.'

'Luckily for me.'

'I'm glad it worked out.' *You have no idea how glad.*

'My son told me you wouldn't take any money.'

'No. It didn't seem right.'

'Hmm.' I couldn't tell if it was a disapproving noise or not. 'My daughter told me you were on your way to a job interview and you missed it.'

'That's right.'

'Found anything yet?'

'Not yet. Still looking.'

'I'll ask around. See if anyone I know has any vacancies. I've got a lot of friends in business.'

I pinched the bridge of my nose, frustrated. 'Thanks, sir.'

'There's one more thing. I'm having a little party to celebrate my sixtieth birthday. It's next week. Would you like to come along? I can introduce you to a few people there. It's always easier to make a good impression in person.'

'That's very kind. Thank you, sir.'

'Give me your address and I'll get my wife to send you an invitation.' He hesitated. 'It's black tie.'

'Yes, sir.'

'Do you have a suit?' It was the question of a man who hadn't grown up rich and knew what it was like to have an unexpected expense thrown in your direction.

'I will have a suit by next week.'

'What I don't want,' he said, showing his steel, 'is to have you turn up in a shitty hire suit looking like a waiter.'

'I'll do my best to avoid that.'

'We can send you a suit. As a thank you.'

'Please don't.'

He chuckled, slightly unexpectedly. 'You have your pride, don't you?'

'Pride, but no suit.'

'Well, sort it out.' He sounded warmer. 'Consider it a test. We'll see how you do. If I'm impressed, I'll make sure we look after you.'

4

In the ordinary course of events, there was no way I'd ever have been allowed across the threshold of Wintlesbury Manor. I'd looked it up beforehand, curious about the venue Geraint had chosen for his party. The hotel was a golden-toned Cotswold mansion with a spa and an award-winning eighteen-hole golf course. I was glad I'd prepared myself as I drove through the grounds and parked my battered car between a Porsche 911 and a Ferrari.

The suit I'd found fitted me as if it had been made for me, and I'd spent the remainder of my budget on a crisp evening shirt. Before I left my flat, I'd looked at myself and thought I looked all right. No one would pick me out. Even so, I felt highly conspicuous as I jogged up the steps to the front door and arrived in a marble-floored hall that was full of elegant women and men in immaculate black tie. Huge flower arrangements stood on every surface and an enormous chandelier had dim enough bulbs to cast a flattering light. A competent but fierce woman with a clipboard and a professional smile took my name and passed me on to one of a fleet of waiters armed with trays of champagne. I took a glass to hold as I moved through the party. For many reasons I wanted to keep my wits about me, and I had the excuse that I would be driving home on dark and narrow country roads.

The rest of the guests were far less inhibited, knocking back their drinks. There didn't seem to be any limit on the amount of champagne being served: the waiters emptied bottle after bottle. No one was particularly interested in me and I tried to look as if I wasn't memorising faces and matching descriptions with individuals. Opal had made it clear that I was to come back with a full list of guests. I was just wondering whether there was any chance of charming the clipboard dragon lady into giving me her list when there was a shriek in my ear.

'You came! You came! I'm so glad.' Juliet flung her arms around me and kissed me full on the mouth before I could move away in time. I must have looked startled because she blushed. 'Sorry, I couldn't help it.'

I laughed. 'You just surprised me, that's all.'

'We are basically strangers.' The dimple appeared. 'I feel as if I know you though.'

I felt the same way, but that was probably because I'd been studying her family for months. 'You look beautiful.'

She did, too: she was in a strapless pink dress that showed off tanned shoulders and a good few inches of cleavage. Her hair was swept up and diamonds that were certainly worth more than my car and *possibly* more than the flat dangled from her ears.

'Thanks. You're not looking so bad yourself.' She frowned at my suit. 'Did Dad send you that?'

'This? No. I bought it.'

'Where?'

'Oxfam in Swindon. Twenty quid.'

'Fuck off.' She rubbed the sleeve, fascinated. 'Look at the material. That's got to be designer.'

'You know your fashion, don't you?' I opened the jacket and showed her the label. 'Ralph Lauren. Someone's weight gain was their loss.'

'You lucky git.'

'I do feel as if my luck has changed lately,' I said lightly. She blushed. *Don't cause trouble*, Opal's voice said in my head. Flirting was strictly off limits. It wasn't fair to Juliet, and anyway, it wouldn't do me any favours with Geraint. 'Where's your dad?'

'Making a big entrance with Mum in a couple of minutes.' She turned to look in the direction of the stairs. 'Why do you think we're all crammed in here? They want everyone to see them before we sit down for dinner.'

'Makes sense.'

She frowned. 'Does it?'

'This is all about people appreciating how far your dad has come, isn't it? He wants to impress all of his guests. He can't just wander in and start mingling – people might not see him.'

'How do you know all that?'

'Because he was terrified I'd turn up looking like a tramp.' I grinned. 'Don't worry. I didn't take offence. I think your brother was unimpressed by what I was wearing at the hospital.'

'Well, I thought you looked fine.' She put her arm through mine and squeezed, rubbing the soft curve of her breast against me. 'But you look even more handsome now.'

'Er, thanks.' I needed to move the conversation onto less dangerous ground. The ethics of undercover policing were complicated but one thing was clear: emotional involvement was a definite no. I was seriously considering a discussion about the weather when a bell rang and a member of staff stepped forward to bellow, 'Ladies and gentlemen, please welcome your host, Mr Geraint Carter, with his lovely wife, Adele.'

26

A soft murmur of applause and appreciation ran through the party as the two of them appeared at the top of the grand staircase. Mrs Carter was slender in silver sequins. She had ice-blonde hair arranged in a sort of bird's-nest style, and spiky eyelashes. Beside her, Geraint looked somewhat diminished by his recent experiences. His jacket seemed loose and the skin on his neck was slack. He was smiling broadly, though, and he moved easily as he came down the stairs.

'I *told* her to wear red lipstick. She looks like a ghost,' Juliet murmured, more to herself than to me.

'Your dad looks better than he did the last time I saw him.'

'He was basically dead the last time you saw him so that wouldn't be difficult,' Juliet pointed out. 'But he's been on the sunbed since he got out of hospital. He's been toasting himself to try to look healthy.'

'How is he now?' I asked with real concern. Geraint dying would put a crimp in my plans.

'Better. The doctors say he is, anyway.' She shrugged, but her eyes were liquid with unshed tears. 'You know how it is. Once something like that happens, you never know when it might happen again. If you hadn't been there—'

'Don't think about it,' I said quickly. 'Not now. Not here.'

She sniffed, and took a gulp of champagne, and lifted her chin. 'It's all right. I'm not going to cry.'

The bell rang again and the waiters started to shoo us into the dining room, a vast space lit with candles and more dimmed chandeliers.

'You're sitting with me,' Juliet said when I paused to look at the seating plan by the door. I followed her, hovering as she kissed her parents' friends and had brief conversations with the sort of people I'd have liked to talk to myself in a more formal setting, like an interview room. One had a police file two inches thick, I happened to know, and I gave him my

27

blandest, most forgettable smile when Juliet introduced me. Most of the guests seemed to have heard about Geraint's near-death adventure and looked at me with undisguised curiosity. The women took a particular interest, muttering comments to Juliet that made her giggle. I succeeded in keeping my ego under control: it wasn't anything to do with me. It was the tag of 'hero' and the dinner jacket that gave me a wholly spurious glamour in their eyes. I was younger than most of their husbands, who tended towards middle-aged spread, and the fact that I was also much poorer didn't matter for what they had in mind. I had joined the select group of personal trainers and ski instructors who were regarded as fair game for a fling. I was polite, but deaf to the loaded remarks they made.

Eventually Juliet led me to a table at the front of the room. Den Blackwood was already sitting there, along with a woman who bore a strong resemblance to Adele Carter as she might have been thirty years before. Cassandra, the other daughter.

'All right, Mark?' Den turned to the woman. 'Cass, this is the guy who saved your dad.'

'Call me Cassie.' She jumped up and shook hands with me. An inch-thick diamond-and-sapphire bracelet slid up and down on her narrow wrist. 'I've heard so much about you. Especially from *Juliet*.'

'Shut up, Cassie.' Juliet pulled out her chair and sat down with a thump. 'Come here, Mark. This is your seat.'

I sat down, aware that Den and Cassie were grinning. What Juliet wanted, Juliet got. There were still four empty places at the table. 'Who else are we waiting for?'

'Carl and his little girlfriend, if they can be bothered to show up.' Juliet pulled a face. 'This isn't really his kind of thing. And then Bruno is supposed to be sitting here too.'

'Where is he? I haven't seen him yet.'

28

'No idea.' She leaned across the table. 'Den, have you seen Bruno?'

'He's just got here.' Den pointed and I turned to see Geraint's heir stalking through the dining room with an expression like thunder. Naomi trailed behind him, delicate in pale green, her eyes focused on the floor.

'Where've you been?' Juliet hissed as they reached us. Bruno glared.

'Mind your own business.'

'Dad was looking for you.'

'I'm here now.' He sat down, his chair pushed as far back from the table as he could get. He looked around the room, his eyes cold, and nodded to a few people who waved at him.

Naomi slipped into the seat next to me.

'Hi again,' I said.

She smiled, then looked at Bruno and shrank. I glanced in his direction and got a glower for my trouble. It was probably kinder and wiser to ignore Naomi, I thought. I wondered what the long sleeves on her evening dress were hiding.

Geraint and Adele made a triumphant entrance, coming to the table nearest ours where their friends clapped and cheered. Someone started to sing 'Happy Birthday' and the whole room joined in. Geraint looked delighted; this was everything he had wanted from his big night.

'You'll have to introduce me to your father,' I said to Juliet. 'We've never met properly.'

'I forgot about that! So strange.' She narrowed her eyes, considering it. 'They're doing a tour of the room between courses. I'll do it then. I don't want to interrupt him at the moment.'

I could see why. He was already deep in conversation with the man next to Adele, a red-faced, white-haired bull of a man. Geraint didn't really do deferential but he wasn't far off it, leaning across, nodding earnestly. 'Who's he talking to?'

29

'Max Burniford.'

The name didn't mean anything to me. 'Who is he?'

'Why do you care?' Bruno raised his eyebrows. 'You're not here to make friends. You're here because Dad wanted you here for his big night. When this is over, you're gone.'

'I'm sure you're right,' I said before Juliet could explode. She was quivering with outrage beside me. 'I'm very grateful to him for inviting me.'

Bruno snorted, unimpressed. He had been hoping for a fight, I thought, and felt a deep sense of foreboding about how the evening was going to pan out.

A couple of hours later, I had relaxed. Bruno remained sulky but he had kept a lid on his temper, for the most part. The food was superb. One course followed another with seamless efficiency and everyone was far too busy eating and drinking to cause any trouble. The only awkward moment came when a waiter put a plate down in front of Bruno and started to move away.

'Hey. Hey, come back.' He clicked his fingers. 'I'm not having this. Take it away.'

'What's the matter, sir?'

'It's had your filthy thumb in it.'

The waiter looked horrified. 'No, indeed not, sir.' He was Sri Lankan, with a heavy accent and a gentle manner.

Bruno flushed. 'Are you calling me a liar?'

'Bruno,' Juliet said. 'Leave it.'

'I'm not eating this.' He shoved the plate away from him so the food slid all over the pristine tablecloth. 'Clear this up.'

The waiter wisely decided not to argue. He cleaned up the mess as best he could. Bruno waited until he had turned away again before he said, quite loudly, 'Fucking P***.'

Den and Juliet started talking at the same time, more or less at random, and Bruno drained the contents of his wine glass defiantly. The waiter pretended he hadn't heard, but he must have been aware of what Bruno had said. He didn't come back to our table again. I couldn't blame him.

Geraint toured the room as Juliet had predicted. On his final round, he stopped beside me.

'Mark, is it? Good of you to come.'

'Thank you for inviting me. It's been an amazing evening.'

He looked at me with keen interest, assessing me, and I tried to imagine what he saw: a very ordinary thirty-something, dark hair, blue eyes, fairly fit, unremarkable in almost every way. After what felt like an eternity, he nodded and moved on to embrace Juliet. I caught Bruno's eye again and regretted it: he was smirking.

When this is over, you're gone.

Maybe he was right.

After the last course was served, before coffee, Bruno got up and went out. I assumed he was going to the men's room, but the minutes passed and he didn't return. Naomi turned around in her seat and stared at the door with the wide eyes of an abandoned animal.

'Where's he gone?' I asked.

'I don't know.' She was biting her lower lip and her hands were twisted around one another.

'Do you want me to go and look for him?'

Her look of gratitude would have melted stone. 'Would you?'

'Sure. Back in a minute.' I headed out to the hall, not hurrying, glad of an excuse to look around. I paused by the seating plan and took a couple of discreet pictures of it so I could send them on to Opal. Then I went down the hall to the men's room, and found no trace of Bruno there. I wandered outside where the smokers had gathered and couldn't see him. I should have been reassured but it bothered me; he wouldn't leave in the middle of his father's big night, would he? So what was he up to?

I was outside for less than a minute, but when I went back the civilised elegance of the evening had been shattered. Two men were reeling across the marble-floored hall, locked in the kind of staggering brawl that no one is going to win. Bruno was one of them, inevitably, and the other was Den. The staff were looking on, horrified. So far, only one or two guests seemed to have noticed the fight, but those who had weren't attempting to intervene. Even as I took the measure of the situation, Bruno managed to get a hand free and delivered a short jab that caught Den full on the nose. It started to bleed as if he had turned on a tap.

'Fuck,' Den spat. 'You bastard.'

Bruno hit him again, this time in the stomach, and Den responded with a headbutt that sounded like two watermelons colliding. The two of them broke apart for a moment. Before they could start fighting again I took three steps forward and got a shoulder between them. I faced Bruno, because I didn't trust him and I wanted to be able to see him.

'Give it a rest. This isn't the place for a scrap.'

'Fuck off,' Bruno managed, and swung a fist at me, as I'd expected. I ducked out of the way, caught his arm and pushed him away. He came back at me, his eyes bloodshot and his jaws working, too coked up to hide it. I brought my knee up sharply just as he came within range. It hit him squarely in the crotch. He crumpled to the floor. I backed into Den so he moved away from Bruno and gave him a warning look over my shoulder.

'This is over.'

Den sniffed and dabbed at his nose with the back of one hand. 'Fine by me. He started it.'

Bruno had got to his feet again, his eyes hot with anger. He balled his hands into fists and came towards me, and I didn't want to fight him but he wasn't exactly giving me a choice.

'Don't do this.'

'Get fucked,' Bruno snarled.

I dropped my voice so only he could hear me. 'Your dad will never forgive you if you ruin his night.'

That was true enough to stop him, at least for a moment. 'All right?'

An eternity passed before he nodded.

'Good.' I took Bruno's arm and held on to him as Cassie came to retrieve her husband and towed him away, clucking about putting ice on his nose. 'Just stay here with me.'

Bruno shook himself free and started to dust himself down, tugging his clothes back into place. He had a huge red mark on his forehead where Den had headbutted him.

'What was all that about?' I asked.

'Mind your own fucking business.'

'Fine.' I put a hand out to stop him as he started towards the dining room. 'Not in there. Go somewhere else. Cool off.'

I expected him to argue with me, or start fighting again, but he did neither. He stood for another moment, breathing heavily, then turned and started up the stairs. The family had reserved rooms, Juliet had told me coyly, with more than a hint of invitation. I hoped Bruno was going to bed.

When I turned back to go into the dining room myself, I realised why Bruno had gone without causing any more trouble. His father was standing behind me, watching, his expression grim. A prickle of unease raced over my skin: had Geraint worked out who and what I was?

His next words were the opposite of reassuring. 'I want to talk to you.'

5

I followed my host down the corridor, past the bar, to a room I hadn't been in before. It was an old library, or at least decorated to look the part of an old library. The books that lined the walls seemed to be authentically old but unread, a random selection bought by the yard for their bindings and jammed in tightly. Heavy brocade curtains hung at the windows and low pools of light illuminated individual chairs. Harry Dillon was sitting on a leather sofa by the fireplace, as out of place as a knuckleduster in a church. He eyed me unenthusiastically. Geraint jerked his head towards the door.

'Step out, Harry. Make sure we're not interrupted.'

'Everything all right?'

Geraint made a noise in the back of his throat that made Harry's eyebrows draw together.

'Need me to do anything?'

'Not at the moment. It's handled.'

Harry flicked another look in my direction and I wondered if I should assume I was the problem Geraint had been talking about rather than the solution. Harry didn't say anything else, though, stomping out through the door and closing it behind him. His dinner jacket had to have been tailored specially for him to allow it to fit across his shoulders, I thought irrelevantly, ridiculously. That was fear. One way in and out of the room, and it was blocked by Harry Dillon. I was going to have to talk my way out of this. It was all too likely that Geraint had worked out I was a police officer from the way I'd handled the fight between Bruno and Den – even the language I'd used had been straight from the big book of street policing. I shouldn't have intervened. I should have let Bruno batter seven shades of shit out of his brother-in-law and done nothing . . .

'You'll have a drink.' Geraint crossed to a silver tray and poured an inch of whiskey into a cut-glass tumbler. He held it out to me without adding a mixer or asking if I wanted it and I took it; there was a time and a place for moralising about drink-driving but this was not it. Besides, if the conversation went sideways, I'd need a drink to get me through the unpleasant aftermath. It would be administered by Harry Dillon. There was no way Geraint would get his own hands dirty when he had an expert in pain at his beck and call.

You need to watch out for him, Opal murmured in the back of my mind.

Thanks for the advice, boss.

Geraint had poured a matching drink for himself and swallowed half of it on his way over to the sofa Harry had vacated. He held out a hand and gestured at the chair opposite. 'Sit.'

I sat.

'What is it about you, Mark?'

'What do you mean?'

He ran his tongue over his teeth, considering it. 'Once again you happen to come along in the nick of time and know exactly what to do.'

'I might have looked like I knew what I was doing, but it was just luck.' Geraint snorted and I went on, 'Anyway, I don't think either of them really wanted to fight.'

'You're wrong about that. It's been a long time coming. They're usually at each other's throats.'

'Why?'

'Family business.' He gulped another mouthful of whiskey and pulled a face as it went down. 'They don't see eye to eye about strategy.'

'Must be difficult.'

'It can be. It can be useful.' He looked straight at me, his eyes cold. 'I would put a stop to it myself if I wanted to.'

'Of course you would.' *Shit, shit, shit.* 'I'm sorry. I shouldn't have intervened.'

'I didn't say that.' He turned the glass, rolling it between his palms. 'This wasn't the right place for a fight. They should both have known better than to start scrapping in front of my friends. The trouble is, Bruno's always had a temper. He can't control it, and Den doesn't have the sense to back down now and then. You can't win with someone like Bruno if you fight them all the time. You have to know when to give in.'

'It's not easy.'

'Den thinks it's a sign of weakness to handle Bruno gently.' The pale blue eyes were fixed on me again. 'You know different, don't you?'

'I don't mind backing down. You've got to keep your own temper and keep your goal in mind. Lose the battle and win the war.'

'So you think you could sort Bruno out, is that it?'

'No. I wouldn't want to try.' I put my glass down on a small table at my elbow. 'I didn't think about it before I stepped in. I just wanted to stop them from causing a scene, that's all.'

'You shut him up and sent him to bed.' A smile showed off Geraint's expensively crafted teeth. 'I couldn't have done better myself.'

'He'd had enough. I came along at the right time.'

'Timing is half the battle.' He looked down at his drink, brooding. 'That's the second time, Mark. It makes me think I should pay some attention to you.'

I sat very still and hoped my expression was revealing nothing more than polite interest, rather than the blank terror I was feeling. *Pay some attention* wasn't necessarily a positive remark. While I was wondering how to find out what he meant, Geraint changed tack.

'Where did you get the suit?'

'Charity shop.'

'Second-hand?'

I nodded. 'Sorry. Best I could do.'

'You're the only person here in someone else's clothes, I'll tell you that much. But you look the part and you talk the right way. You act quickly when you need to. You don't wait for instructions.'

'I do if I'm supposed to. I'm not exactly a maverick.'

'You're your own man. I like people who want to be independent. People who stand on their own two feet. People who would rather go and buy an old suit from a charity shop than accept a gift they fully deserve.'

I ducked my head, embarrassed. 'There was no need. I didn't want to take anything from you.'

'Most people, if they got in with a guy like me, would be thinking about what they could get out of it.'

'That's not how I work.'

'I can tell.' Geraint smiled again. 'That's why you're living in a one-bed shithole, though.'

'You looked it up?'

He waved a hand; Geraint wasn't the sort of person to jump to Google Maps every time they came across a postcode. 'Juliet did. She was horrified.'

'I can imagine.'

'Don't you want more for yourself? Don't you have any ambition?'

'Of course I do.' I would never dare to snap at Geraint Carter, but I came close to it then, as if I really was Mark Howell, and worried about my prospects, and aware I was one small step ahead of financial disaster.

'Then why aren't you trying to make something of this?'

'All I have is me,' I said slowly. 'I have to be able to live with myself. If I tried to persuade you to help me – to give me money, or opportunities – I'd hate myself for it. I'd rather earn my chances. Even if it doesn't make sense financially, I have to do what I think is right. It's not necessarily what other people would think was sensible, but it's how I live.'

'Very moral.'

I laughed. 'Not necessarily. I'm no angel, Mr Carter.'

'What does that mean?' He looked intrigued. 'Ever stolen anything?'

'When I needed to.'

'Ever beat someone up?'

'When I needed to,' I repeated.

'Regret anything you've done?'

'Loads of things,' I said with feeling. 'But mainly because they didn't work out.'

Geraint leaned back in his chair. 'You seem like the sort of person who would be useful to have around. Do you still need a job?'

'Yes.'

'Would you work for me?'

'Yes.'

38

He grinned. 'You haven't even asked what the job would involve.'

'That's not as important as who I'd be working for. I could work for you, I think.'

'I think you could.' He nodded. 'I think you'd like it.'

I hesitated. 'Having said that, what sort of work did you have in mind?'

He laughed out loud. 'I can't tell you that now. I'll find something for you to do, don't worry about that.'

'And . . . what would you pay?'

'Enough.' His eyes were bright: he was enjoying this. 'Come and see me tomorrow. Do you know the address?'

'No.'

'Haulton House, near Bourton-on-the-Water. Anyone local can tell you how to get to it.'

'That's not what I meant. I'm not going to come to see you tomorrow.'

'Why not?' The ice was back in his voice, instantly. You didn't just say no to Geraint Carter . . .

'You're not going to want to have a meeting with me tomorrow. You'll be tired.'

'Is that a diplomatic way of saying hungover?'

'It might be.' I smiled, keeping it light. 'I do want to come and see you, sir, more than you can imagine, but I can wait a couple of days.'

'Monday, then.'

'Monday.'

'Ten o'clock all right?'

'I'll be there.'

Geraint stood up. 'I need to get back to the party. They'll be looking for me.'

'Of course.'

'Thank you again for dealing with Bruno.'

'It was a pleasure,' I said truthfully and Geraint chuckled.

'Try not to show it too much. He doesn't have a sense of humour about that kind of thing.'

As he spoke he crossed the room and opened the door. Harry turned and gave him a look I couldn't read. In the distance, I could hear singing from the dining room, but I couldn't make out the tune or the words. Geraint swung back to me. His manner was business-like now.

'You must be exhausted. You're not staying here, are you? No? Then let Harry get you a car to take you home.'

'I was planning to drive myself home, actually.'

'Good for you.' He patted Harry's arm. 'See our friend to his car.'

Harry nodded grimly.

I checked my watch: just after eleven. It seemed early to wind up the party.

'I should say goodbye to Juliet.'

'Better not,' Geraint said. 'Leave her be.'

I might have an invitation to Geraint's house, and the prospect of a job, but he wasn't going to encourage me when it came to his younger daughter, which I thought was dead right as well as useful in the circumstances.

The music swelled from the dining room, a chorus sung with more vigour than musicality. I didn't recognise the song: a football chant? Something with filthy lyrics? Could that be what was making Geraint look flustered? But he wouldn't care about a nobody like me hearing something like that, even if it was sung by the rich and powerful people at his party.

'Come on.' Harry gripped my elbow, pinching the nerve unerringly so my hand went numb. 'Let's find your car.'

There were trials of strength I could win; this wasn't one of them. I hastily thanked Geraint for inviting me and promised again to see him on Monday, and not before. I turned to go

40

back to the hall and the front door but Harry dragged me in the opposite direction.

'This isn't the way,' I protested mildly.

'It's quicker.' He shouldered open a fire exit that led directly into the car park. 'Which car?'

'That one.' I pointed.

A grunt of disapproval. 'Should have guessed.'

'It doesn't sound as if the party's over.'

'It is for you.' Harry took the car key out of my pocket and opened the door for me. 'Get in.'

I got in.

'Go away.'

'I'll see you on Monday.' Some evil inclination made me add, 'Your boss has offered me a job.'

For an instant, he looked surprised. 'Don't count on him sticking to that when he sobers up.'

'You could put in a good word for me,' I suggested, and his craggy face broke into a smile.

'Fuck off.'

It wasn't quite a hero's send-off, but I grinned as I drove away.

6

I was prepared to turn up at Haulton House the following Monday and get sent away. It was one thing for Geraint to promise me an opportunity in the middle of his birthday party, when he was weak with relief that I'd stopped his son and son-in-law from making a scene, but quite another for him to follow up on it two days later. He didn't really need me, I thought, shaving with extra care, and he wasn't the sort of person to feel he had to live up to his promises. He might even have forgotten all about it as the night had worn on.

But I'd done him a disservice. When I found Haulton House behind huge electric gates and a high wall, I pressed the intercom and announced myself.

'Bang on time.' I recognised Harry Dillon's gravelly voice. 'Good start.'

The gates slid open and I coaxed the Golf up the long, winding drive, through grounds that were mainly parkland. Every few hundred metres there was some feature or other: a pergola, a rose-covered arch, a fountain, a pair of Greek statues, a folly. The beautiful scenery wasn't enough on its own; it didn't say wealth and taste and whatever else Geraint wanted you to think as you progressed towards his house. The grass undulated into the distance with the emerald perfection you got on the better kind of golf course. It was a huge estate, I realised, and I'd known he was wealthy but seeing it spread out in front of me was different.

The house was beautiful from the front: an eighteenth-century country mansion in red brick – not huge, but elegant. As more of it came into view I saw that there were considerable additions lurking behind the original structure: I would find out that the two wings that stretched behind it cradled a glass-walled extension. Beyond that lay a swimming pool, garages and stables, and in the distance a tennis court. There was an indoor pool too, I would discover, and a gym, and a home cinema – all the trappings of the ultra-rich – but on my first visit I didn't get the full tour. What I could see from the drive was enough: Geraint was a very wealthy man indeed.

I parked by the front door, aware that I was lowering the value of the house just by leaving my car there. The door swung open before I could knock.

'Mark. Welcome.' Geraint jogged down the steps to greet me, moving well for a man who had been on the wrong side of death's door the first time I encountered him. He was wearing chinos with suede loafers and a pink cashmere jumper, perfect for drinks in Cannes or a quiet day at home in the country. I had thought long and hard about what I should wear and settled on my best jeans and an open-necked navy shirt. A suit felt too formal. More to the point, it made me look too much like what I really was. Casual clothes made me look needier, and younger, and hungry for an opportunity. 'Nice to see you again.'

'And you.' His handshake had a decent amount of force to it today: his recovery seemed to be on track. 'How did the party go the other night after I left?'

'It went well. I was pleased.' He looked smug. 'We're still opening presents. The kitchen looks like a florist's shop. People were very generous but of course it was a big occasion for me.'

I stared as I followed Geraint into the hall. 'This is amazing.'

It was indeed amazing to discover that the back of the house had been carved away to allow for the glass extension that housed the kitchen and a living room and a marble-topped table surrounded by expensive designer chairs. The older part of the house looked unchanged, with high double doors standing open to reveal a formal drawing room with a traditional dining room beyond it, all gleaming mahogany and gilt-framed art. On the right, beside the grand, sweeping stairs, there was a large study. I couldn't believe the planners had given them permission to slice off the back of the house, though. Geraint took my shock as the appropriate level of awe and looked smug.

'I'm glad you like it. Cost me a fair bit. This place was a ruin when I bought it.'

'It's incredible,' I said, truthfully, and Geraint practically purred.

'Come into my study. Harry?'

Harry Dillon appeared instantly, as if he had been waiting to be summoned.

'No interruptions.' Geraint turned to me with a faint smile. 'I like to keep my family close to me, but they can be a bit too close sometimes.'

'Do they all live here?'

'My children all live in the house or on the estate. Apart from the youngest, who's at university, or supposed to be. He seems to spend most of his time in Camden spending my money on God knows what.' He led me into the study and gestured to a pair of sofas that faced each other on either side of a massive fireplace. 'Sit. Coffee?'

'Thanks.'

There was a tray on the table with a pot and two cups. Geraint poured some coffee into one and sat down opposite me.

'Help yourself.'

I did as I was told, hiding a smile at the degree of welcome I was being accorded: he had come out to meet me and he was providing refreshments but if I thought Geraint Carter was the kind of man to serve me my coffee I had another think coming.

'Thanks for asking me to meet you. I appreciate the opportunity.'

Geraint looked pleased. 'Well, least I could do. And it's not all for your sake. Like I said the other night, when I see someone who could be useful to me I like to make use of them.'

'I said I'd work for you and I meant it.' I ventured a smile. 'I'd probably need to know what the job would involve, though.'

'Do you know what I do? What paid for this place?'

Two very different questions with very different answers, I thought. 'You have a few different businesses, Mr Carter. Locksmiths, warehouses, beauty salons, dry cleaners, painters and decorators, plumbers and electricians. You're an investor in various property businesses and a chain of pubs. You had a travel agency but you sold it four years ago and that put you on the *Sunday Times* rich list for the first time.' *But you could have been on it years before if you'd been able to declare your illegal income . . .*

He smiled. 'You've done your homework.'

'I looked you up, when I knew I was coming here.' I had, too. I wanted to know what an ordinary person should be able to find out about Geraint Carter – what you would make of him if you took his public reputation at face value. I'd found a couple of carefully worded articles that hinted at the truth as I knew it: the legitimate businesses that laundered cash for the vast illegal empire he ran, catering to the economy that existed in the shadows and centred on drugs, sex work, violent crime and fraud. 'It's an incredible achievement to have built up your fortune from where you started.'

'One shop.' Geraint leaned back and locked his hands behind his head. 'That's all it took.'

That and being prepared to break the rules, and his competitors' skulls.

'If you can see a role for me in your organisation, I'd like to work for you, sir. It would be an honour.'

Geraint dropped his arms and sat up straight. 'The thing is, Mark, I could put you in somewhere as a manager. Nothing could be easier. Give you a few people to look after, see how you do with the business side of things.'

'I'd do my best.'

'I know you would. But I think I'd be missing a trick.'

I hoped my relief didn't show on my face. I did not want to end up managing a warehouse for Geraint Carter, dealing with him by email or on the phone and seeing him once a year, if that.

'What appeals to me about you, Mark, is that you're effective. You see a problem and you sort it out without waiting to be told what to do. I like that.'

'Thank you, sir.'

'Call me Geraint.' He was watching me, his eyes unnervingly sharp. 'I was impressed, at the party, when you broke up that fight between my son and my son-in-law.'

'I just assumed you wouldn't want them scrapping in front of your friends and family.' I was treading carefully, all the same.

'You assumed correctly. As I told you the other night, I find it useful to let Den and Bruno butt heads. It's effective as long as there's someone around to rein them in, but I can't be here all the time, and I shouldn't have to act as a referee. Also, there's a time and a place for that kind of thing. I want someone around who doesn't have a personal stake in deciding who wins when the two of them argue – someone who won't get drawn in. Now, I can't advertise that as a job, and most people wouldn't be able to do it anyway, but you have the right approach, from what I've seen. You stand up to them but you don't get fussed. I talked to you on Saturday after you'd sorted them out and you weren't even out of breath. You're a cool customer.'

My heart had been racing, even if it hadn't been apparent to Geraint, but that was because of the threat he posed to me. 'I just had to get in the way and slow them down.'

'No one else stepped in.'

I grinned. 'No one else was stupid enough to do it, maybe.'

'Stupid is all right. I don't need you to think about what you're doing. You seem to do well enough by acting on instinct.'

'So what you're suggesting is that I just . . . hang around and wait for trouble?'

He laughed. 'We'll find jobs for you to do, don't worry. Whatever I need you to do, when I need you to do it. How does that sound?'

'I don't want to step on Harry's toes.' Because he would break me into many tiny pieces, I thought, but didn't say.

'Harry knows his job. He's here to look after me, and he does it well. He's not going to be threatened by you, believe me.'

'OK.'

'I'm not interested in benefits and sick leave and what have you. I'll pay you per day you work and I'll put a roof over your head and give you a decent car to drive.'

'You want me to live here?'

'Why not? We've got plenty of bedrooms.' He stretched his arms along the back of the sofa. 'And it's not a nine-to-five job. It's mornings and evenings and weekends. I don't want to have to hang around for you to get here from somewhere else. I'll own you, but I'll make it worth your while.' He named a daily rate that was generous by any standards.

47

'Yes.'

'Is that it?' He raised his eyebrows. 'You don't want to negotiate?'

'I'm keen to work for you.' It was the truth; he didn't realise how much I wanted this. 'You're offering me an opportunity that I'd never dreamed of. I'm not going to put that in jeopardy by quibbling about the details.'

'Good lad. You can trust me, you know.'

I nodded, not quite able to bring myself to agree in words. 'When would you like me to start?'

'As soon as possible. Give notice on your flat and get rid of everything you won't need. I don't want you bringing that car here either – scrap it. You'll be able to buy a new one soon enough and in the meantime I've got a few cars you can use. Bring exercise gear. I want you to get fit and stay fit. There's a gym here, a pool, horses you can ride.'

'I'd have to learn.'

Geraint grunted. 'I don't ride, myself. I don't like anything that goes that fast and doesn't have brakes. What about tennis?'

'I'm all right at it.'

'Good. Clean driving licence?'

'Yes.'

'Criminal record?'

This was a question that Opal and I had discussed over and over again. She could have faked a record on the PNC without thinking about it, and wanted to. I'd thought it was one lie too far.

'No, by sheer luck, basically.' I hesitated as if I was weighing up the risks of being honest. 'I've got away with a fair bit in my time.'

'I like people who look clean and know how to play dirty.' Geraint was looking positively benign. 'You know, I think this is going to work out well for both of us.'

7

'Morning.'

I looked up from the fruit I was chopping. 'Good morning.'

'What are you making?' Juliet shuffled into the huge kitchen, her fluffy slippers scuffing over the marble floor. She was squinting against the sunshine that streamed in through the glass roof, and her hair was tied back in a messy bun that had shed strands around her face. She looked somehow unprotected without the heavy make-up she liked to wear, her eyes small and easy to read, her mouth pale.

'Kale and avocado smoothie. Want one?'

'Ugh. No.' She stretched and I looked away from her, studiously ignoring the way her skimpy pyjama top slid up. She wore incredibly brief shorts too: subtle she was not. But after two weeks, I was used to it, and used to the morning routine. The kitchen was the hub of the house, and it was where every day began.

'Can I have a bit of banana?'

'Get your own.' I pointed the knife at the fruit bowl. 'There are plenty.'

She reached past me and took a chunk off the chopping board anyway, grinning at me. 'Sorry.'

'I doubt that.'

'What time is it?'

'Just after seven.'

'Early.' She yawned, not covering her mouth, and went to a cupboard to get a mug. 'Why are you up?'

'I went for a run this morning.' I had gone all around the estate, casually checking out the lie of the land. It was what I did, four times a week, so I could keep up with Geraint's demands of fitness while keeping an eye on what was going on. I'd found Den and Cassie's house, built on land to the left of the main property, and a building site on the right that would be Bruno's home when it was finished. He had already gone through two architects and three builders. The site currently sat idle: a few walls standing in a sea of churned mud. It meant that he and Naomi were living in the main house, in the family wing, along with their little girl, Tessa, with no prospect of moving out. I spent most mealtimes trying to pretend I didn't notice him glaring at me. Bruno had not been pleased to discover I had a new job that came with a roof over my head. I'd overheard him confronting his father as I came down the stairs one day, early on.

'Why does he have to be in the house?'

'Because I want him here.' Geraint had sounded irritated.

'What about Neil's place? It's empty.'

'Mark's not a chauffeur. Anyway, Neil's flat isn't ready yet. You know it still needs sorting out.'

'What do you mean, Mark's not a chauffeur? He drove Mum into the village yesterday.'

'That's not all I want him for.'

'What else?'

'Jobs,' Geraint had snapped, and I'd carried on into the kitchen.

Neil was the chauffeur who had left, and I still didn't know where he had gone or why. I'd asked Adele when I drove her, but she had been vague to the point of rudeness. I really, really wanted to get a look at the chauffeur's flat but I hadn't been able to work out how without looking suspicious. What needed sorting out? What had happened to make him leave? They weren't the most pressing questions on my mind, but I stored them away for future consideration.

'Are you busy today?' Juliet perched on a high stool at the breakfast bar and watched me tip ingredients into the blender.

'No idea. Your dad hasn't told me what I'm doing.'

'Don't you mind not knowing?'

I shrugged. 'He warned me before I took the job that it wasn't going to be predictable. As long as I can do whatever he asks me to do, I don't mind.'

'You're so easy-going.'

'Just compared to your family.' I glanced at her. 'Bruno's wound tight, isn't he?'

She rolled her eyes. 'That's the understatement of the century.'

'Has he always been like that?'

'More or less. He likes to throw his weight around.'

'And his fists.'

'What do you mean?' There was an edge to her voice and I looked up, surprised.

'He had a fight with Den at your dad's party.'

'Oh. Yeah. They do scrap now and then.'

'What did you think I meant?'

'Nothing.' She gave me a meaningless smile and I switched on the blender, letting it run for a minute. The silence afterwards was loud.

'So are you involved with your dad's businesses?'

'No.'

'How come?'

'I don't need to work.' There was colour in her cheeks and her eyes were bright: I'd blundered into dangerous territory.

'Maybe you don't need to, but don't you want to? You're clever.'

'Dad doesn't think so.' She sighed. 'Carl is the baby of the family but I get treated like I am. One day Carl will be running some bit of the business and I'll still be standing around looking pretty.' She was staring into her mug as if the answer to her problems was at the bottom.

'How old are you, Juliet?'

'Twenty-three.'

'You have plenty of time to find out what you want to do in life.'

'I want to get married.' A challenging stare from those blue eyes. 'Does that seem weird?'

'No, not at all. Your parents seem very happy. And your sister and Den have a good marriage.'

'You didn't mention Bruno.'

'I did not.'

'You don't think his marriage is happy?'

His wife isn't, I thought. 'I don't know. It's none of my business.'

'What isn't?' Geraint strode in, his hair wet. I'd seen him ploughing up and down the pool, motivated to keep up with his new exercise regime after his near-death experience.

'The fact that I don't have a job, Daddy,' Juliet said smoothly, and I could have kissed her for lying so well. 'Mark has been asking me why I don't.'

'My daughters don't work.' He kissed her on the cheek and ruffled her hair, then gave me a cold look. 'My wife doesn't either. I don't have any interest in pushing them into areas that don't concern them.'

'Fair enough.' I held up my hands. 'Nothing to do with me, as I said.'

'Don't be mean to him, Daddy,' Juliet said with a pout. 'He was trying to encourage me to take an interest in your businesses.'

Was that what I'd done? I didn't think the conversation had gone that way, but Juliet was turning it to suit her own ends. She leaned against her father and wound her arms around his neck.

'I don't even know what you do – not really.'

'Just business, darling.' He patted her arm distractedly.

'What kind of business?'

'You know. Where you get your hair done, where you get your nails done, where you buy your clothes. That's all mine.'

And money laundering? I wondered. Organised crime? Protection rackets? It wasn't all legitimate, not by a long way. I didn't expect him to tell her the ins and outs of it over break-fast, but I would have loved to hear his version of it.

'You're so clever, Daddy.'

He smiled at her indulgently. 'What do you want, Juliet?'

'A piece of toast. And a new pair of boots.'

'Go on. No one's stopping you.'

'Can Mark drive me to Oxford to go shopping?'

'Tomorrow. Not today. Today I need him here.'

I put down the smoothie I'd been drinking. 'Why, what's going on?'

'I've got some associates coming for a meeting. You're not going to be joining us but I want you nearby. I might need you.' He looked around as one of the housekeepers came in carrying a pile of ironed sheets. 'Malee, I'd like eggs – poached – and coffee.'

She nodded, smiling. She was Thai, as was the other house-keeper, and I didn't think either of them spoke English well. It had occurred to me that it was a deliberate choice on Geraint's part; the less they understood, the less they could say about what they saw and heard at work. I had thought about trying to ask them about comings and goings at Haulton

House but the language barrier made it impossible. Opal could have found someone with a Thai background to develop a casual friendship with them if either of them ever left the estate, but they seemed to spend their days off in seclusion in the staff quarters.

'Good morning.' Naomi came in with Tessa in her arms, her eyes trained on the floor as usual. She was pale. A pink dressing gown covered her from her neck to her ankles.

'Morning, darling. Where's that son of mine?'

'Still asleep.' She put Tessa down inside a playpen that stood in the corner and stretched out her arms with a wince as if they ached from carrying the baby. 'I didn't want him to wake up, so I thought I'd come down here with Tessa.'

'Have something to eat. Malee is making me a proper breakfast, or Mark can whip you up one of his horrific vegetable drinks that look like pond scum.'

'My smoothies taste better than they look,' I protested.

'So I'd hope.'

'I don't want anything.' Naomi put a hand up to the neck of her dressing gown and held on to it tightly, her knuckles shining through her skin.

'You have to have something. Most important meal of the day,' Geraint said.

'Not for me.' She tried to smile. 'I'll have some tea or something.'

'I'll make it for you.' I got as far as taking a mug out of the cupboard when Naomi lifted it out of my hands.

'It's fine. I'll make it.'

'No trouble.'

'I'd rather do it myself.' That sharp note of panic; would Bruno really mind so much if his father's employee made his wife some tea?

'Let her do it herself.' Juliet set her own mug down with

54

more force than she needed. 'She can manage. It's not as if you insisted on making tea for me.'

'I was busy.' I was going to say something bland to take the heat out of the conversation, but as I glanced at Naomi, I saw the neck of her dressing gown had come open. There was a ring of dark bruises around her throat, as if someone had grabbed her. So it wasn't only Den who got the benefit of Bruno's fists, I thought, and swallowed my anger. It sat like a cold hard lump of metal in my gut.

'I'd like to make the tea myself. I want to make a cup for Bruno in case he wakes up.' Naomi smiled without meeting my eyes and turned to the boiling-water tap.

Geraint went over to the playpen and started cooing at Tessa, who beamed back. She was an engaging child, blue-eyed and cheerful, and Geraint was utterly smitten. 'Who's my princess? Who's my little girl?'

'I am,' Juliet said through a mouthful of toast.

'My *other* princess.'

'You spoil her.'

'I spoiled you first,' Geraint said without looking round, and Juliet slid off her stool.

'You haven't finished your breakfast,' I pointed out, but she kept moving towards the door.

'I'm not hungry.'

The kitchen door slammed behind her and I made a move to follow her.

'Let her go.' It wasn't quite an order, but the look on Geraint's face told me it was more than a suggestion. 'It'll do her good to learn her place.'

'I shouldn't have brought Tessa down here.' Naomi was literally wringing her hands, her anxiety obvious.

'It's not your fault, Naomi,' Geraint snapped. 'Christ, stop being such a victim.'

'Sorry.' It was a whisper. She dropped her head, blinking hard against the tears that swelled along her lashes.

He gritted his teeth, obviously irritated. Naomi's vulnerability brought out the bully in him rather than any instinct to protect his daughter-in-law. The bad temper that was so obvious in Bruno ran through the family like a seam of toxic ore; they were all dangerous, especially for someone as gentle as Naomi.

The worst thing I could do was come to her defence, I reminded myself, so I said nothing, and pretended I hadn't noticed the unpleasant undercurrent in the room, and hated myself for it.

8

The cars began to arrive on the stroke of 10.45, rolling up the driveway in convoy. There were three of them, all large and expensive, all driven by big men with short hair and watchful eyes. They parked at an angle to the house and the drivers got out with synchronised efficiency to open the passengers' doors. I memorised number plates and distinguishing marks as best I could while welcoming the visitors to Haulton House. I recognised one of the men from Geraint's birthday party but didn't know his name: he was small, with slicked-back dark hair, a black silk bomber jacket, knife-pleat slacks and an expensive watch. He was perhaps sixty, hoping to pass for fifty, and his wife had been one of the younger women at Geraint's party, lacquered in make-up. I recalled a gravity-defying dress that barely veiled breast implants as round and firm as beach balls. The second was Max Burniford, the big man who had been at the top table the same night. He walked with a stick, his movements ponderous, and his driver hovered near him until he was safely inside the house. The third man was bearded, with grey hair curling on his collar, and I'd never seen him before. He wore an open-necked shirt, jeans and trainers.

Geraint had decided he would receive his guests in his sitting room and I acted as a sort of butler, ushering them inside one by one. They greeted Geraint warmly, hugging him. Burniford slapped him on the shoulder, hard, and I saw a grimace flit across my employer's face for an instant. Who was in charge here? Who was the leader?

Harry Dillon appeared and took up his usual place outside the door with his hands folded in front of him: I could forget about loitering out there and listening to the conversation. Slightly to my surprise, Den Blackwood sauntered past us into the room and shook hands with the three new arrivals. They knew him and he knew them – there were no introductions. Den sat down and propped one foot on his knee. He looked relaxed but the ceaseless bouncing of the foot told a different story.

'You're the one who saved Geraint's life, aren't you?' The man with slicked-back hair was looking at me. 'What are you doing here?'

'Mr Carter's given me a job.'

'Has he?' A glance at Geraint, who was looking amused. 'Well, that's interesting. I'm Phil Boxton.'

I shook his hand, trying not to betray that I recognised the name: he owned a nationwide chain of gyms that were just short of a cult among the membership. He had started out with one boxing gym in a rough part of East London and boxing was at the heart of the business still: *Box on, Boxton* was the slogan and it appeared on everything from T-shirts to water bottles and weights. Phil Boxton had fought as a featherweight but in financial terms he was a proper heavyweight.

'What's this?' The bearded man looked interested. He had a strong Glasgow accent.

'I had a little episode last month. Fine now.' Geraint shook his head, dismissing the entire incident. 'Mark here came to the rescue.'

58

'Mark Howell.' I held out my hand and the bearded man shook it after a moment's consideration.

'Ivan.'

The penny dropped for me with a clank that was practically audible. Ivan Manners, who had made a vast fortune from mobile phones in the 1990s and currently spent a huge chunk of it on researching and developing new satellite technology. I'd never seen a picture of him but he was a big name, famous for his fabulous wealth above all.

Whatever Geraint was doing with this group of men, it involved money, and lots of it.

'Are we ready to start?' Burniford's voice was low, a growl.

'Not quite.' Geraint caught my eye. 'Go and find Bruno, would you? He's late.'

Yeah, why don't I do that. I nodded and went out, ignoring the smirk on Harry's face as I passed him and headed up the stairs. I hadn't seen Bruno yet; it was a safe bet that he was still in his family's suite of rooms. And that meant he was in the family wing, a place I hadn't dared to visit. I had express permission from Geraint to go and find him – I'd have the chance to look around properly . . .

Juliet was in the stables with Naomi and Tessa, I thought. Cassie was still in her own home with her kids, twins a year older than Tessa. I'd left Adele in the kitchen. The housekeepers were an unknown quantity, but otherwise the only person I had to worry about meeting was Bruno himself.

I turned left at the top of the stairs instead of the usual right and walked confidently down the hall into the family wing. There were windows on the right, overlooking the glass extension at the centre of the property, and the rooms were on my left. The first door hung open, revealing a palatial room with a four-poster bed hung with silk curtains. Adele's, I thought, spotting her shoes where she'd kicked them off on the thick carpet.

The room next door would be Geraint's – he liked the old-fashioned tradition of sleeping apart from his wife, I knew. Juliet had told me, most disloyally, that Adele snored. Geraint was an early riser whereas Adele liked to stay up late, drifting around the house in the small hours, her make-up smudged, her eyes vacant. I suspected she drank and knew for certain she had a major tranquilliser habit.

The third door was open too – Juliet's room, I knew without looking, because her perfume hung on the air. Clothes were heaped on chairs and the bed was unmade. The dressing table was chaos: open bottles of foundation and palettes of make-up left splayed, smudged pieces of cotton wool, spilled eyeshadow, brushes, tissues, hair ties and clips. Too much of everything, excessive like Juliet herself. I moved on quickly, counting rooms. Naomi and Bruno shared a large room at the very end of the wing. Tessa's bedroom was beyond that, and I knew it had been decorated for her at great expense, with giant stuffed animals and a hand-painted mural and bespoke furniture. Geraint doted on her, to the exclusion of everyone else, including Cassie's children. I wondered what she thought about that, and whether they ever argued about it. There were fault lines in the family that wouldn't stand up to a lot of stress. Geraint believed in the patriarchy, which was why it was Cassie's husband rather than Cassie herself who was sitting downstairs in the meeting with the multi-millionaires. Cassie might have resented her brother and his child, but did she dare to say it?

I knocked lightly on the door of Bruno and Naomi's bedroom, which was closed.

'Who is it?' Bruno yelled from somewhere inside.

'Mark,' I said.

Silence.

'Your father sent me to fetch you,' I said to the door. 'It's time for the meeting to start.'

More silence.

What did Geraint expect? Should I go in? Drag Bruno out and shove him downstairs? Returning without him wasn't an option.

The handle turned and Bruno yanked the door open. He stood and swayed, his shirt unbuttoned and his hair everywhere. His eyes were hostile and red-rimmed. His nostrils looked raw.

'What do you want?'

'Your dad sent me to find you.'

'And here you are.' He put the back of his hand to his nose and rubbed it.

'You missed a bit.'

'What?' He looked uneasy.

'You have something white on your face.'

'Shit.' He wheeled around and headed for the bathroom. I walked into the room after him, without waiting for an invitation.

'Looks more like coke to me.'

'Fuck off.' A tap swished water into the bathroom sink and I heard splashing: from the sounds of it, Bruno was dunking his entire head. 'How long have I got?'

'They're waiting for you.'

'Fuck.' He towelled his head vigorously and came to the bathroom door. 'Find me a clean shirt, would you?'

'No problem.' I went into the bedroom and found I couldn't quite look at the bed Bruno shared with his pretty, delicate wife. I flicked on the light in the walk-in wardrobe. 'Any preference?'

'There's a blue one hanging up.'

There were four blue shirts: Bruno did not believe in stinting himself. His clothes took up three quarters of the generous space in the wardrobe. Naomi's clothes were neatly folded but there weren't many of them, less than any of the other women in the family. High necks, long sleeves, low hemlines: Bruno liked her to look modest and she went along with it. Her choice – she was an adult, after all, I reminded myself. She could leave him if she didn't like it.

She *should* leave him, I found myself thinking.

I pulled a blue shirt off its hanger and my foot touched something that jangled on the floor. It was one of Tessa's toys, a soft rabbit with a bell inside it. As if Naomi had explained it to me herself, I got it: Geraint would never let Tessa go, and Naomi would never leave without her daughter, so she had no choice at all.

'Here.' I pushed the bathroom door back and handed Bruno his shirt. There was a white smear beside the sink and some powder on the floor. 'Want me to clean that up?'

'The housekeeper will do it.'

'You don't mind her knowing about it?'

He laughed. 'What's she going to do? Report me to the cops?'

'It would be awkward if she did.'

'She wouldn't dare.' He shrugged the shirt on and started buttoning it, his fingers trembling. 'You can clean up if you want but I'm not going to give you a tip or put in a good word for you.'

'I might leave it then.'

He looked up with quick interest. 'If I told you to do it, would you clean it?'

'Probably.'

'Because my dad would want you to do what I tell you.'

'Because it would be easier than saying no.' I shook my head. 'I don't think your dad cares whether I do what you want or not. He wants me to do what he tells me to do. Beyond that it's between me and you.'

'Is that right?' Bruno murmured. 'I wonder what you wouldn't do. I wonder where you'd draw the line.'

'Maybe we'll find out one day.' I said it flippantly, without any premonition that it might become an issue.

'Are you coming to the meeting?' Bruno was tucking his shirt into his trousers with rapid movements.

'I don't know.'

'Then you're not.' He ran a brush over his damp hair, eyeing himself in the mirror. 'Which is as it should be. You haven't earned the right to be there.'

'What does that mean?'

'It means Dad doesn't trust you yet.' He looked at me briefly. 'And neither do I.'

'OK.'

'You're going to have to do a lot more work to impress us if you want to make it through the door.'

I said nothing and he laughed, pleased.

'Tell you what, why don't you start by cleaning this room up? There's water everywhere, and toothpaste on the mirror, and the rest. I want it spotless when I come back.' The grin widened. 'In fact, why don't you do the whole bedroom? The housekeeper will tell you where to find the dusters and the vacuum cleaner. They might even lend you a pair of rubber gloves.'

He swung out of the bathroom, chuckling to himself, and I waited until his footsteps had faded away before I relaxed my hands from the fists they'd become. Having unsupervised access to Bruno's room was an opportunity I couldn't pass up, but it still took me a minute before I could bring myself to start cleaning up Bruno's mess.

9

It was a positive pleasure to be given the chance to drive Geraint Carter's fleet of cars, and it *was* a fleet. He had replaced the Mercedes with an identical model except that this one was silver instead of black. Not superstitious, I had thought, before I noticed that he chose to drive his Porsche when he was on his own, and one of the three Range Rovers when he was driving someone else around, while the Mercedes sat in the garage, unloved. I switched between an Aston Martin (when I was driving Adele) and one of the Range Rovers (when I was running errands or driving anyone else) and I regarded it as one of the best things about my current situation.

Today, I had the Range Rover I always used out at the front of the house, freshly washed and vacuumed, gleaming in the winter sunshine. I rested my back against the car and felt almost at ease. I was never going to relax around Carter or anyone in his family, but I was beginning to know when to step forward and when to fade into the background. Harry Dillon had a habit of catching my eye and giving me a nod when I needed to disappear, and I appreciated it. He had started to accept my presence in the house even if he didn't like me much, and I made it my business not to get in his way. Geraint was his territory and I left him to it, concentrating on looking after the women of the family.

After ten minutes of standing around waiting, with diminishing enjoyment of the sunshine and vanishing patience, I leaned in through the driver's window and hit the horn.

'Sorry, sorry, sorry.' Juliet scampered out of the house, a risky strategy when she was teetering on high, high heels. As she approached the car she stumbled and fell against me.

'Oh!'

'Careful.' I set her back on her feet, maintaining a decent distance between us.

She shot me a look through silky false eyelashes. 'Thanks.'

'A decent pair of trainers would probably be more sensible if you're going to run everywhere.'

'Sensible but boring.'

She climbed into the passenger seat and put her seatbelt on but made no effort to shut the door; that was my job. I closed it gently, went back to the driver's side and got in. 'When is your appointment?'

'Twelve, I think.'

I checked my watch and winced. 'You haven't left a lot of time, have you?'

'They'll wait. They never mind when I'm late.'

'They wouldn't dare.' I headed down the drive at what I considered to be the maximum safe speed, sending birds winging away through the trees.

She giggled. 'Look, I don't take advantage of Daddy owning the place very often.'

'Only when you want an appointment at the last minute.' I eyed her hair. 'It looks fine to me. What are you getting done?'

'Balayage.' She showed me a picture on her phone when I stopped to wait for the gate to open.

'It looks like that already.'

'Don't be silly. You'll see the difference when I come out.' She looked pleased, though, and crossed her legs, showing off approximately a mile of toned, tanned legs. 'Doesn't your girlfriend get her hair highlighted?'

'Don't have one.'

'Really? What about a boyfriend?'

'I really don't have one of those.'

She sighed. 'You're impossible. You never tell me anything about yourself.'

'What do you want to know?'

'When did you break up with your last serious, proper girlfriend?'

'A while ago.' Longer than I realised, when I counted it up. Two years? More than that?

'And why did you break up?'

'She didn't love me.'

'Seriously?'

I shrugged. 'No one's fault. I just got tired of waiting for her to feel the same way about me that I felt about her. I had to accept it was never going to happen.'

'So she broke your heart.'

'Pretty much.' I frowned into the rear-view mirror. There was a black car behind us, two vehicles back, that I was sure I'd seen before. An Audi RS3, fast-paced but unobtrusive, and it was where I would have been if I'd been following the Range Rover. There were two men in it and they were so big they were wearing the car like an overcoat.

'That's sad,' Juliet said, oblivious. 'Have you got over it?'

'Pretty much,' I said again.

'Ready to date again?'

'Maybe. If the right girl comes along.'

'Maybe she has already.'

I couldn't help laughing. There was no way I was going to encourage Juliet to flirt with me – and Opal would skin me alive if I did – but I liked her.

For once the traffic was light and I got her to the hair salon with two minutes to spare. The black Audi was still behind us but when I pulled in it slipped past, the two men staring straight ahead as if they had no interest in us. Maybe my instincts were wrong.

'I'll find somewhere to park. What time are you going to be finished?'

'No idea. Hours and hours.' She flapped a hand at me. 'I'll phone you.'

I sighed and she giggled as she slammed the door. I watched her walk to the salon, hips swaying, big sunglasses in place, every inch the princess. Once she was safely inside I left the car in the small town-centre car park and went to get a coffee. I'd already discovered there was absolutely nothing to do in the local town on some of the previous occasions I'd driven the female Carters to hair appointments, and I'd also discovered just how long a hair appointment could be. The combination of extreme boredom and constant tension was a wearing one; I wasn't sleeping all that well, despite the exercise and the long hours of waiting to work. Coffee was just about the only thing keeping me going.

It was a long three hours before my phone hummed with a text from Juliet to say that she was ready to be picked up. I was already sitting in the car. I'd learned very quickly not to keep Geraint or his family waiting. When I got to the high street, though, there was a hold-up: a van that was blocking the road while the driver had a long, leisurely argument with a man on a motorcycle.

Juliet was enough of her father's daughter to have lost patience; by the time the salon came into view, I could see she was standing outside. Her attention was on her phone and sure enough, the next second my mobile vibrated.

Where are you

Look left, I texted back.

It took her a minute to spot me. I didn't get a smile. She took her sunglasses off the top of her head and pushed them into place so they hid her eyes, then swished her hair around so it fell in waves around her face.

Hair looks nice, I sent.

A glance at her screen. The suspicion of a smile appeared on her face. She started to make her way towards me, not hurrying, and I thought about what it was like to have nothing to do and nowhere to go, every day, except shopping or the gym or a spa or the hairdressers. It seemed to me there were all kinds of prisons in the world, and some of them came in the form of luxury country houses and fathers who would give you everything you wanted in life except independence.

I wasn't consciously thinking about any threat to Juliet's safety, or to mine, but when the two men from the Audi stepped out of a side alley and flanked her I felt nothing like surprise. Some part of me had been expecting this all along. For a couple of seconds that felt like years I watched the little scene unfold in front of me: Juliet's expression changing to horror, one man holding her arm and shouting into her face, the other looming behind her, full of menace. He was looking over the top of her head to check that they weren't being watched, that no one was planning to intervene. His head swivelled slowly, working from left to right, which was lucky for me because I was the last thing he would see.

No time to think of a clever plan. I was outnumbered, quite possibly outgunned and certainly a lot less bulky than either one of the meatheads who were looming over Juliet. What I did have was the car. I swerved out of the line of traffic and around the van on the wrong side of the road. There was just enough space to get back on my side before a car sped by with a blare of the horn that I barely heard. Without hesitating I mounted the kerb and drove along the pavement for a couple of feet, until I collided with the shouting man, slamming on the brakes as he pitched out of sight under the bonnet. I undid my seatbelt and had the passenger door open the next second.

'Juliet, get in.' She turned a white face towards me, stunned, and didn't move. '*Juliet*.'

The second man was bending down, peering at his friend in shock. But shock wasn't going to distract him forever. *Come on, Juliet.* I couldn't get out of the car to put her in it; that would take another few seconds that we didn't have.

She took a step towards me at last, and another. I leaned across, stretching to the absolute limit, and managed to drag her into the car by the arm. Her movements were slow and uncoordinated: shock, I thought, and dived back across her to shut the door.

'Seatbelt.' I reversed off the pavement and slammed the car into gear, the tyres screeching as I sped away. As I put my own seatbelt back on, my attention was half on the road and half on the rear-view mirror, where the enormous man was still lying on the ground. His companion stood beside him, staring after us. I hoped the guy on the ground wasn't dead; I didn't think he was, but you never knew. The entire incident had taken seconds, so quick that no one around us had a chance to react. The traffic was still stalled, the onlookers struggling to work out what they had seen. Confusion was guaranteed with that kind of scrap, but that didn't mean I could assume they would all be bad witnesses, or that no one was filming, or that there wasn't a dashboard camera or CCTV nearby.

Juliet was shaking badly as she tried to fasten her seatbelt. Without taking my eyes off the road, I put my hand over hers and slotted the metal tongue into place.

'Just take a moment to catch your breath. You're OK now.'

She was completely silent for the next few minutes, staring out through the windscreen, unblinking. I concentrated on driving as fast as I could without actually breaking the law.

'I – those men. I thought—'

'It's all right. You're safe.' We were making good progress and there was no sign of a car pursuing us. I was roughly as worried about the police showing up as I was about the men we'd left behind. Some do-gooder could have called them. As a way of drawing attention to myself, ramming someone with a car in the centre of town was fairly effective. 'Who were they?'

'I don't know. They wanted me to g-give a m-message to my d-dad from their b-boss.' Tears were streaking her cheeks and she smudged them away impatiently. 'But they d-didn't get a chance to say what it was.'

'I did interrupt.'

'If you hadn't been there . . .'

'But I was.' Not a second too soon, the gates of Haulton Hall loomed up on the right. I turned in and waited for the security staff to notice that we were there, jabbing the button on the intercom impatiently.

'What's the rush?' Juliet asked. There was more colour in her face. 'We're almost back.'

'I want to be the other side of these gates in case someone followed us.'

The gates began to open slowly.

'But they wouldn't.'

'They might. Or the police might.'

I drove through the gates and up the drive, my eyes on the rear-view mirror to make sure no one slipped in behind us before the gates closed. When they were finally shut I gave a heartfelt sigh of relief.

The house dreamed peacefully in the afternoon sunshine, looking exactly as it had when we left, which was jarring in the circumstances.

'Here we are,' I said unnecessarily as I stopped in front of the door. Juliet was still shaking. I pressed the catch on her seatbelt to release it, then went round to open her door. She slid out of the car and straight into my arms.

'Oh, *Mark*. It was so *awful*.'

'I know. But you're safe. Everything's fine.' This time, I knew she wasn't pretending to need my support. Her whole body was trembling.

'What the hell is going on?' Geraint barrelled out of the house and down the steps, his face red. 'Mark, get off her.'

'Daddy!' Juliet peeled herself away from me, but only so she could move on to her father. She wrapped her arms around Geraint's neck and pressed her face into his shoulder. 'Daddy, some men attacked me.'

Geraint went completely stiff, like an angry dog. 'What?'

'Mark saved me.' She sniffed, leaning back so she could see his face. 'He was amazing, Daddy.'

Daddy glowered at me. 'What happened?'

'I'll tell you in a minute.' I was heading back to the driver's door. 'We need to get rid of the car.'

'What? Why?'

'I used it to ram one of the thugs who grabbed Juliet. Someone could have taken note of the number plate.'

'But you were saving me.' Juliet sniffed. 'You won't get in trouble.'

Geraint frowned. 'No. He's right. Harry?'

At the sound of his name the big man appeared in the doorway.

'We need to ditch the car. Take it round to Andy's office. Leave it there with the keys in it. I'll get him to change the plates and take it away.'

Andy was the estate manager, a mild-mannered fifty-year-old who spoke slowly and rarely. He had come with the property when Geraint bought it. He seemed thoroughly decent and I doubted he knew what his boss did for a living.

'I can do it,' I said.

'You'll be busy.' Geraint's eyes were cold. 'You have more important things to do, like explaining to me what the hell just happened to my daughter.'

10

I followed Geraint and Juliet into the house, where we ran into Cassie. Geraint tipped Juliet into her arms without ceremony.

'Take her into the kitchen and look after her, will you? Give her a drink or something.'

'What's wrong? What happened?' Juliet's older sister was taller than her and far more reserved. She held Juliet awkwardly, as if she wasn't all that keen on physical contact. Juliet clung to her like an orphaned monkey.

'Someone scared her,' I said.

'What?' Bruno steamed out of the study, his hands balled into fists. 'What happened?'

'That's what I want to find out.' Geraint nodded at the study. 'In there, Mark. Now.'

Bruno started to follow me but his father stopped him. 'Not you. I don't need you.'

'But I want to know what happened.'

'You'll find out, I'm sure. Ask Juliet.'

'I don't want to ask Juliet. I want to hear what Mark has to say for himself.'

Geraint gritted his teeth. 'Not now, Bruno. I said no. Get lost.'

Even Bruno wouldn't dare argue with Geraint when he was looking so grim. He settled for giving me a dirty look, turned on his heel and stomped away towards the kitchen. I hoped he would be nice to Juliet.

I hoped Geraint would be nice to me.

He came in and slammed the study door behind him. 'Tell me what happened.'

I told him what had happened since we left the house, including the fact that I'd noticed the two large men in the Audi on our way to the hairdressers.

'I kept an eye out for them when I was waiting for Juliet. No sign of them or the car. I'd decided I was wrong about them.'

Geraint grunted. 'But you weren't. How did they get hold of her?'

'She called me to say she was ready to be picked up. By the time I got there, she'd already come out of the salon. They were on her before she could get to the car.'

'She should know better than that.' He had been standing with his hands on his hips. Now he moved to the sofa and sat down, rubbing his hands over his face as if he was exhausted. 'I sent her on a course. One of those anti-kidnapping ones. You know the type.'

I nodded. 'They can be useful.'

'Only if you follow the rules.'

'Were you worried about her being kidnapped?'

'Why do you think I have you driving her everywhere?'

'I'm not a trained bodyguard.'

'No, you're better than that. A trained bodyguard would have got himself beaten up and she'd be gone. You're enough of a thug to do it your way.'

I had remembered an incident when I was a very new response officer and my sergeant had used our car to mow down a suspect with a knife. 'Thug' was a description that would have fitted her very well, I thought, and tried not to smile.

'You rammed him with the Range Rover,' Geraint said. 'Weren't you worried about killing him?'

'A bit.'

'You could have been arrested.'

I shrugged. 'A risk worth taking, I thought. Once the cops didn't turn up at the scene or behind us, I stopped worrying about it, to be honest with you. We need to get rid of the car – tell them you sold it at the weekend, if anyone asks. But . . .'

'But what?' His eyes were sharp.

'I don't think they'll make a complaint to the police. What are they going to say about what they were doing? "We were intimidating a young lady when her companion drove at us." That's going to cause them a lot more problems than it solves. Especially if they're working for someone who doesn't want to be bothered by the police. I was worried that one of the witnesses might call it in but if they did, it hasn't come back to us yet. And if the victim doesn't cooperate with the police, which I'd assume he won't, it'll go nowhere.'

Geraint nodded slowly. 'I don't think they'll be cooperative at all.'

'Do you know who they were? Or who sent them?'

'I have some suspicions. I have a number of competitors. People who aren't on my side, if you know what I mean. Toes I've stepped on.'

I nodded.

'Some of them are very keen to talk to me. Some of them are looking for ways to influence me.' His mouth tightened. 'Maybe I should have warned you about this.'

'I was expecting something might happen.'

His attention sharpened. 'Why is that?'

'You have full-time security guards on the estate. The fencing around the boundary is electric with barbed wire top and bottom. You have about fifty CCTV cameras around the house and grounds. Most of it is invisible, unless you know what you're looking for, so your family probably aren't even aware of the amount you're spending on keeping them safe.'

'How did you spot it?'

'I used to work for an alarm company that specialised in big properties,' I lied. 'Otherwise I might have missed it.'

'You don't miss much,' he said heavily.

'If I hadn't been there, what would have happened to Juliet today?'

'Probably nothing.'

'She said they wanted her to pass on a message.'

He managed a kind of smile. 'I've got it, all right. The message is that she's not safe and I shouldn't assume I can keep her safe. But you looked after her, didn't you? You were outnumbered and caught on the hop and you went and got her.'

'I was just doing what I knew you'd want.'

'No one cares that much about keeping a job, Mark. No one would put themselves in harm's way like that – take that kind of risk – for a job.'

I shrugged, at a loss. It was hard to explain that I would have done anything I could to stay in his inner circle, and not give myself away. 'Look, it's not about the job for me. I feel grateful to you. You gave me a chance when no one else would. You looked at me and saw someone with possibilities, not a failure. I was in a pretty big hole when I met you, I don't mind saying. I wasn't in great shape. I was desperate.'

Geraint nodded. 'I recognised it.'

'You've changed my whole life. I owe you more than the clothes on my back and the roof over my head.' I swallowed as if I was fighting down a strong emotion, stronger than the mild nausea I was feeling at my distinctly overstated praise for my master. 'You gave me some self-respect again after I lost my job. No one wanted me. I felt worthless until you came along. So if you're asking what I'd do for you, the answer is I'll do whatever you need me to do.'

'Anything?' A calculating look had come into his eyes.

I nodded. Christ, what was I getting myself into?

'Up to now,' Geraint said, choosing his words carefully, 'this has just been a trial run. I wanted to know more about you before I trusted you, Mark. I hope you understand that I have to be wary.'

'Of course.'

'The way we met – you couldn't have made that happen. It was pure chance.'

It was all that. I nodded.

'That helps. That makes me feel you're being straight with me.' He leaned forward. 'If I find out you're not, I will kill you, Mark. And no one will ever find your body.'

I blinked, as if I hadn't already been aware he was ruthless enough to make good on his words. 'I'm being straight with you, I swear it.'

'I want to take you into my confidence, Mark. Not about business. About something much more important to me than business.'

Interesting. I stood very still, waiting for him to go on.

'You saved my life and you helped my daughter. I trust you. I want you to be involved in what I'm planning. But I'm not going to lie to you; it's risky. This is your last chance. If you have any reservations, now is the time to say so and go.' He flicked his fingers. 'No hard feelings. I'll let you keep your clothes.'

And my life. I cleared my throat. 'That's very generous of you . . . but I want to stay. And I want to help with whatever I can, however I can.'

'Sit down.' Geraint motioned to the sofa opposite him and I

77

sat, obedient as a dog. 'Tell me again about how you lost your last job.'

I went through the story again, grateful that Opal had trained me in adding in enough detail to be credible but not so much that I got confused. The characters lived in my mind, so familiar that I could picture them: the pot-bellied boss who played favourites, the cousin from Pakistan who was patently terrified to offend his relatives, the way I had been let go without ceremony. I was careful not to go on for too long. Geraint was more of a talker than a listener.

When I got to the end, he stretched. 'That's what I thought. And I'm guessing, Mark, you're not a fan of all of these people coming to our country, are you? Taking English jobs from good English boys like you.'

And good luck to them, I thought. It couldn't be easy. What I said, though, was, 'I'm not exactly keen on them.'

'It bothers me how easy it is. Just an open door. Any of them can come and set up here and what do we do? Make space for them. Give them council houses and school places and free medical care so they can pop out a few more little kids who'll grow up and start looking for the same things their parents got. We're mugs. And I don't like being a mug.'

I nodded.

'The thing that really winds me up – the thing that really gets my goat, Mark – is that they're not even fucking grateful. They come here for money but they hate us. They fucking hate us and they want to obliterate us. They want to shove us aside and take over from us and turn our schools into places where they don't even speak English. They want to make our women wear veils and hide away. They hate everything we value, Mark, and I hate them for it.'

'You're right. But what can we do?'

'It's not easy to get rid of them. Not easy at all. They're like

78

that horrible knotweed – they've burrowed down into the foundations of this country and they're working on splitting it apart. But you can root it out, if you work hard enough. You can play them at their own game.'

'How? I don't follow.'

'It's about finding support from people who think the way we do, and then persuading more people to admit they feel the same way. Then you can bring in proper legislation. Politicians will change things if there's a vote in it for them. If the whole country turns against the Muslims, we can get rid of them. We can close down the mosques and the faith schools. We can turn the tide, Mark – if there's enough of us who are willing to take the risk, that is. I've got some friends who feel the same way as you and I do, and they're helping to fund our efforts.' He leaned back, pleased with himself. 'And then of course there's a dividend for us when they sell up. We're ready to buy their businesses and properties. It'll be a fire sale – they'll be desperate to go. Oh, we won't lose, when it plays out. We wave goodbye to them and take back what should be in British hands.'

I thought of the meeting I hadn't been allowed to attend – the wealthy, powerful men who had come to the house, who seemed to have nothing in common apart from their friendship with Geraint. I remembered the crowd at his sixtieth party and how every single guest had been white. I remembered Bruno picking a fight with the Sri Lankan waiter, and the singing that was too faint for me to hear, that wasn't suitable for anyone who hadn't been vetted, that now sounded more sinister than celebratory.

'But how do you persuade people to turn against them? Publicly, I mean.'

Geraint smiled. 'That's the genius part of it. We have a plan that can't fail.'

'OK,' I said warily.

'Come on.' He stood. 'I'll show you.'

11

Because I'd been playing it safe, especially given Geraint's fondness for hidden security cameras, I hadn't searched the house as thoroughly as I would have liked. There were many places I hadn't been yet, and one of them was the attic room that ran across the entire front of the house. But even if I'd wanted to venture up the last flight of stairs that led to it, I wouldn't have been able to gain access, I discovered now. Geraint had installed a proper keypad lock by the door. I stood well back, where I had a good view of the numbers, but he made a point of shielding them from me as he tapped them in.

'Sorry. Not that I don't trust you.'

'You're better off not trusting anyone completely.'

He gave me an approving look, then pushed the door open. 'Come on. What do you think of this?'

I don't know what I had been expecting to find at the top of the stairs, but a private museum was not it. The long room was filled with cases and display tables. The first thing I saw was an enormous Nazi flag, the swastika in the centre. It was framed on one wall, and took up most of it. 'Jesus. Where did you get that?'

'The internet.' Geraint smiled. 'You can get anything on the internet, you know. This flag was flown at Nuremberg. It has a certificate of authenticity.'

'Wow.' I put as much awe into my voice as I could manage. 'Is all of this stuff from World War Two?'

'No, not at all. I keep that memorabilia at this end of the room.' He pulled back a cloth and showed me a full SS uniform under glass in a display table. 'Beautiful, isn't it? Such attention to detail. I wanted to put it on a mannequin, but the dealer advised me not to. It would get dusty, he said, and the fabric would wear. If you want to preserve something like this you lay it flat in a controlled temperature environment and you protect it from moths, because they would go through it for a snack. Uniforms like this are not all that easy to come by anymore. I've got British and American ones too, but this is my favourite.'

'It's amazing.' I swallowed, trying to keep a lid on my imagination; evil seemed to seep out of the glass case that contained the uniform.

'I've tried to find out more about the officer who wore it, but the records aren't readily available to the public. You have to be a proper historical researcher.' Geraint pulled a face. 'I'll get a student to do it sometime. I'm not the kind of person who wastes their life in a library or an archive, but I want to know more about him. We're the same size.'

'Have you tried the uniform on?'

'The dealer made me promise not to.' Geraint lowered one eyelid in a grotesque wink. 'But it's mine now.'

'So you did.'

'Just once. I couldn't resist.'

'No, I can imagine.' I felt like being sick, then and there, at the idea of him play-acting as an SS officer. There had been times I had almost liked Geraint. It was probably good to remind myself what he really was.

As if he realised it was a line that shouldn't be crossed, he said, 'The thing is, Mark, I'm not a neo-Nazi, or whatever they're called now. I do respect the Nazis. I respect how they went about their business. They had this incredible machine and they used it so effectively. Nothing was left to chance. No detail was too small. If Hitler hadn't overreached himself, they would have achieved everything they set out to. He was too ambitious, too greedy. He was in too much of a hurry. If he'd taken his time, I believe he'd have established a powerful enough empire to take over the rest bit by bit. Countries would have been queueing up to join the Third Reich. But he was in a hurry.' Geraint drew the cloth over the glass case with care. 'I don't happen to mind about Jews. My accountant is Jewish. I've always got on with them. Jews are all right.'

'I'd agree with that,' I said slowly, as if I'd ever considered the alternative was worthy of consideration.

'What I do think, though, is that they should have left when Hitler gave them the nod. They weren't wanted. He gave them fair warning. The ones who stayed . . .' Geraint shrugged. 'Nothing was going to shift them, was it? And I think a country has a right to decide what kind of people it wants to live in it. If the authorities don't control immigration at the borders, you see, these people get in and start to burrow out of sight. Much harder to get them out than to stop them from coming in the first place. But as the Nazis discovered, if you make it very unpleasant for people – hostile, that's the word the politicians use these days, isn't it? – then they make different decisions about where they want to stay. They don't get such an easy ride. You're left, like the Nazis were, with the ones who can't or won't leave. Then what you do is up to you.'

'The final solution?'

'It was a bit radical, don't get me wrong. I wouldn't agree with death camps and all of that.' Geraint shook his head, disapproving.

'That's a relief,' I said, truthfully.

'Anyway, I don't think you could get away with it in this day and age. From what I've seen they're managing to do something of the sort in China, but the Chinese are big enough and scary enough to do what they like. No, you'd need to be a lot more subtle. Just make it impossible for them to survive here. Go the political route, so it's all official and above board. Recruit people at a grassroots level so that place by place, community by community, you can make it clear to the Muslims that you want them gone. Boycott their businesses. Raise their rents. Start a few little fires. Eventually they'll get the message and go off to Afghanistan or Syria or Pakistan or whatever shithole country they came from.' He sighed. 'Except they don't, do they? They get a taste for a decent life. They'll move on to another white Christian country and start trying to change it to suit themselves. They won't be happy until all the women are afraid to go out in public and we're all praying to Allah six times a day.'

He was wandering around the room, picking up his treasures and putting them down. With a flourish he showed me a table full of swords, nestling in velvet.

'That one is Tudor. This is a replica of a Viking weapon, but it was made by a master swordsman. Weighs a ton. That's a cavalry officer's sword from the British army in the Boer War.'

'Nice,' I said, and he grinned.

'Not your kind of thing? Never mind. What about these?'

He opened a cupboard that folded out like a concertina and showed me an array of classic firearms, from old muskets and rifles all the way up to a collection of handguns that would have got him a ten-year sentence any day. I looked for permission to pick one up and got a nod. I chose a Glock handgun, checking the magazine was empty before I did anything else with it. There were boxes of ammunition stacked up at the base of the cupboard, so the fact that it was empty wasn't all that reassuring. It was viable, from what I could see, and he had the means to make it lethal.

'You know your way around a pistol,' Geraint said approvingly.

'Don't tell anyone.' The weapon I was holding was illegal in the UK and had been since 1997. If I wasn't a police officer, I'd have to be a serious criminal to have any familiarity with it.

'That's a G43. It's designed to be slimline so you can conceal it easily. Single-stack magazine. You get six rounds to play with. It only weighs twenty ounces when it's fully loaded. Just over five hundred grams, you'd probably say. I still measure in imperial.'

Of course you do.

I held it as if I was going to fire it, with a two-handed grip, squinting through the sights. My reflection pointed the gun back at me from mirrors throughout the room. 'Six rounds should be enough. God, that's nice.'

'I had to bring it in from the US.' Geraint shook his head. 'The regulations here are ridiculous.'

'Do you ever get to fire these?'

'I've got an indoor range. There's a barn beyond the main paddock. I keep it locked, in case of busybodies.' He took the gun from me and slotted it back into place with care. 'Some time I'll let you pick a couple of weapons and we'll do some shooting.'

'I'd like that.' I hesitated. 'You've got quite the collection here. Are you planning a war?'

Geraint chuckled. 'Not exactly. These are just a hobby. They're not part of the grand plan.'

I felt the clawing tension release its grip on me a little. 'So what is the plan?'

'All in good time, Mark. All in good time.' He shut the door of the weapons store and locked it carefully. 'I wanted you to see all this so I could get an idea of your attitude. You weren't shocked by any of it, were you?'

'Not really.'

'No. You may not look it but you're tough.'

I looked down ruefully at my body, which was about twenty pounds heavier since I'd been working for Geraint, and all of it muscle. 'Thanks.'

He laughed at my tone of voice. 'You'll do, is what I mean. You're what I need, as I thought.'

'But I still don't know what you're going to do.'

'It's a brilliant plan. Brilliant. I don't think there's any chance we can fail.' Geraint's eyes were bright. 'The thing is, Mark, they're a violent bunch. Muslims want to burn us to the ground and they've been vocal about it. The way to defeat them is to use their own violence against them.'

'Right,' I said slowly. I still didn't know what he was implying. So far he was long on rhetoric and short on facts.

'We need to convert the fence-sitters into allies. We need to do something so extreme – so extraordinary – that there's no chance of smoothing it over. We need to make it absolutely clear that having all of these Muslim immigrants in our midst is suicide, pure and simple. We're putting our own heads on the block and asking them if the axe is sharp enough. That's got to stop.' He walked up and down, too wound up to stand still. 'It used to be you couldn't say any of this stuff. You'd get shouted down. We're using the internet now to recruit people who think the way we do, but you've got to be subtle about it. You've got to lead people away from the received wisdom. You've got to stop them from accepting what the mainstream media sells as acceptable. They're sleepwalking towards disaster.'

'What can you do that would make people wake up?'

'You lay the foundations. You give them somewhere to speak freely, somewhere safe. You create a community. Then, when the shit hits the fan, there's somewhere for them to go. That's when you lay out the plan, when they're ready to start questioning what they've always accepted. They have questions and you have answers for them. It's all about guiding them to where they can hear the truth. When you've got enough people listening and believing in what you're suggesting, you can make it happen. You just have to make it safe for them to speak up without being called racist or prejudiced rather than honest, and scared, and second-class citizens in their own fucking country.' His voice had risen, and he was breathing heavily. He touched the back of his hand to his mouth. 'Sorry. I get a bit upset.'

'I'm not surprised. Not surprised at all.' I hesitated. 'So it's a two-part thing. You've got the online recruitment. What's the incident that's going to drive them to find it?'

'Now you're asking, Mark, my friend.' He clapped his hand on my shoulder. 'You'll find out, don't worry. You're going to be playing a very important part. And it's going to be spectacular.'

12

'That was the word he used? "Spectacular"?'

I nodded. 'But he didn't give me any more details. He said I'd find out in good time.'

The woman sat back in her chair, a frown denting the skin between her eyebrows. She was thin and intense, her face devoid of make-up, her eyes small behind thick glasses. Her pale hair was scraped back from her face and secured in a long, narrow plait which gave her the air of an earnest student. She was utterly nondescript, from her drab clothes to her undyed hair, and I thought she was probably one of the cleverest people I'd ever met. We hadn't been introduced properly, so I had no idea of her name or anything else about her.

'This lady is an expert,' Opal had said, and had taken the only other chair in the small, dingy hotel room she'd chosen as our meeting place, so I had had to sit on the edge of the bed. 'Tell us everything you've found out. Don't leave anything out.'

I'd spent the previous hour running through what I knew and what I suspected. Opal listened in silence, her face grim. She hadn't wanted to meet me; it was too risky, she had protested. I'd insisted. Someone needed to know what I knew, in case the spectacular turned out to be a human sacrifice with me as the main attraction. Geraint would get a kick out of lining me up to play that part, I thought with a shiver. He wanted bloodshed and it wasn't going to be his, or anyone in his family. From Opal's point of view her neat little investigation into a highly successful criminal had suddenly turned into an anti-terrorism operation. We would be supported by the security services, she had told me, but allowed to run with it, given my position in Geraint's household. Lucky her. Lucky me.

It had taken some effort to find an excuse to leave the estate, and then I had taken a roundabout route to the small hotel that was just off a motorway, a place that was designed for single-night stays rather than holidays. The windows were sealed shut against the noise of the traffic thundering along fifty metres away, and the air conditioning wasn't working properly. It was stuffy beyond belief, and grim, and I would have given a lot to stay there in safety rather than returning to the luxury of Haulton Hall.

'The three men who came to the meeting with Carter and his son and son-in-law. They're interesting.' The woman tapped her fingers against her mouth, considering it. Her nails were trimmed and not painted. She looked so different from Juliet Carter it was as if she belonged to another species. 'Phil Boxton came up the hard way. He's got an awful lot of money by legitimate means through his gyms but that's not where he started. He has links with organised criminals across the south-east. He was almost pulled in during an investigation into gunrunning about five years ago, but they couldn't get anything on him specifically and he had the lawyers to get himself out of trouble. He has associates in prison for everything from murder to armed robbery. We know he's funded various legit-imate political campaigns going back as far as the Save the Pound campaign in the nineties and early oughts. He campaigned for Brexit and contributed approximately a quarter of a million pounds to pro-Brexit organisations. He puts his money where his mouth is.'

'What about Max Burniford? I'd never heard of him.' There was something about the big, red-faced man that made me uneasy.

'He's an old-school right-winger. He made money from carpets, would you believe, but he sold up about twenty years ago. He had a shit-hot financial adviser who managed to get him into technology in a big way – he invested in YouTube and Google long before anyone else realised it was a good idea, for instance, but he's made a fortune from the invisible side of the tech industry too, investing in the infrastructure so he's not dependent on what's popular with consumers.'

'And what does he do with all that money?'

'He's funded right-wing politicians across the UK and in Germany, Hungary and Poland – he's really committed to pushing an anti-immigration, anti-EU line. He made a few unwise statements about wanting a race war, or a race war being inevitable, and basically embarrassed some of their more plausible political candidates so he was banished to the back room. He's rich enough and unaccountable enough to do whatever he likes. He's been on a buying spree in the last two years that's been concerning to us: regional newspapers, regional radio stations and a TV channel that's devoted to news and current affairs – all with a right-wing agenda. The newspapers aren't worth much but he's developed very flashy websites to go with them, using the names so there's local brand recognition and trust. Some of the stuff on there is straight from the conspiracy theorists in the US. Facts aren't important but ideology is.' She frowned again, considering it. 'The other thing that worries me is that he funds quite a few online discussion sites.'

'This is what Geraint was talking about, isn't it? Providing safe spaces to say and hear the unthinkable.'

'Exactly. It's a tried and tested way of shifting public opinion. If you think everyone else thinks the same as you, you're more likely to be open about your feelings, when you vote if nowhere else. Sadly, there are quite a lot of racist people out there. And there are more people who are just disappointed in their lives and wish things were different. They're sitting ducks. You sell them a dream where all the money stops draining away from them and starts filling their pockets instead. It's impossible to counter a dream with reality. The truth doesn't seem like a very appealing alternative to being told your problems aren't your fault.'

'So we've got a crime connection through Carter and Boxton, and the media controlled by Burniford. What about Ivan Manners?' Opal said. 'What's his role?'

The expert's mouth twisted. 'I have to admit, he wasn't on our radar before now. I knew of him, of course. For someone so wealthy he's extremely low profile.'

'I didn't recognise him when I met him,' I said.

'I don't think I'd know him if he walked in now,' the expert said meditatively. 'But I'm interested. He fits the profile – he's wealthy, he's bored, he's white, he's middle-aged. The country has changed a lot since he was young. People don't like change. People with money think they can control their world. If they don't like something, they aren't prepared to tolerate it.'

'What Ivan Manners does have is access to technology.' I was putting it all together, but slowly. 'If you wanted to be able to organise the technical side of . . . let's say a bomb, for argument's sake, you could do a lot worse than bring in a billionaire with his own staff who are trained to be secretive and who were recruited to solve problems with complicated mechanisms. Even if they weren't in agreement with Manners

90

and Carter and the rest of them, they could still be strong-armed into doing the work. They needn't be told what it's for. Someone like Manners owns his staff. He pays them well enough that they can't take the risk of losing their jobs. It's wiser to turn a blind eye.'

'And then you have back-up from a small-scale media tycoon for your grassroots recruitment,' Opal said.

'And someone who is deeply involved in organised crime to handle acquiring the illegal components you might need.'

'With Geraint Carter at the heart of it all to come up with the plan and bring the three of them together.' The fair-haired woman smiled thinly. 'Without him, they would never have found each other.'

'I think Carter is planning to take an active role in executing whatever it is they're planning,' I said. 'I get the impression that he's agreed to provide the muscle.'

'Not Phil Boxton?'

'They're going to want people who are completely loyal, aren't they? Carter doesn't really trust anyone except his own family.'

'And you,' Opal said slyly.

'So far.' I was thinking about it. 'When he asked me to work for him it was specifically to stop his son-in-law, Den, and his son Bruno from fighting. They were both in the meeting with Boxton, Manners and Burniford. There's no real reason for them to be involved unless they're part of the plot. Bruno is a massive liability, though. He's a cokehead and he has serious anger issues. What I think is that Geraint is petrified one or other of them will let him down. Den can't manage Bruno at all.'

'And you can?' The thin-lipped smile again from the expert: politely dubious was the nicest way I could describe her.

'I've been lucky so far. He's backed down every time, or I haven't needed to make it into an argument so it wasn't an issue. But I think Geraint sees me as his insurance policy. I'm supposed to make sure whatever they're planning goes without a hitch.'

'You think it's a bomb?' As a rule, Opal didn't do panic, but the way she was chewing her bottom lip was the equivalent of another person's screaming hysterics.

'It would fit. They want something huge, something head-line-grabbing – something that everyone is afraid of. They'll have looked at the spike in anti-Muslim sentiment after the 7/7 attacks.' The expert's eyes were wide. 'It all hangs together.'

'But we can't stop it unless we know the details,' Opal said. 'This is all conjecture. We don't know where, when or what they're planning. We've got no evidence. If we can't get a handle on the plan in time, you're going to have to try to head it off on your own.'

I shrugged. 'All I have to do is stop it without them suspecting anything. Not a problem.'

'Do you know anything about bombs, Rob?' she asked, eyebrows high.

'Not a thing.'

'I'll see if I can find someone to give you a crash course.'

'There might not be time,' I said soberly. 'From the way Geraint was talking, it's going to kick off any day now.'

The expert had melted away to her own room, where she was staying for two nights. Opal only had to endure another couple of hours after I left before she could flee to London. It was all about blurring the outlines of what was happening, she had explained to me. Never go directly from one place to another. Never arrive at or leave a meeting at the same time as the people you're meeting. Never look as if you're in the same place at the same time for the same purpose. If the people you're meeting are dressed casually, you wear a suit.

You separated yourself from what you'd been doing in distance and time, and in other people's perception of you, and unless the people watching you were very good, you tended to get away with it.

The trouble was, I had no idea how good Geraint and his crew were.

'Give me your phone,' Opal said, holding out her hand. 'I don't want you taking it back to them in case they trace me through it.'

'Unlikely.' I gave it to her anyway.

'Not impossible. Ivan Manners has access to a lot of technically knowledgeable people. Do you really think they couldn't crack our security?'

'I suppose I don't.' I felt uneasy, though, to be handing over the only way I had to contact her. 'Was it worth taking the risk of having this meeting?'

'Definitely. But make sure you have a cover story in case someone saw you.' She smirked. 'You're not going to want to suggest we're sleeping together, are you.'

'Only because they're horrible racists and I'm supposed to be one too,' I said gallantly. 'Otherwise it would be an honour and a privilege.'

'Oh, gimme a break.' Opal threw a pillow at me. 'What's the real story?'

'What I thought was that you owed me money.'

'Nice.' She went to her handbag. 'You'd better have some. How much?'

'A couple of hundred.'

'Whew. For what?'

'Services rendered.' I took the notes she was holding out to me. 'Gardening, I thought. Some sort of manual labour.'

'I wish you would come and mow the lawn. Derek never does it.' Derek was her husband, a large and friendly Ghanaian.

'When all this is over, I will.'

'I'll hold you to that.' She nodded at the cash. 'For two hundred quid you're going to need to do it for the whole summer. I'm going to want my money's worth.'

13

I'd thought I didn't have much time before Geraint put his plan into action, but I'd expected to have longer than a couple of days. It was a Wednesday evening, the weather damp and drizzly. I'd been in the gym, and I was heading upstairs with nothing more taxing on my mind than a shower when Geraint called my name from the study.

I went to the door and discovered that Bruno and Den were there already, with Harry brooding massively in the corner. 'What's up?'

'Come in. Shut the door.' Geraint was sitting at his desk which was unusual, and even more unusually he was fidgeting with the things in front of him. He looked excited and nervous, and I tried to hide the sinking feeling I had as I turned to close the door behind me. 'Sit down, Mark.'

Den shifted to one end of his sofa, making room for me. Bruno glowered at me, as he tended to. Did he think that sitting on the same piece of furniture as Den meant that I was taking his side? Was it possible for even Bruno to be so pig-headed? Probably, I concluded, and focused my attention on Geraint.

'I've been talking to Mark about our plans, boys. I've decided that I want him to be involved.'

Den nodded slowly. Bruno's knuckles flared white briefly as he clenched his fists.

'You've got to be very sure you can trust him, Dad.'

'I do. I've looked into him. Everything checks out. He's trustworthy.'

I nodded my thanks at Geraint, thinking of Opal and her absolute attention to detail. She'd promised me my background story would hold up. My life depended on it.

'Mark thinks the way we do. He's just as determined as we are to see some changes in this country. He's got fast reactions and he's a problem-solver. He's exactly who we need as the last member of the team.'

I wondered if he was trying to persuade them or himself. I was aware of Harry's scrutiny from the corner of the room, and I tried to make sure my expression was conveying nothing more than enthusiasm, determination and a little bit of puzzlement. The last part was no effort. What the hell were they planning?

'Mark, I've told you the basic principle of our plan – that we need to shake people out of their complacency with some-thing big. Before we do that, we've got a little bit of work to do. We're going to do it ourselves, because I don't want to bring too many people in at this stage. Operational security is key.'

'OK.' I was relieved at the implication that we weren't yet at the point where the 'spectacular' was going to take place. His next words made me reassess how comforting that was.

'What we're going to do – or what you're going to do, to be more accurate – is in the nature of a trial run. We need to prove ourselves to the people who are putting their money and expertise into our plans. We need to show that the plan works on a small scale before we go for the big one.'

He was talking about Boxton, Manners and Burniford, I thought, and nodded instead of saying anything that might reveal I'd thought about the three of them at all.

'It's all part of the strategy too. Raising people's fear levels.' He angled his hand like a plane taking off, sending it up towards the ceiling. 'Making them anticipate trouble. Then when trouble comes, they're already in the right frame of mind to act on it.'

'It's psychological war,' Bruno said. 'Call this a warning shot.'

'So what are we going to do?' I asked.

'We're going to trick people into thinking their lives are in danger. A prank, nothing more than that. Harmless.' Geraint was leaning back in his chair, drawling his words. It was a giveaway that he was lying, I thought with a prickle of unease.

'What sort of prank?'

'We're going to set off some small explosive devices on the Underground.' Den sounded completely reasonable. 'They're smoke grenades. Completely non-toxic. Not dangerous. They're sold for films, theatrical productions, displays – you can get them in all kinds of colours. They give off smoke for about thirty seconds. They're legal.'

'Not the way you're planning to use them,' I pointed out. Smoke grenades on the Underground . . . 'That's going to cause pure panic, isn't it?'

'That's the idea. That's exactly it.' Geraint rubbed his hands together. 'The idea is that you, Den and Bruno take them into London. You set them off. Then we let the public take charge from there. They'll assume that it's a bomb, of course, or a fire.'

'There'll be mayhem.'

'Exactly.' He leaned forward, lacing his fingers. 'You aren't shocked, are you? Not having second thoughts?'

I tried to force my face into a smile. It felt stiff and awkward. 'No, of course not. I'm excited. I think it's a brilliant idea.'

'Good. What we're thinking, you see, is that it's relatively low risk. If one of you gets stopped by the police, you can explain you're transporting the grenades to a photoshoot.'

'I have actually arranged one,' Den said with a grin. 'Booked a photographer and a model and everything. Nothing like being thorough.'

'That's the way,' Geraint said approvingly. 'You'll all have the address. It should be a good enough cover story. It shouldn't arouse any suspicions if one of you does get stopped so we won't put the rest of the plan in jeopardy.'

'Good,' I managed. 'Great. But what if we're seen detonating the grenades?'

'They're easy enough to hide. The train will be crowded. You'll have a prearranged time to set off your grenades, in a station, then you hang back. Let the other passengers get off the train before you follow. I expect there'll be a certain amount of chaos. You'll want to lose yourselves in the crowd. And don't try to meet up afterwards. You need to distance yourselves from each other so no one connects the three of you. Obviously if questions are asked you can say you were travelling together and got separated – that does happen at busy times.'

'So you're planning to do this at rush hour.'

'Of course. No better time.'

'No.' My throat was dry. I had to find some way of warning British Transport Police so they knew what to expect. A rush-hour train crammed with people, pulling into a station with a full platform of waiting passengers, and more moving through the tunnels behind them . . . the panic would be a killer on its own. And Geraint would know that. I hoped I was keeping my thoughts off my face. Geraint would know that this was a plan for murder. Shedding blood was not a problem, as far as he was concerned. He needed to impress his major-league collaborators. Rich though he was, he was a minnow compared to the sharks he was swimming with. He needed to prove himself. A mild scare, a couple of small injuries – that would prove nothing. He had promised them deaths, front-page headlines, a terrorised public who would be ready and willing to lash out at whoever got the blame. And Max Burniford would be behind the scenes, orchestrating the media response to it, shifting the public mood with dog-whistle racism. Maybe even overt racism, if enough innocent people died. Maybe it would be enough on its own to turn the tide of public opinion for a week or a month or longer.

Maybe it would be the small shock that started an avalanche.

'How many of us are involved?'

'Directly? You, Den and Bruno. You and Bruno will be together – you have one grenade and Den has the other. Den will be at the other end of the train. You'll set off your grenades at the same time. That will confuse people even more.'

'I don't need a babysitter.' Bruno's voice was harsh. His father ignored him.

'Harry will drive you into London. As I said, you'll be finding your own way back. Take your time. Den, make sure everyone has the address for the photoshoot, just in case, but there's no need to go to it unless you're worried about being followed by the police.'

'They won't be following us,' I said. 'They'll be struggling to control the crowds first and foremost, and then dealing with any injuries. If we don't get arrested immediately, we should be absolutely fine.'

'So don't get arrested.' Geraint smiled at me to take the sting out of it.

'If we do,' I said slowly, 'are you going to sort out a solicitor for us?'

'No. If you get arrested, you're on your own.'

'Does the same go for all of us?' Bruno's voice came out as a squeak.

'I'm not getting involved.' Geraint held up his hands. 'We can't take the risk. If I get implicated in all of this and they start looking more closely at what we're doing, we might not be able to do the main event. That requires a lot more in the way of planning and hazard. We've got to acquire the materials. There's a risk in that anyway. If the authorities are looking at me already, it'll be impossible. You've got to sort it out for yourselves if you get arrested. Don't do anything stupid like writing down your solicitor's details. Memorise a name if you want to, but don't make it look as if you were expecting trouble.'

Bruno grunted, obviously unhappy.

'When is this happening?' I asked, my mind racing. I would have to come up with some reason to leave the estate and contact Opal. She could warn the Met and BTP that we were on our way, and for what purpose.

'No time like the present.' Geraint smiled at the expression on my face. 'Eight o'clock tomorrow morning sounds like a good time, doesn't it?'

'But that's fourteen hours from now.'

'Exactly. No big build-up. No time to get nervous.'

'I'm nervous already,' I said, and Den laughed.

'You're not the only one, believe me. I think we should get it over with. Rip the plaster off.'

'You're going to be leaving early tomorrow morning. Three o'clock, we thought, didn't we, Harry? You want to have plenty of time to get into position. No one needs to be stuck in rush-hour traffic.'

'Be ready to go at three on the dot.' Harry came out of his corner, moving like an old bulldog, all bandy legs and broad-chested swagger. 'I'll have everything you need.'

The other two nodded and I found myself standing up at the same time as them, dismissed.

'Get some dinner. Then go to bed. Take it easy,' Geraint ordered. 'Don't start drinking to take your mind off it.'

I started towards the door with the others. Three o'clock in the morning. That didn't leave much time but maybe—

'Mark, hold on. I want a word with you.'

Shit. I stopped and let the others file out. Harry gave me an unreadable look as he passed me. Geraint waited until the door was closed behind him.

'Do you recognise these two?' He handed me a newspaper, folded over. Two balding, bull-necked men glared out at me from what were obviously mugshots. Their names were printed underneath: Angelo de Luca, aged 28, and John Bianchi, aged 31.

'They're the ones who tried to bother Juliet the other day.'

'Good.'

I flipped the newspaper so I could see the article's headline. TWO MEN DIE IN READING HOUSE FIRE. 'They're dead?'

'Unfortunate,' Geraint said smoothly. 'Live by the sword, and so on and so forth.'

'You did it?'

'Now, now, Mark. Obviously not. Obviously, it's just a coincidence.' He lowered one eyelid in what might have been a wink.

'You weren't even sure it was them.'

'Well, quite. I wasn't sure. But someone took care of them, so I don't need to worry, do I? And neither do you. They won't be making any complaints about the incident the other day.'

'No, I suppose not.' I put the newspaper down on his desk, numb with shock.

'Stay out of Juliet's way this evening. Get something to eat and then go back to your room. You need to concentrate on what you're doing. I don't want you heading off on some wild goose chase for her.'

'OK.'

'You'll do all right tomorrow. Strictly between us, I'm counting on you to make sure Bruno doesn't fuck it up.'

'Great.' I said it with perhaps a little too much feeling and Geraint glared.

'If you're not happy to—'

'No, I am. Of course I am.'

'I know he's not easy to manage.' Geraint turned away. 'Maybe you think it would be wiser not to involve him, but I want to give him the chance to prove himself.'

To his father or to the conspirators, I wondered.

'This job,' Geraint went on, 'he's got some real responsibility. It's down to him to make it work. All this time I've been protecting him when I should just have let him be a man. He'll be taking over from me one of these days. The heart trouble made me think about the future.' He tapped his chest. 'I'm not going to go on forever. Time for Bruno to show what he's made of.'

But you don't trust him enough to send him on his own. That said it all, even if Geraint couldn't admit it to himself.

I made myself smile. 'He won't let you down. And neither will I.'

14

We were all silent on the journey to London, by choice. Harry had flatly refused to put the radio on when Bruno asked him to, so Bruno subsided into a deep sulk. In the back seat, Den was dozing beside me, his head tipped back. His Adam's apple bobbed now and then: he was having bad dreams, it seemed, given his occasional convulsive movements and the flicker of expressions passing across his features. I knew Den was nervous and I also knew he would go through fire to prove himself to his father-in-law. If Bruno let Geraint down, Den was poised to take over as his heir.

Geraint had been standing in the hall when I came down-stairs, ready to wave us off.

'Did you sleep?'

'A bit,' I said. The stale alcohol on Geraint's breath told me that he hadn't gone to bed. He was shifting his weight from foot to foot, too excited to stand still.

'I wish I was coming with you. I wish I could be there.'

'You can watch it on the news.' I knew it would be tele-vised. Imagining the footage made me feel sick. CCTV from the train and the station platform; phone-filmed video from the passengers trying to record what they were seeing – the entire event would be played and replayed over the next few days, complete with whatever part I managed to play in it. A face in the crowd, more than likely, insignificant and unidentified. Not a villain, but probably not a hero either. I couldn't expect to be a hero, in the circumstances, when it was my first responsibility to survive.

You have other priorities, I reminded myself.

Geraint had a very different idea of what those priorities should be. 'You're there to back up Bruno.' He glanced out through the front door to make sure his son was safely shut away in the passenger seat of Harry's car, out of earshot. 'He's the one with the smoke grenade, not you. If he can't set it off, it's your job to detonate it.'

'I'll do my best.'

Geraint's eyes were steady on mine. They were threaded with red veins and puffy underneath. He looked like a man who had been in hospital recently, which was far more truthful than the healthy and vital image he'd been projecting ever since. 'I will hold you responsible if he fails, or gets hurt, or if he's arrested.'

'I'll look after him.' I tried to sound both confident and calm. I didn't want Geraint keeling over with another heart attack – not until we'd got enough on his powerful accomplices to put them behind bars.

'He can't know that I've asked you to mind him.' That terrible, tearing anxiety in Geraint's voice. He really minded Bruno being useless, I thought with a twinge of something like pity.

'Of course not.'

'He wants to do it on his own.' Geraint's face was touched with tenderness for a moment. Then it changed. He glowered up the stairs. 'What do you want?'

104

'Where is Bruno going?' Naomi's voice shook as she asked the question. Her face was white, her eyes hollow. She was still lovely, but with her hair tied back and without make-up it was easy to see how gaunt she had become.

'None of your business,' Geraint snapped.

'Is it dangerous?' She came down a step, trembling so much that the hem of her dressing gown was vibrating. 'Did you say he might get arrested?'

'No. You misheard.' Geraint's face was rigid with anger, as if it was carved out of granite. 'Go back to bed.'

'He didn't say goodbye.' Her eyes brimmed with unshed tears.

'He'll be back before you know it,' I said, with a kind of false heartiness I detested. 'Don't worry, Naomi. We'll look after him.'

'Go on. Go.' Geraint folded his arms and stared at her until she retreated back into the shadows at the top of the stairs. I thought she was probably still standing there, out of sight, straining to hear anything else that might tell her if her husband was likely to come home or not.

What I mainly wondered was whether she was hoping he'd be back, or if she was praying he wouldn't return.

In the car, I thought about whether I could have got word to Opal about the plan. I'd decided it was impossible – far too risky, even if I could think of a way to get off the estate, which I couldn't – but as the miles disappeared under the Range Rover's wheels and London edged closer, I started to worry that I'd done the wrong thing. I'd put my own safety and the investigation's security ahead of the public's welfare. I was under no illusions about what would happen if we detonated the grenades underground. The smoke would dissipate, but not until people had fled in panic. In major disasters like fires, it

105

was often the panic that killed more than the smoke or the flames. I had seen too many pictures of bodies piled high in narrow doorways.

Tell someone. Warn someone. Find a way to disable the grenades. The options spun uselessly in my head.

I cleared my throat. 'Are we stopping anywhere along the way?'

'No.' A complete answer, Harry-style.

'Not even for a piss?' Bruno glanced round at me. I could see far too much of the whites of his eyes. He was sweating, and he was clearly in the grip of extreme tension. Any decent copper would wonder what was wrong with him, if they saw him like that.

'Harry, we need to stop.' My voice was urgent. 'We need to get our heads right before we go on the Underground.'

'No.'

'People will notice if we don't look like other commuters. We all need to know exactly what we're doing today, and we need to be in the right frame of mind. It's still early. We can stop and have a cup of tea and go through the plan properly. It will take what – twenty minutes? You can spare twenty minutes. There are services coming up, look.' And I could slide away to a telephone, I thought, or even buy a pay-as-you-go SIM card and a cheap phone, to make contact with the authorities. I wished I'd used the phone I carried, which Geraint had given me, even though I guessed everything I did with it was monitored. Not safe to use, not protocol. Better than the alternative. I should have done it earlier if I'd wanted to, but I had hesitated, fatally.

Harry shook his head. 'I've got my orders. They don't include stopping.'

'I really need a piss.' Bruno was practically squirming in his seat. 'Come on. There won't be anywhere to go when we get into London.'

106

The sign for the services flashed up again: half a mile to go. A quarter of a mile. A hundred yards.

Harry cursed under his breath and indicated for the exit. 'Just a piss, though. We're not stopping for longer than that.'

I sat back in my seat, trying to hide the relief that was making me feel weak. Services. If I slipped away, would any of them notice? Even at this time of the morning the place was busy with commercial vehicles. There would be people, noise – distractions. It was a chance.

Harry cruised through the car park, passing empty spaces.

'That one's close to the door,' I said. 'On the left.'

'Not going in.' He kept driving until we reached the back of the car park, well away from the buildings, where he stopped. The engine was still running. 'There you go. Trees. Nature's solution to needing a piss.'

'This is where people exercise their dogs,' Bruno said with disgust.

'Same difference. They piss here, you can piss here. Now get on with it. You've got two minutes until I drive off.'

Fuck, fuck, fuck.

I got out and followed Bruno into the trees, acutely aware that Harry was watching from the driver's seat of the car and that he'd see me sending a message. Den got out, stretching and yawning, and came stumbling towards us.

'I thought we weren't stopping.'

I ignored him, too angry to speak. The main building glowed against the darkness like a spaceship. It was just as inaccessible as if it had been orbiting a distant star.

And after that, there was nothing I could do but sit in the back seat and wait for Harry to park the car. He would send us on our way, like little robots doing Geraint's bidding, without a thought in our heads except the task that lay ahead of us.

*

107

Hounslow doesn't make it into many guidebooks to London but it was Hounslow where Harry stopped, near the entrance to the Underground station.

'Right. You're getting the Piccadilly line. It's always busy, even this early in the morning,' Harry said, accurately. The station was a couple of stops away from Heathrow and the line hummed with confused, weary travellers at all times of the day and night. 'We're going to wait until rush hour when the maximum number of passengers are using the Underground. You want to be on the 07.26 to Arnos Grove. That will get you to Piccadilly Circus at 08.04. You'll change to the Bakerloo line heading north. As it comes into Oxford Circus, which is the next station, you will detonate your grenades. Wait until the train is alongside the platform, but do it before the doors open. We're not giving you a specific time in case of delays, but you need to be on the same train, the three of you, and you need to trigger them at the same moment. Mark and Bruno are at the front of the train and Den, you're at the back. When the doors open the platform will fill with smoke from the carriages. The passengers should run into the people waiting to board the train. It's a busy station.'

'Isn't there an interchange at Oxford Circus?' I said. 'The platforms for the Bakerloo line and Victoria line are side by side.'

Harry's craggy face split into a smile. 'That's why we picked that particular station. Two sets of passengers waiting, two sets of passengers in transit. The smoke will cross to the Victoria line platform very quickly.'

I nodded enthusiastically, and felt sick. This was getting worse and worse the more I thought about it. You could fit over a thousand passengers on a rush-hour tube train. Add in two crowded platforms and the possibility of another train on the other line and you quickly reached a volume of people that was unmanageable if just about anything went wrong.

'Tickets?' Bruno said.

'No. You can tap in with your bank cards.'

'They'll know we were on the train,' Bruno objected.

'Yes. You're not trying to hide anything. You're all going to the photoshoot for—' Harry broke off and looked at Den expectantly.

'Oh – they're promotional shots for the hair salons. The studio is in Edgware Road.' Den took out his phone and fiddled with it. 'I'm sending you the address now.'

'You don't want to look as if you're trying to hide, you see,' Harry explained to Bruno, slowly, as to a child. 'They will track you down if you seem suspicious. You came to London for the day and left the car here instead of going in and paying the congestion charge.'

'How do we end up at different bits of the train?' I asked.

'Den gets held up. He can't find his bank card or he spills his coffee. Something. Anything.'

Den nodded.

'He just makes the train by the skin of his teeth, but at the wrong end. You're planning to meet up at Edgware Road.'

'All right,' I said. 'And we have two grenades.'

'One for Bruno, one for Den.' Harry passed them to the two men in brown paper bags with handles, the kind used in sandwich shops for substantial take-aways. 'Also includes a breakfast croissant for each of you. No, don't eat it now.'

Bruno let his slide back into the bag. 'Why not?'

'It's your reason for carrying a bag, if the cops spot you on CCTV afterwards and ask what you had in there. You can get a coffee on your way to the station. No one will think anything of it.'

'It's too heavy,' Bruno protested.

'Then don't let anyone else carry it. Make it look as if it's light.' Harry turned to me. 'Look at the grenade, Mark.

Familiarise yourself with the mechanism. The others have tried it out a few times back at the estate.'

'It's like a fire extinguisher,' I discovered. 'Pull out the tab and push the lever down.'

'That's right. You don't have to hold it down either, once it's triggered, not that you would want to hold it. The canister will get hot. Stick it on the floor but don't make it obvious. And take it out of the bag, in case they work out what it was contained in. Hide it behind a newspaper. You can pick up a free one at the station. Remember, they will be looking at the CCTV footage from the carriages when they're trying to work out what happened, but the train will be crowded. If you don't look as if you're doing something dodgy, they'll find it hard to pick you out. Act casual, then shocked.' Harry looked around at the three of us. 'Hang back a bit, won't you? Don't get caught up in the crush. The last thing we want is for any of you to get hurt.'

'We won't.' Bruno sounded supremely confident. 'Should we go?'

'Not yet.' Harry checked his watch. 'Soon. You can go in a bit early and get your coffee.'

Silence fell again. I watched the clock tick forward inexorably, as the street became busier and busier. I knew that I would be getting on the train with them, as instructed, and putting ordinary members of the public in danger.

There was no way out.

15

I will say this for Harry: his timings were spot on. We queued together for coffee at a small shop near the station, then headed into the station itself, not hurrying, chatting among ourselves as if it was an ordinary day and we were ordinary people. I tapped my card and passed through the barrier, listening for the beep behind me that was Bruno following on my heels. On cue we turned to laugh at Den, who was juggling his bag and his coffee cup while patting his pockets. The stream of commuters parted to flow around him incuriously, giving him a wider berth when he found the card and simultaneously spilled the coffee.

'Catch up with us, all right?' I said, when I judged that enough time had passed for us to be able to move on.

Den nodded and waved.

On to the train, finding our way down the platform together. Standing back to let the first train go – 'too crowded,' Bruno said to me, and I nodded, although it wasn't really too busy. The second train was the one we needed. I looked back down the platform and saw Den's lanky frame moving forward. It helped that he was taller than most of the other passengers, though I remembered not to say that to Bruno; at least some of his loathing for Den was because the other man had a considerable height advantage. We boarded at the same time and found seats opposite one another, which suited me fine, because the idea of making conversation with Bruno all the way into London was not appealing.

The train inched through the suburban stations, though I was so focused on what we were doing that I only noticed about half of them – Osterley and Boston Manor in zone four, Acton Town and Chiswick Park in zone three, then Hammersmith and Earl's Court in zone two . . . all too soon we were in zone one. The weight of passengers had increased with every stop, people crowding on to the train, filling all of the standing room in the carriages. It was a struggle for the passengers to get off at each station now. I gave up my seat to an older man with a stick and moved to be closer to the door so that I was in position to get off at Piccadilly Circus. As I pushed through the crowd I caught a glimpse of Bruno, who was still seated, his arms folded, his eyes fixed on the map above the door that listed each station.

The change at Piccadilly Circus was seamless. I had done it thousands of times; I could do it without even thinking. Bruno followed me, obedient as a dog for once. He wasn't used to the Underground, he had mentioned to me, and he didn't have the same instinct as me for shortcuts or those opportunities to save a second here and there that came naturally to Londoners; I had to slow down so he could stay close to me. London's commuters yawned and ate and stared into space around us, moving through the station in their own world. Many had headphones on: all were intent on where they were going rather than where they were at that moment. This was a journey most of them made all the time and therefore it didn't require any thought – a journey that was instantly forgotten as they rose to the upper air of central London and a day at work.

They would not forget this journey, I thought, and neither would I.

We arrived on the platform for the Bakerloo line train heading north. It was busy, as Harry had expected, and I made Bruno wait while I checked that Den had made it too. Two trains passed by before I saw his balding head in the distance. He had found a different route to the platform so he didn't have to walk past us for no reason. I caught his eye over the heads of the commuters who filled the platform, and we moved away from the wall, getting into position to board the next train.

When it arrived, it was crowded but not unduly so. A handful of passengers alighted, the rest of us standing back with barely concealed impatience before flooding on. I looked around, casually, assessing the other passengers. Most of them were young, or on their way to work, in suits. There were students – four of them, clustered together, talking animatedly in German. It was too early for tourists, at least, but a gap on the other side of the carriage made me frown, and crane to see: a woman with a buggy, the child in it a dark-haired toddler who was angelic, huge-eyed. My stomach knotted even further. I opened my mouth to shout the warning that was pushing against the inside of my skull, and the doors slid closed.

Piccadilly Circus to Oxford Circus – a short hop, one stop. It felt endless. Bruno dropped his hand into his bag and took out the canister, invisible in the thicket of upraised arms from the commuters around us. I turned my back to him, scanning the carriage, trying to decide what to do. The seconds wound down.

'The next station is . . . Oxford Circus,' the automated announcement cooed. 'Please mind the gap between the train and the station platform. Mind the gap.'

The darkness of the tunnel slid past the windows, and then

light: the platform slipping by, crowded with people who were pressed together, jostling to reach the train.

Bruno was sweating. He was staring down at his hands, his whole body trembling.

Maybe he wouldn't be able to do it. Maybe—

The driver braked, and we swayed forward, then back, obedient to the forces of gravity. The doors were on the point of opening. It was now; he would never . . .

Bruno moved his arm with a single, convulsive jerk, then threw the canister at knee-level so it landed as far away from him as possible. It clattered into the middle of the carriage. There was a second of stillness before a cloud of greyish white smoke began to billow out of it. The smoke and the panic swelled at the same time, and I moved, elbowing past the passengers who were forcing their way to the door so I could grab hold of the buggy, standing over the child to keep her safe as the people around her scrambled for safety.

'It's all right. It's all right. It's not a bomb,' I said urgently to the mother. 'Just wait until the others get off. The smoke will blow away. It won't harm you.'

I had no idea if she could hear me. Her attention was on her child, anyway, as the smoke filled the air and the three of us started to cough. I stepped back as she bent to undo the straps and lift the little girl out of her buggy, and almost lost them both in the smoke. Seconds had passed and yet the entire carriage was now clouded, so much so that I couldn't see the door. I shut my eyes for a moment and thought about how many paces I had taken, and in which direction.

'Come on.' I took the woman's arm and she stumbled beside me, tripping over abandoned bags and coats and even a couple of shoes. The doorway loomed up out of the mist and I peered out of it, on to chaos. A dark sea of people surged along the narrow platform, reacting to their panic rather than any actual guidance. I looked in vain for a member of Underground staff, or better yet British Transport Police. The air was full of screaming and the station's evacuation alarm, so loud that it was hard to think.

But what I mainly thought was that the conspirators had made a mistake. The platform they had chosen for their chaos had many, many exits, some to the network of tunnels that moved passengers around the station and some a straightforward ten-step walk to the other platform where the Victoria line passed through Oxford Circus. There were platforms in smaller stations where there was one entrance and one exit and a whole lot of blank tiled wall between them, with nowhere for people to go. Here, they could have been flooding away from the train and the smoke that was already beginning to clear.

I hopped back up onto the edge of the train carriage, to get a better view of the platform and the milling passengers. What I saw chilled me to the bone.

Of course they had decided not to take any chances with us. Of course they had hedged their bets. Geraint wanted us to be the ones who triggered the smoke grenades, to prove to his conspirators that he was absolutely committed to his plan – to the point that he would risk his own son and son-in-law, but we were not alone. In addition to the three of us there were at least five men, all white with short hair and heavy muscle, all tough-looking, spaced out along the platform. They stood close to the exits that led to the Victoria line, and they were steering passengers away from them, and safety, towards the exit at my end of the platform, which happened to be a flight of stairs.

Bethnal Green.

The two words came into my head along with a host of unwelcome images: a wartime panic, a crowd of people rushing into the station for fear of attacking German bombers, a woman and child falling on the stairs and causing an obstruction that turned into a fatal crush. A hundred and seventy-three people died in the narrow stairwell, mere feet from safety.

There was nothing to stop it from happening again here.

I had no time to contemplate the evil genius of Geraint's plan.

'Stay here,' I shouted to the woman with the toddler. 'Stay on the train. The smoke is clearing. You're safest here.'

She nodded at me, her eyes wide, the child pressed into her body as if they were one entity. I hoped she would do what I said; anyone could see that the platform was unsafe.

The smoke at either end of the train had made the passengers bunch together in the middle of the platform, so that my end was relatively clear – it was probably less than a minute since we'd triggered the grenades, though time was meaningless, as so often in a crisis. I jumped down and ran across to the entrance to the stairwell in what remained clear space. People were starting to head that way, in ones and twos, stumbling and choking. I let a few go past and then pulled my phone out of my pocket. I held it in the two-handed grip familiar to everyone who had ever watched an American police drama, in a way that said *gun*, and I pointed it straight at the people who were spilling towards me.

'GET BACK. GO TO THE OTHER PLATFORM OR GET BACK ON THE TRAIN. DO NOT COME THIS WAY.'

Impossible to know if they heard me, but they saw me, and I must have looked as if I meant business: dark clothes, confident stance, shouting, a point of determination in a sea of confusion. The crowd checked and reversed and this time they took no notice of the men who were waving them away from the other platform, filing through with unstoppable weight of numbers. I put my phone away and started working my way through the people nearest me, shoving them towards the staircase.

'One at a time. Do not run. Take your time. Get moving.'

They went, obedient as sheep, and I looked along the platform to see the crowd unknotting itself harmlessly as people chose their route to safety. The big men had disappeared, and at the other end of the platform I saw the gleam of high vis jackets that meant proper help was on its way. I dived back to the first carriage and found the woman. She was shaking, and her toddler was crying.

'Come on. Let's get you out of here.'

I ended up carrying the child, who was heavier than she looked but enchanted by the jolting she got as we half-walked, half-ran through the station's labyrinth of tunnels. Reassuring numbers of the emergency services were going the other way at a brisk jog-trot. I turned my head away from the police officers and obeyed all of the instructions from shocked-looking station staff, who were trained for this but not on a Thursday morning – not on *this* Thursday morning.

As we came through the barriers into the ticket hall, I looked around, on edge. Paramedics looking calm, civilians with what seemed to be minor injuries, no bodies yet. No one I recognised, either. The tension slackened, very slightly, and I came back to myself to realise that the woman I'd helped was thanking me through her tears. I handed the child back to her and brushed off her gratitude, moving away before she could insist on getting my name and telephone number.

'There's no need to thank me, really. Safe home.'

I left her staring after me and cut away through the crowd, making for one of the exits that led onto a side street. I needed to put clear air between me and the incident. Daylight glared palely from above me as I jogged up the stairs, eyes down, my whole focus on being as unobtrusive as possible so I could

117

slide away into the milling crowds and make contact with Opal. I stepped out onto Argyll Street and turned left, as I'd planned. What I hadn't planned was walking into a wall of solid police officer, well over six foot and broad with it. He smiled down at me.

'Hold on a second, my friend. What's the hurry?'

'No hurry, I just don't want to get in the way.'

'That's him.' It was one of the men who had been at the front of the crowd, who had gone wide-eyed with terror when I pointed my phone at him. 'He's the one with the gun.'

I had enough time to put my hands up before the implacable force of London's finest hit me like a truck.

16

I'd known it was a possibility but there was still something soul-destroying about being cautioned, and cuffed, and searched, while onlookers made all too audible comments about me. I stared stonily into the middle distance, ignoring pretty much everything, including the Met officers who had arrested me. Outside the station, on the street, I was on Met ground. They would handle my arrest and custody instead of BTP, which I imagined the BTP officers would be quite happy about. They had enough to do today.

While they searched me, the officers kept up a steady stream of questions.

'What are you doing here? What was the purpose of your journey?'

'What did you do with the gun?'

'Did you set off the explosives?'

'Not feeling chatty?'

'I'll talk at the station,' I said quietly at last. 'I'm not going to go through my personal business here on the street. But all I did was try to help.'

'What did you do, then?'

I shook my head.

'Let's stick him in the van,' the skipper said to two of the PCs and they lifted my wrists behind my back so I had to bend forward at the waist, a classic tactic for controlling difficult prisoners.

'I'm not going to fight,' I said mildly to the ground, and they ignored me. 'Where are you taking me?'

'Charing Cross,' one of them said, and I thought about that while they guided me into the back of the van, which at least had the advantage of hiding me from curious eyes. It was a station I knew well from my time on the other side of the fence. What worried me about going there was being recognised.

'Hey,' I said as one prepared to shut the door of the van. 'Is anyone else under arrest?'

'Oh yes. More than a few of you.'

'Thanks.' *Fuck*. That meant that I'd be in a queue to be presented to the custody sergeant on my way into the station. It would be a disaster for someone who knew me to greet me with a cheery *Hello, Rob, how's it going, haven't seen you for a while, did you transfer out of the flying squad?*

And I had to decide what to do if Den or Bruno was one of the other people under arrest. Should I speak to them? Were they going to stick to the cover story about the photo shoot? Somehow I doubted it. I also didn't believe Geraint when he said he wouldn't arrange for legal representation for us; I might be on my own but they could expect the most expensive criminal solicitors in London to be at their disposal. Den and Bruno would hang this around my neck if they could get away with it, and feel no kind of guilt about it.

I kept my head down on the way in to custody, staring at the floor, and discovered no queue. They were bringing arrested people in one by one from the vans rather than letting us queue in person, and mingle, and potentially interact with accomplices.

Not as much of a comfort as it might have been; I had clearly been prioritised for processing. When I reached the custody sergeant I glanced up and away immediately, not betraying any recognition of the big bull of a man behind the desk. A sheen of sweat glossed his bald head and he'd put on enough weight to make his uniform strain across his belly, but I knew him: Millsy, who had been one of the PCs at the first nick where I'd worked. And he knew me.

Fortunately, he knew how to take a hint too. He sniffed. 'Who's this?'

'Mark Howell.'

Nothing, not a flicker betrayed any surprise. I stood still while they took off the handcuffs and answered the custody sergeant's questions as if I'd never heard them before (and, in fairness, I'd never had them addressed to me): no, I had no injuries, no, I wasn't suicidal, no, I wasn't addicted to anything.

'Can I make a phone call?'

'In a bit.' He didn't even look away from the screen where he was typing the answers – all professional, distant, competent. There was an atmosphere of suppressed tension in the station, and I could understand that since they were processing everyone arrested at the scene. The tactic seemed to have been to lift everyone who might have any involvement in the attack, and then sift through whatever CCTV they'd got to match us up with any actions reported to them.

'Do you understand why you've been arrested?' Millsy asked.

'A misunderstanding,' I said, as an innocent person would. 'I was just trying to help.' That part was true, anyway.

'All right.' He turned to the other custody sergeant behind the desk. 'Let's arrange for Mr Howell to have that phone call before he goes to his cell, all right? We're going to get swamped here and it might be a while otherwise.'

She nodded, and after I submitted to being photographed,

fingerprinted and swabbed for DNA (nerve-racking, except that I knew I'd been taken out of the Met's database when I started working undercover) she stood next to me while I dialled the number I knew by heart.

'Yes?' The volume of the phone was loud enough that I didn't really need to hold the receiver to my ear, which I knew was deliberate. I softened my voice, allowing a little emotion into it, but talking fast so I couldn't be interrupted.

'Hey, honey, I'm so glad you picked up. It's Mark. Look, I don't want you to worry but I'm at Charing Cross Police Station. I've been arrested.'

'What? What's happened?' Opal's voice was so shrill I winced and caught a sympathetic look from the custody sergeant.

'Did you see the incident at Oxford Circus tube?'

'Yeah, it's all over the news. Baby, are you OK?'

'I was there. Just passing through, you know, but someone thought I was involved in whatever happened. Can you believe that?'

Opal sniffed as if she was overcome with emotion. 'Yeah, I can actually, Mark. It's so typical of you to get caught up in this kind of shit.'

I knew she meant it as a dig. 'I'm sorry, sweets. It's just a misunderstanding.'

'Yeah, of course, but they won't believe that.'

'They will. I'll be out of here soon.' I didn't quite manage to sound confident. 'Look, can you get hold of a solicitor for me?'

'I can try.' She sniffed again and I knew she was playing for time while she thought it through. Sending in a solicitor wasn't ideal. They had to be prepared to lie about who I was, or they had to be kept in total ignorance, which had its own implications. 'I'll see if there's any way I can help. Don't worry, babe. I'll sort something out. You might have to wait a little bit, but—'

'I want to get out of here.'

'I bet you do. I want you out of there too. I want you home.'

Home was Geraint's house, not anywhere Opal would be. The longer I spent cooling my heels in the police station, the more I would miss of the aftermath of this first foray into terrorism.

'Leave it with me,' she said after a tiny pause, which for Opal was long enough to plan an entire strategy. 'I'm going to see if anyone can help. I'm owed a few favours.'

That was interesting. I wondered what she was planning. 'I know you'll do your best,' I said.

'It'll be OK, I swear.' More sniffling. 'I can't believe it, Mark. What a thing to happen. And you're OK?'

'I'm OK. Not hurt. I don't think anyone else was hurt much either.'

'That's good, that's good.'

'I think you've had long enough,' the custody sergeant said with a glance out of the room. 'They're going to need this room. We've got another customer coming in.'

'Got to go, sweetheart.'

'OK. I love you.'

Fucking hell, Opal. 'Yeah. Me too,' I said guardedly, and hung up. I caught a flash of amusement from the custody sergeant. She was blonde and very pretty, and in other circumstances I would have been exerting myself to be charming. There was something about having your shoes and belt confiscated – not to mention having to coo at your hard-as-nails boss down the phone – that took the edge off your confidence.

And if that wasn't enough to take the wind out of my sails, the next thing the custody sergeant said would have done it.

'We're going to need your clothes, I'm afraid.'

*

123

Time passed slowly in a busy police station, at least if you were locked in one of the cells. Every so often someone peered in through the wicket in the door and offered me a range of things: a book to read, a cup of tea, a hot meal. I couldn't complain that they weren't looking after me. What I could complain about was the custody tracksuit I'd had to put on, which was on the short side, and the custody slippers that completed the outfit. I didn't have access to a full-length mirror but I had a feeling that the cheap grey cotton tracksuit was making me look more like a criminal than any CCTV footage they'd managed to find. My clothes were in an evidence bag, just in case they needed to go for forensic analysis. I had liked those jeans, I thought, and felt irrationally angry about losing them.

The custody area was noisy. It made sense that they had grabbed hold of anyone who was even vaguely of interest. You didn't want to find out you'd waved a terrorist through a police cordon so that someone had to go to the trouble of tracking them down again. Even if the terrorist attack had proved to be more of a prank than a violent act, it would be investigated the same way as a proper bombing. They would be interviewing everyone they'd scraped up, panning for evidence, specialist anti-terrorism officers taking the lead. I hadn't seen anyone I knew in the station – but then again, I hadn't seen anyone at all. Millsy came down himself to apologise that there wasn't going to be an opportunity to take me out for exercise yet.

'You're not a smoker, are you?'

'No.'

'Yeah. Well, you're stuck here for a while longer.'

'How long is it going to be?' I allowed myself to sound frustrated, because I was, and Millsy lowered one eyelid deliberately.

'You're waiting for a couple of detectives to get here. They're bringing in some extra help to handle the interviews and you're number one on the list.'

'Thanks for that,' I said. Nothing that anyone could overhear and find suspicious, but it was helpful for me to know what wheels were turning. Who were the detectives, I wondered. Opal herself, in her professional capacity? Someone else from the team, scrambled to conduct a formal interview with me so that anyone watching would be fooled? I deliberately hadn't used Opal's first name on the phone in case she made an appearance herself, but was that too risky? She liked to keep her distance, did Opal, and I appreciated it most of the time but I'd have given a lot to see her waiting for me in the interview room.

I went back to sitting on the fold-down bed with its squeaky wipe-clean mattress, trying not to think about all the dedicated criminals who had sat there in their time. I knew I was on camera, displayed on screen so the custody skipper could watch me except for a modesty square over the cell's toilet that gave the illusion of dignity. My every movement was being studied for signs of distress, or guilt, or incipient violence. I sat with my legs bent, elbows on knees, and thought bitterly about all the places I would rather be.

I must have dozed off, sitting upright with my head against the wall, because when the door opened it woke me up.

'Mr Howell? You ready for an interview?'

'Yes.' I jumped up, stretching cramped limbs. 'Is my solicitor here?'

'No.' The pretty blonde bit her lip. 'Do you want to wait, or—'

'No, let's get on with it.' I stretched and tilted my head left and right. 'Sorry.'

'Take your time.' She smiled at me.

I was probably more polite than the usual prisoner who made it into her custody suite but I wondered if Millsy had hinted to her that she should be nice to me. He wouldn't, I thought with a chill of nerves. This only worked if everyone played along.

Maybe it was just that she liked me.

I shambled down the corridor as she walked behind me, directing me to the interview room where I'd been on the other side of the table a couple of times. I tried to look wary and uncertain and a touch outraged, in case anyone was watching. Too relaxed would be a giveaway. Too jumpy would be out of character. The Mark that Geraint knew would be watchful, his mind working overtime to get him out of trouble. And since that was exactly what was happening in my head, it shouldn't have been hard to act that way.

'Here you go.' She let me into the interview room and waited while I sat down. 'They're just coming.'

Footsteps in the corridor: I folded my arms across my chest and leaned back in the chair, one foot tapping under the table.

'Thanks, we've got it from here.' A man's voice, and I looked up in genuine surprise to see him saunter in, his hands in his pockets, tall and broad in an immaculate suit that I envied. He took the time to give the custody sergeant an appreciative look as he edged past her, and was unsubtle enough about it that she blushed, but then that was pretty typical, I thought.

'Mr . . . Howell.' He sat down opposite me and gave me a piercing look. 'I'm Detective Inspector Josh Derwent.'

I know.

'I'm going to be interviewing you regarding the incident on the Underground this morning.'

'Are you from British Transport Police?'

A grin appeared on his face and disappeared just as quickly, which I took as a compliment to my acting. 'No. Actually, my colleague and I aren't usually tasked with this kind of thing. We've been called in because there are so many suspects to process.'

'Your colleague.' I looked at the empty chair beside him and raised my eyebrows.

His expression was deadpan, unreadable. 'She should be here any second.'

I had absolutely not enough time to process that before the door opened.

'Sorry, I got held up.' She slipped into the room and shut the door behind her, and I felt my throat tighten as she sat down opposite me, her attention on the folder she was holding, her eyes fixed on it even though I was willing her to look up.

'As I was saying, this is Detective Sergeant Maeve Kerrigan,' Derwent said silkily. 'At long last.'

17

I'd imagined Opal pulling off all kinds of things, but getting my old colleagues to interview me wasn't even on the list. It made sense, though – they had no connection with my current role, they knew exactly who I was, and they were Tier 5 interviewers who were qualified to help an over-stretched Counter-Terrorism Command. I wondered if she had known that one of them – the one who was reading something fascinating in her folder, the one who hadn't actually looked at me yet – was my ex-girlfriend. It wouldn't have stopped Opal, but she might have requested video footage of the interview.

'As I said, I got held up. And speaking of at long last,' Maeve said, her voice soft and clear as she turned to Derwent, 'when are you going to fix the kitchen tap? The drip is getting worse and worse.'

That sounded domestic. I swallowed: if this was how I was going to find out Maeve and Josh Derwent were living together, it was going to be hard to look as if I didn't care.

'I'll get around to it,' Derwent said, bored.

'You are just the worst landlord. I hope you know that.'

Landlord. I could have cheered.

He flashed a grin at her, then looked at me. 'Sorry about that. Let's get on with this interview, shall we? Try and be a bit professional?'

Colour washed into Maeve's face and I realised that she had been as pale as paper when she came in. This had to be hard for her too. I had walked out without any warning, because the job required it, and because I couldn't think how to say goodbye, but I knew it had hurt her. She looked the same: maybe a little bruised under the eyes, as if she hadn't been sleeping well. Still beautiful enough to make you catch your breath. Her hair – a reliable indicator of her general frame of mind – was pinned into a knot, a sleek wave across her fore-head softening the effect. *This is business. I am here for professional reasons and nothing else.*

Fair enough, I thought, and longed to touch her.

Derwent occupied himself with the preamble for the inter-view, for the benefit of the tape, stating who was in the room and that I had waived my right to legal representation. Maeve looked up at me at last while he talked and I held her cool grey gaze, trying to convey everything I couldn't say.

I'm sorry.

I didn't want to see you again like this.

I can't be anything other than Mark Howell at the moment so I can't say anything that gives me away.

You look beautiful.

I missed you.

I'm *really* sorry.

'So, Mark, tell us about this morning,' Josh Derwent said. 'You were arrested outside Oxford Circus tube station. Tell us what happened before that.'

'I was on my way to work.'

'Where?'

'We were going to a photoshoot.' I gave him the address Den had given me, and he wrote it down.

'Where did you start your journey?'

'My boss's house.' I recited the address for Haulton House too. I limped through the cover story that Geraint had given me, explaining who I had been with and what we had been doing, and how we had got separated early on and I hadn't got close to Den. Derwent took the lead in asking the questions; Maeve barely spoke. She was listening, though, and watching me – presumably coming to her own conclusions about how I looked and sounded. More than ever I resented the custody tracksuit I was wearing.

Derwent took me through the entire story, right up to the moment when the first explosion went off.

'And what did you see?'

'Nothing.' I shrugged. 'I was looking at the people who were waiting to get off and hoping I'd get a seat. Then there was a bang and the carriage filled with smoke.'

'And what did you do?'

'I thought about jumping out of the carriage. There was a woman with a child in a pushchair – I was worried that people would trip over the pushchair and injure the child. I stopped to help her.'

'Did you know her?' Maeve asked.

'No.'

'Get her name?' Derwent's eyebrows were raised.

'No, and I didn't get her phone number either.' I was genuinely irritated by his tone of voice. 'I told her to stay on the train until the platform was safe, which it wasn't at first, and then I helped her through the station. That was all.'

'That wasn't quite all.' Maeve took a printed picture out of her folder and slid it across the table to me. 'Tell us what was going on here.'

I looked at the image of myself at the top of the stairs, pulled from CCTV. Blurry and distorted as it was, it was recognisably me, facing down the crowd of people who were approaching.

'They were heading for the stairs. I thought there was the potential for a significant loss of life if that many people tried to take one exit from the platform, especially in their panicked state of mind, when they would be rushing. There was considerable chaos on the platform itself. I wanted to persuade them to try the other exits that seemed less appealing in the moment, because I knew they were safer options. The station staff were responding but at the time there wasn't anyone else to organise the evacuation.'

'And that's not a gun,' Derwent said, circling it on the image with the end of his pen.

'It's my phone. There wasn't time to persuade people to listen to me. I thought the phone would look enough like a gun that it would be an effective deterrent. My expectation was that the crowd would veer away instinctively, given that they were scared anyway. It wouldn't have fooled anyone up close but they were thinking of terrorists and saw something dark in my hands.' I shrugged. 'It worked.'

'Wasn't that quite risky?' Maeve asked, not looking at me. 'They could have stampeded. You were right in their path.'

'It seemed like the right thing to do.'

'We have a couple of very full witness statements describing the gun.' Derwent leaned back in his chair and grinned. 'Bit of debate about whether it was a Glock or a Sig Sauer, but they were absolutely certain that you pointed a handgun at them.'

'Just an iPhone. People see what they want to see.'

'Indeed they do.'

'Have you been looking for a gun in the station?' I asked.

'Not personally.' Derwent smiled. 'They haven't found one.'

'I never had one, and I didn't see anyone else with one.'

'OK.' Derwent glanced at Maeve. 'Anything else to ask?'

She shook her head.

'Then all we need you to do is write us a statement, if you would. A *full* statement.'

'Am I still a suspect?'

Another look sparked between the two of them; I really envied that easy wordless communication they'd developed.

'We're treating you as a witness. You'll have your belongings returned to you and then you'll be free to go on your way.'

'Are you happy to write your own version of events?' Maeve asked. 'I can write something for you to approve if you prefer.'

'No, I'll do it.'

She slid a few sheets of paper across the table and I started writing, concentrating first on the version of events that Geraint had supplied. It didn't take long. Then I moved on to a separate sheet and wrote a note for Opal: what had happened, the men blocking the access to the other platform, my suspicion that either Geraint didn't trust us or his conspirators didn't trust him. I added descriptions of the people I thought should be of interest, knowing that Opal would be able to pick them out from the CCTV if she had enough detail. The other men had stood out to me, with my heightened state of awareness during the incident, but I wondered if they would look like innocent passengers to anyone who hadn't been there. I was certain I'd identified them correctly.

I finished off by pointing out that we needed some failsafe way to communicate in similar circumstances. The worst part of the day – aside from the tracksuit – had definitely been not being able to warn anyone in advance. It was risky for me, but the next time this happened – and there would be a next time – I wanted to be the one taking the risk, not the innocent civilians who'd blundered into the path of Geraint's obsessions.

132

I slid the note for Opal behind the bland statement that would go on file with Mark Howell's signature at the bottom and passed it back to Maeve.

'Thanks,' she said, reading through it. 'That's all we need, I think.'

'Can I go now?'

'You'll need to go back to your cell, I'm afraid.' Derwent didn't actually manage to sound sorry about it. 'Just while we get the paperwork processed.'

'Right. Can I have my clothes back?'

Amusement narrowed his eyes. 'I'll see what I can do. You might have to leave dressed like that.'

'I'd rather not.'

'I'm sure.'

Casually, I looked back at Maeve, to see that she was watching me again. She held my gaze for a beat longer than she might have, then stood.

'I'll go and sort out the paperwork.'

No, wait. Stop. I need to talk to you. I tried to make sure my face was impassive, but I kept my eyes on her until the door closed behind her and cut off my view, leaving me on my own with Josh Derwent, his raised eyebrows and an atmosphere that was suddenly heavy with unsaid things.

An hour later I was dressed in my own clothes. I would never take them for granted again, I thought.

'Ready?' Derwent was standing in the doorway of my cell. 'Bet you can't wait to get out of here.'

'Yeah. Thanks for sorting this out.' I started towards him and he held up a hand, checking over his shoulder.

'Wait.'

There was a mild commotion in the corridor. I looked past Derwent to see Den being returned to his cell. He caught sight of me and his expression changed.

'Hey. Hey, Mark.'

'Don't talk to him.' Derwent put himself between me and Den, blocking his view very effectively, and glowered at Den.

I turned away, clasping my hands behind my head as if I was frustrated, but really wondering if I'd given myself away. I hadn't been being friendly with Derwent – not exactly. And he had hardly been smiling at me. I was under no illusions about his feelings about me. He had chosen his side early on, and it wasn't mine.

'Come on,' Derwent said finally when the cell door had closed behind Den. 'Back to the skipper.'

I followed him, head down, looking fed up and sullen. I had been hoping that Maeve might be at the desk too, but there was no sign of her. Derwent handled the processing of my belongings with grim efficiency, and Millsy looked through me as if he had no reason to be pleasant.

'Total waste of time,' I said quietly as I slid my watch back on.

'I wouldn't say that.' Derwent leaned on the counter, signing a form. Casually, he said, 'Do you know where you're going?'

'I'll work it out.'

He nodded, and said goodbye with grim professionalism.

I found myself back on the street in busy, bustling central London, as if nothing had happened. I walked away, not too fast but with decision, and it wasn't until I was sure I'd lost myself in the crowds at Covent Garden that I allowed myself to take out the folded sheet of paper that was in the pocket of my coat.

It was an address, I saw, scrawled in Josh Derwent's writing. Nothing more.

It was all I'd wanted.

*

134

Three hours later I stood outside the front door of a Victorian maisonette at the end of a quiet residential street, after taking elaborate and careful precautions to ensure I wasn't followed as I made my way across London. I rang the doorbell. My heart was thumping as if I was on speed. I knew I was allowed and even expected to turn up – I wouldn't have had the address otherwise – but I wasn't sure what kind of reception I was going to get, and I braced myself as the door opened.

This time Maeve's hair was down, a soft and gleaming cloud around her face and shoulders. A big jumper, narrow jeans, bare feet: her off-duty uniform, and it was so familiar it made my heart hurt.

'Hi.'

'Maeve.' I hesitated, trying to find the words, and she came to the rescue.

'I presume you've come to fix the tap.'

'The tap,' I repeated. 'Yes, I thought I should take a look. I mean, I'm not an expert. But I probably won't make it worse.'

The smile started in her eyes. 'You'd better come in, then.'

18

'So this is Josh Derwent's place.' There wasn't room for both of us in the tiny galley kitchen, where Maeve was cooking. Like the rest of the flat the kitchen was immaculate, freshly painted and neatly designed, with every inch of space put to good use. The old Maeve had lived in a constant state of mild chaos, but that had changed. I felt it wasn't the only difference. She seemed a stranger, somehow, in a way that wasn't just down to the way I'd left or the time we'd been apart. It was as if something was missing that I'd taken for granted. 'How did you end up here?'

She gave me a sidelong look. 'Are you sure you want to ask that question now?'

'Why not?'

'Well, after you left without any warning whatsoever, I stayed in our flat for a while. Then I got bored with being there on my own. But I didn't want to leave in case you came back.'

And I hadn't. 'Ah.'

She was stirring the pasta sauce with great concentration. 'And then Josh moved out to live with his girlfriend and her son—'

'Wait.'

'—so this place was empty.'

'Josh Derwent has settled down?'

She gave me a flash of a grin. 'More or less. He turned into a proper family man.'

'I did not see that coming.'

'Neither did he, I think. But he fell in love.'

'Must have, if he took on a kid as well.'

She laughed. 'I think he fell in love with the kid first. They're proper partners in crime. My parents look after Thomas now and then. He's brilliant. And Josh likes being a father figure.'

'That surprises me.' I leaned against the door frame. 'But he was looking good earlier. It gave me quite a shock to see him.'

'And me.'

'And you.'

She was smiling to herself as she turned down the heat under the pasta. Cooking in itself was remarkable because the Maeve I had known was able to handle the toaster with reasonable competence but anything else had been a struggle. 'I could tell you were shaken. Imagine how we felt when we got sent to CX to interview you.'

'At least you had some time to prepare.'

'Years.' She gave me another ironic look and I winced.

'OK. I know. I'm sorry. But I had to go that way. And I wasn't allowed to tell you where I was going. The less you knew, the better.'

'And I take it the story about you joining GMP was complete rubbish too.'

I'd let it be known I had moved to Greater Manchester Police, a force big enough to hide in, and close to where I was from originally. 'A cover.'

'And you didn't get engaged.'

I blinked. 'That was definitely not something that happened.'

'It was Josh's invention, I think. He wanted to come up with something that would make me forget about you.'

'I thought you'd do that easily enough,' I said it lightly, but she looked at me, serious.

'No. I didn't find it easy.'

'I – I didn't know.'

'No. I don't think you knew me at all.' She focused her attention on the food, as if what she'd said had no significance. 'What I gather is that you've been doing a fair amount of dangerous undercover work since the last time I saw you, and the only time you've made contact with me was when you were scared.'

I winced. 'Mainly boring undercover work rather than dangerous.'

'Mm. That would be more convincing if I hadn't had a chat with your boss before I got to Charing Cross today.'

'Opal? What did she say?'

'Enough to make it clear that we had to convince anyone who was watching that you were exactly what you're pretending to be. She said the people you're dealing with would kill you without hesitating.'

'True,' I allowed. 'But only if I make a mistake.'

'Or run out of luck.'

'Or that.'

Maeve looked up, serious again and we stared at one another for a long moment. Then she turned away. 'This is ready, I think. Are you hungry?'

'Ravenous.'

'If you want to help, you could lay the table.' She took out wine glasses and cutlery. 'It's in the sitting room.'

I hesitated. 'Can you go first, to close the blinds?'

'Sure.' She sidestepped me. I heard her moving around in the sitting room, and the clatter as all three blinds slid down to cover the bay window. She came back. 'Done.'

I gathered up the glasses and cutlery. The sitting room was as tidy as the rest of the place, though I recognised a poster on the wall and two of the cushions on the sofa as having belonged to her before. It felt like a home, which was new for Maeve. Thoughtfully, I laid the table and then crossed the room to peer out at the street through a tiny gap, checking for anyone who shouldn't be there.

Maeve came in carrying a bottle of wine and a basket of garlic bread. She set them down and tilted her head, watching me. 'You're worried about being followed.'

My first instinct was to laugh it off; my second was the truth. 'All the time.'

'How can you live like that?'

'I don't think about it unless I have to.'

'What do you get out of it?'

'That's a big question.'

'Let me get the pasta and then you can answer it.' She smiled at me before she left. *No getting out of this one, Rob; she's the last person on earth to let you change the subject, even if the question isn't to your liking.*

As soon as she came back, I blurted out, 'I feel as if I'm doing something. Achieving something.'

'Go on.' She put my bowl down in front of me and sat down herself, her attention apparently on the wine she poured with a steady hand.

'Usually, we get called after a crime has happened. We pick up the pieces as best we can. We make sure the right people get locked up, but that doesn't really make up for whatever they've done. You've seen the pain and misery, I know you have. And that goes just as much for ordinary burglaries and robberies as for murder. The damage it does – the way people lose their trust in others . . .' I trailed off.

'I do know what you mean.'

'When I left the murder team, I thought it would be better.' I put my fork down, remembering. 'I thought it was a different kind of work. Not emotionally demanding. Just crimes about money.'

'And it wasn't.'

'No.' I drank some wine. 'I didn't want to talk to you about it. I was disillusioned. Fed up. You were still in love with the job.'

'I've never been in love with the job.' Her eyes were bright.

'It's not a bad thing, Maeve. It makes you care. I mean, it won't love you back, but that doesn't matter to you at the moment.'

'Stop talking about me and tell me what changed for you.'

'Do you remember I went on a course in America? Debbie Ormond arranged it.'

Maeve's mouth tightened. 'I remember. Two weeks with the FBI, and she went too.'

I remembered too late that Maeve hadn't liked Detective Inspector Ormond at all – and that as far as she knew, I'd slept with Debbie right after I left her for the last time, which I hadn't. They'd made it look as if I had, and I'd gone along with it in the stupid, reckless frame of mind that had jolted me out of my old life.

'Yes, well, we weren't in America. I was going through a recruitment and assessment process. It was very, very secret, and part of the test was me not telling you where I was or what I was doing.'

'How would they have known?'

'I assume they know everything. Opal can find out just about anything she wants.'

'Your current boss.'

I nodded. 'They offered me an opportunity. Get in first. Gather evidence of crimes before they happen. Head off the worst trouble – like today. No one was seriously hurt, and no one died. Some of that was probably because I was there.'

'Undoubtedly.' Maeve leaned back and folded her arms. 'We watched the CCTV. Do you know how long the incident took, from the first smoke to the last passenger being evacuated?'

I shook my head.

'Twelve minutes and twenty-four seconds. Do you know how long it took for any emergency services personnel to respond?'

'It felt like forever.'

'Three minutes, fifty seconds. During that time you, the train driver and a single member of platform staff were the only guidance for hundreds of people who were being directed towards danger. The train driver was moving through the carriages, checking for casualties. The guy on the platform was completely overwhelmed. You made all the difference.'

'I thought it was longer.' I was reviewing my memory of it. 'I lost all sense of time.'

'I'm not surprised.' She looked down at my food. 'If it's not good, we can order pizza.'

'No, it is good. It's excellent.' I ate, genuinely enjoying it. 'When did you learn to cook?'

'I've got five recipes that I can do.' She looked mischievous. 'It's a start. I made myself a promise that I'd start behaving like a grown-up.'

'I'm impressed.'

She dropped her gaze, blushing, and I felt the old familiar ache at my heart, even if it was fainter now.

'Anyway, that's why it's worth doing the job, dangerous or not,' I finished. 'And don't get the wrong idea. It's mostly not dangerous at all.'

'I can understand that.' She was still looking down, toying with her food.

141

I'd told her the truth, and it wasn't enough. I cleared my throat. 'I hated leaving you the way I did. Going, without saying anything. Looking back now, I don't know what I was thinking.'

She nodded, silent, not looking at me.

'We had a row, as I recall. They had told me—' I broke off and regrouped. 'They had told me to take the next opportunity to go. It had to be believable, they said. A reason for me to walk out of my life.'

'You walked out of *my* life,' Maeve said quietly. 'And I didn't get a say.'

'I didn't think you'd mind.'

She looked up at that, and I almost flinched at the heat in her eyes. 'How can you say that?'

'Because you didn't feel about me the way I felt about you, and you never would.' I knew she wouldn't deny it. 'That wasn't your fault, and it wasn't mine, but it was something I couldn't deal with.'

'I loved you.'

'Not enough.'

'As much as I could.' She was on the edge of tears, holding on to her composure but only just.

'I know. But it wouldn't have worked out. I could see that. You were keeping things from me – not in a bad way. Not to hurt me, or mislead me. But I talked to Josh and I know that you were going through stuff that he knew about and I didn't.'

'Did you talk to him about what happened with my last boyfriend?' Her voice was sharp.

'No. I meant back when we were together.' I frowned. 'What happened?'

'I – I went out with someone. I trusted him and – and I shouldn't have.' Her mouth twisted. 'I don't have great judgement when it comes to men.'

Thanks for that, I thought. 'Did he hurt you?'

'I'm all right. You can unclench your fists.'

'Does he need dealing with?'

'No.'

I didn't know why I was asking; Josh Derwent had probably pulled out his spine through his nostrils for daring to upset Maeve. 'I know it's not my place—'

'I said no.' She looked amused, back to her usual composure instead of the raw emotion I'd just seen. 'I noticed you'd beefed up but I didn't know you'd become a proper thug.'

I winced. 'Harsh. And the muscle is what the current target demands. He likes his employees solid.'

'It suits you.'

I cleared my throat. 'Look, Maeve—'

'Are you finished?' She looked pointedly at my plate which was still half-full.

'No. Not even nearly.' I went back to eating, focused this time, and she sat on the other side of the table, sipping wine, her expression unreadable.

It was time to steer away from tricky emotional territory, I thought. We talked about neutral subjects for a while, slipping back into the old rhythm, understanding each other without any need for long explanations. There was something on her mind though, something that made her lose track of what she was saying once or twice, and I waited for it to become so pressing that she had to blurt it out, which she did after a second glass of wine.

'The night you left.' She was concentrating on her glass. 'What do you remember about that night?'

'Everything.'

'You'd been drinking.'

'Not as much as you thought I had,' I said.

'So you already knew you were going.'

'Pretty much.'

'I thought – I thought you left because I made you stop when we were – we were in bed—'

'No.' I remembered it vividly. Maeve had pushed me away, losing interest, and I'd thought it was a fitting ending for a doomed relationship. 'But it made me feel I'd been right to think there was something wrong between us that we probably couldn't fix, and that it would hurt us both to admit it. Moving on didn't seem like such a bad idea.'

She blinked, hard. 'I should tell you what had happened to me that day. I should have told you at the time, but I didn't. I was . . . not at my best.'

I listened with mounting horror as she told me about a confrontation in a stairwell, and how she had been threatened, and how the trauma had stayed with her.

'But you didn't say.'

'I know.'

'Did you tell Josh?' I found myself asking, as if that mattered.

'Eventually.' She shook her head. 'He guessed. I didn't tell him, not then. I didn't tell anyone.'

'God, Maeve, if I'd known—'

'Of course. And I should have said.'

My head had been full of my own worries. No wonder she had asked me to stop mauling her. And then I had left her, and let her think it was her fault – on Opal's orders, but of my own volition.

My image of myself as a nice guy was taking the battering it deserved, I thought, and loathed myself.

'You must have hated me.'

'No. Never.' She leaned across the table. 'Rob, it hurts to say this, but I think you were right. I should have been able to tell you about it. I should have *wanted* to tell you. I was always holding back from you, and you deserved more.'

144

I deserved shooting, I thought, and tried to smile at her. 'At least now we both understand.'

'Yes.' She had gone back to staring at the wine in her glass, weighing something up. 'Do you want to stay tonight?'

'Have I been here that long?' I checked the time; late, but not too late. 'I can go. I'll find a hotel.'

'No. I want you to stay.' She risked a glance to see how I was taking it. 'With me.'

'With . . .' I realised what she meant and it made me silent for a second: an unhoped-for chance to make things right. 'Are you sure?'

'I think so.' She laughed a little. 'I know so. I'm sure.'

I thought she was persuading herself into it, though, and I didn't rush as I got up and went around to her side of the table. She stood up, and for a long moment neither of us spoke, or moved, or did anything to break the silence. At last I slid one hand into her hair, and pulled her gently towards me, and I kissed her. It was tentative, on both sides – more of a question than the answer to anything, and when we broke apart she leaned back, grinning.

'Not great. Seven out of ten. I think we can do better than that.'

'I'll do my best.'

This time I kissed her with more conviction. She felt the same in my arms, and not the same. Kissing her was a reminder of all the things I'd missed about her and excitingly unfamiliar at the same time.

'Maeve, I—'

'Don't say anything. You don't need to.' A gleam of amusement. 'And also, I don't want to wait any longer. Come on.' She was pulling her top over her head as she left the room.

There was still a part of me that knew something wasn't quite right with her, but I followed her to the bedroom. I let her take charge, peeling off my jumper, unbuckling my belt, guiding my hands where she wanted them to go, telling me in words and by her reactions how to please her. The same as before, and not the same, but real. Her skin on mine, her breath against my cheek, her heart thudding close to my chest: there was nothing else in the world and nowhere else I could imagine being.

19

I was tired, but sleep was hard to come by. I lay in the darkness and worried. I had plenty on my mind, not least that I wasn't where I wanted to be: in bed with Maeve. The sex had been wholly satisfying for both of us, I was sure of it – there had been nothing fake about her focus, or the catch in her breath when I touched her, or the way she had moved against me. But afterwards I'd looked into her eyes and seen nothing but doubt, and emptiness, and distance, as if she was a long way away instead of lying underneath me.

'What's the matter?'

'Nothing.' She wriggled, pushing me away. I sat up.

'Sorry – did I do something wrong?'

She edged away until there was a foot of empty mattress between us, and no possibility of even accidental contact. She drew her knees up to her chin and wrapped her arms around them. The body language couldn't have been clearer, despite the smile she threw in my direction. 'It's fine. It's not you. Just – I don't want to sleep in the same bed.'

'Maeve . . .' A thud of dismay; if she regretted what we had just done, I would never trust my instincts about women again.

I pushed my ego to one side and thought about what she'd told me earlier. 'What was that – a test?'

'What do you mean? I said it wasn't about you.'

'Not of me,' I said gently.

'Oh—' she put her head down on her knees. 'I'm sorry.'

'Maeve, talk to me. You wished you had told me about what was bothering you before. Maybe I can help this time.' I pulled the sheet over me and sat back against the pillows, and after a moment she sighed.

'Maybe it wasn't fair to you but I wanted to see what it would be like with someone I trusted.' When she lifted her head, her face was grave, and utterly lovely. 'I haven't tried since . . . my last relationship.'

I had the strong impression she had been about to say something else. *Since what?* She raised a hand to her collarbone, and then snatched it away.

'What happened, Maeve? What did he do to you?' I reached out and pushed her hair back. 'You have a scar on your forehead.' I'd seen it when she lay down, not before, and it struck me that the way she wore her hair now was designed to hide it. 'Was that from him?'

'He's gone to prison for it.'

'For how long?'

'He'll be out in two years.'

I did some sums and considered usual sentencing guidelines. 'GBH?'

'With intent.'

I sat up. 'Fuck. Maeve, what did he do?'

'Nothing that didn't heal. And I'll be all right. The scar will fade.'

'Yes, but—'

'But what?'

You can't pretend that everything is back to normal, I wanted

148

to say, and didn't. Instead I reached out and took her hand. 'If this helped, it was worth it, and if it didn't, I'm sorry.'

She looked pensive. 'Because it was you, I felt safe. I could pretend it was the old me, from before. It worked in the moment, but I'm not that person anymore and I have to admit that to myself. I just didn't want what he did to change me.'

'When did it happen?'

'Last year.'

'You have to be patient, Maeve. Give yourself time. Don't rush it.'

'I'm sorry.'

'What the hell do you have to be sorry for?' I lifted her hand to my mouth and kissed the back of it. 'I'm glad you trusted me to touch you. I'm glad we did this. I wish you'd told me before we did anything, that's all.'

She looked away. 'I didn't want you to treat me like a victim.'

And now I was. I couldn't think of anything to say. She turned away from me and curled into a ball.

'If you don't mind sleeping on the sofa, I'd prefer it.'

We had always slept curled around each other, our limbs tangled, lazily companionable.

'Goodnight.'

End of conversation.

I knew better than to push her, but I lay on the sofa and missed her, fiercely. I wished she'd told me everything. It wasn't lost on me that this was exactly what she had done before. Maybe that was the one constant in our relationship, I thought unhappily, each of us on either side of a deep crevasse filled with unspeakable subjects. There was no trust without honesty, and no love without trust. Bleak thoughts, considering the joy I'd felt earlier in the evening.

I must have dozed for a while because it was after one when I heard a noise in the hallway. Someone was moving around, at ease in the dark, but trying to be quiet. Not Maeve, I thought. Someone who had no reason to be in the flat.

I slid off the sofa, feeling at a disadvantage as I reached for my jeans. If I had to have a fight I wanted to be wearing something. After that there wasn't time for anything subtle. I took two steps across the room and yanked the door open, stepping forward to shove the solid figure of the intruder back. He cannoned into the bedroom door frame with an exclamation of surprise and pain. I didn't wait for him to recover, launching myself at him, crossing my fingers there was no knife or gun or second man I didn't know about.

No weapons, no back-up: what he did have was total aggression. He didn't miss a beat, responding with a solid punch in the stomach that sent the breath wheezing out of me, then followed it up with a forearm across my throat. I found myself pinned against the wall for a bad moment until I twisted away from him. I got hold of the collar of his jacket, hauled him off balance and punched him in the face and he swung at me again. This time he missed. I hit him another couple of times, keyed up, on some level glad to have a focus for the anger and uncertainty and tension that had been keeping me awake. He clouted me on the side of the head and jabbed me in the ribs, and the two of us wound up face to face, chest to chest, evenly matched, neither of us able to end it, clinging to one another, until I actually heard what he was saying in a low, furious voice.

'It's me, you twat.'

Josh Derwent.

I let go of him slowly and he stepped away from me, the two of us breathing hard. There was enough light in the hallway that I could see his face, and the lack of friendliness in his eyes. Rainwater glinted on his clothes.

'What are you doing here?'

'Checking up on you.'

'Why?'

He jerked his head towards the bedroom. 'I don't want her to get hurt.'

'By me?' I put a hand to my stomach and winced; it was going to be a hell of a bruise.

'By whoever is sitting in a car on the other side of the road, watching this place.'

'What?' I forgot about how I was feeling. 'Someone's out there?'

'Two of them. In an unmarked car.'

'Job?'

'No way to know. Is it the sort of thing your lot would do?'

'Yes.' But it was also the sort of thing Geraint and his pals would do. I felt cold. I had been so careful. I'd made sure I wasn't followed to Maeve's door, and they had found me anyway. 'Are they just watching?'

'So far.'

'How did you get in?'

'Over a couple of walls and up the back stairs. They didn't see me.'

'Can I get out that way?'

'Yeah, but what if they aren't job, and they think you're still here, and they come in looking for you?' He smiled, without any humour. 'Didn't think of that, did you?'

He was right and I couldn't put Maeve in harm's way.

'Look, it's pissing down,' Derwent began, and stopped. I looked over my shoulder to see what had turned him to stone: Maeve, coming out of her room. She had put on a T-shirt and pyjama shorts, and was pulling a huge cardigan around her. Her hair was in glorious disorder, and the T-shirt was so tight that she might as well have been naked: soft curves, long legs, the sort of vision that detached your brain from its gears for a while. Josh Derwent and I stood there, struck completely

151

dumb, neither of us capable of forming a single coherent thought. She wrapped the cardigan around herself and looked from me to him.

'What are you doing here? Can I put the light on?'

'No.' We said it in unison, and it snapped me out of my daze. 'There's a car outside, someone watching the flat. Josh came to warn me.'

'And you don't know who it is.' Maeve was never slow on the uptake, even half asleep.

'No.'

She rubbed her eyes, trying to wake up. 'I heard you talking . . . I couldn't think what was going on . . .'

'He heard me come in,' Derwent said.

I was realising, belatedly, that he had known exactly who he was punching when he hit me. He glowered at me.

'I thought you'd be in the bedroom.'

'Yeah, I was earlier.'

'Rob,' Maeve said, a quiet protest, and the guilt kicked in. What was I doing, boasting to Josh Derwent about what Maeve and I had done, like a teenager showing off to his mates?

The answer came instantly. He swung around to Maeve, his jaw tight with anger.

'So is all this starting up again? You and him?'

'No,' she said. 'It was the end of it.'

Matter-of-fact. I knew she was right and I knew it was a better ending than I'd deserved but the pain in my chest was worse than any bruise I'd got from Josh Derwent. He flicked another look at me and I did my own version of the sardonic eyebrow-raise I'd had from him when I was in the police station, a few hours and a million years earlier.

'How did you know about the surveillance? How did you know to warn us?' Maeve was catching up. For once, Derwent looked embarrassed.

'I was coming back from that job in Tottenham. It was on my way. I just thought I'd check on you, that's all, and then I saw the car outside. I knew Rob would be here.'

'At one o'clock in the morning?' She raised her chin, defiant. 'Even I didn't know he'd be here then.'

'You're always the last person to know how you feel.' The tenderness in his voice made me look at him again speculatively: it wasn't just that he wanted to sleep with her, as I'd assumed. Maybe we had more in common than I'd thought, but it didn't make me like him more.

'And instead of knocking on the door or calling me, you decided to let yourself in?' Maeve shook her head. 'Just invade my privacy, why don't you?'

'I thought it might be more useful if they didn't know I was here.'

'You still could have phoned,' I pointed out and he glowered at me.

'I could, but that would have been missing a trick.'

'What do you mean?'

'If you don't know who they are, I'm guessing you don't want them following you.'

I shook my head. 'If they're colleagues, I'll find out about it the next time my boss is in touch with me, but they don't have any reason to keep their distance. If Opal wanted to talk to me, she'd have let me know by now. And if they're not colleagues, I really don't want to have anything to do with them.'

Derwent looked me up and down. 'Presumably you had clothes at some point. Might be time to put them on.'

Maeve shivered and looked down at herself: bare legs under the cardigan, not enough for the middle of a cold night. 'I'm going to get dressed too.'

'Shame,' Derwent said, and got a glare as she disappeared.

He turned back to me and the two of us gave each other matching looks of assessment and disapproval and mutual distrust.

'You should go out the back,' he said in the end.

'I thought you said that was a bad idea.'

'Not if they think you've left already.'

'Why would they think that?'

'If they think I'm you.'

I got dressed in double-quick time. Derwent and I had fairly similar clothes, it transpired – dark jeans, a dark jumper, trainers and a heavy jacket. But of course, he had planned that.

'I noticed what you were wearing earlier when you left Charing Cross nick. Didn't think you'd bother to change.'

'Didn't think I'd need to.' I was standing at the window, the blind screening me from view as I peered down the street. 'I don't recognise the car but that doesn't mean much. I can't see the occupants.'

'Mm.' He shrugged himself into my coat. 'Do you want this back?'

'Keep it,' I said, resignedly.

'Not my style.' He tweaked the hood up. 'And you might need it when you go back to your undercover life. Won't they notice if you come back wearing something different?'

It was a fair point. The coat had a distinctive reflector flash on the sleeves. I'd had it for a couple of years and I'd never be able to replace it with something that matched exactly. If it was just Geraint I might have taken a chance but Juliet noticed everything to do with clothes. 'I've got the use of a locker at Euston, on the upper level,' I said. 'It's the fifth one from the left in the first row. The lock has a combination code – eight zero two zero. You can leave the coat there.'

'OK.'

'There's another coat in there – a raincoat. You can keep it.'

He grinned. 'Glad to hear it. I wasn't looking forward to getting home in this weather with no coat.'

'I'll leave this one there in a few hours.' I picked up his Superdry jacket: always that or North Face for off-duty coppers, which was why I avoided those brands. 'You can pick it up whenever it suits you.'

'If you wouldn't mind.' He was settling himself into my jacket, making sure it fitted as if he was used to wearing it. 'Right. I'll be off.'

'You know those people might not have my wellbeing at heart. Be careful.'

A flash of white teeth: genuine amusement. He didn't scare easily. I went down the stairs with him to repeat the code for the locker, and to thank him which he shrugged off.

'I'm not doing it for you.'

'I know.'

He stopped to look at me. 'If you hurt her—'

'I won't.'

'Never mind these guys. You don't want me coming after you. And I will.'

'I have no doubt.'

He swung out of the door and slammed it behind him. I heard quick footsteps walking down the path. I ran back up the stairs to watch his progress.

Maeve was in the sitting room, peering out warily.

'He's gone,' she said without looking.

'Yeah.'

She turned a pale face to me. 'Rob? But I thought – he looks so like you.'

I went to join her and watched the figure half-walking, half-jogging down the street. It was beyond strange to see myself in the distance; he had replicated my way of moving almost exactly.

A car engine started up and lights came on, gilding the hammering rain as the vehicle turned to follow Josh.

'I hope he's going to be OK.' Maeve was fidgeting, tense. 'I didn't get to say goodbye.'

'He won't mind.'

'I mind.'

I looked at her, and wondered – but then, Derwent had been right, she was the last person to guess what she wanted. It wasn't my place to point out that she had been quite calm about me leaving again without a backward glance, but for Josh Derwent she was biting her lip . . . *Anyone but him*, I thought, and knew I couldn't say it.

'What happens now?' she asked.

'I have to go.' I looked past her again at the empty street. 'I don't know when they'll realise that's not me. I want to be long gone before they come back. With any luck they'll think they were wrong about me being here at all once they realise they're following Josh.'

'Hope so.' She shivered. 'I could do without thugs.'

'Lock the doors after I go.'

A quick double-blink, wide eyes. 'Thank goodness you're here. I'd never have thought of that.'

'Yeah, all right. I suppose I don't need to tell you to look out for strangers trying to get to know you either.'

'I'll be on my guard.'

I drew her close and held her for a moment. 'Thank you for tonight. I'm sorry it worked out like this.'

She leaned her head against mine. 'Goodbye is never going to be easy for us, is it?'

'I hate leaving.'

'But you have to go.' She half-smiled. 'You know, it broke

156

my heart when you left, and I still love you – I think I always will – but we're not who we used to be. I'm glad we had tonight, but like I said, this is the end.'

'There's no way back?' The question was almost involuntary, but I needed to hear her say it.

'This isn't what either of us needs,' she said gently. 'It was good, once, and I'm glad we can remember that, and this evening, instead of the last time you left.'

'I hope I helped a bit.'

'Yeah, it was a heck of a therapy session.' She shrugged. 'I have a long way to go.'

'You'll get there.'

'Look after yourself.'

'You too.'

She kissed me lightly, with nothing more than affection. Well, everything had to end sometime. I kissed her back in much the same way, and this time I actually said a proper farewell before I made my way down the back stairs, and lost myself in the night.

20

'Look what the cat dragged in.' Den swaggered into the kitchen. 'Where have you been, Mark? We thought you'd disappeared. I knew you'd been released from the police station before me so I couldn't think why you weren't back already. Geraint was climbing the walls.'

'I know. I've seen him.' I had, briefly, and got a glower and a snapped, 'Later' when I tried to talk to him. He wasn't pleased with me. I assumed he was angry about the failure of his plan and hoped it wasn't anything more serious.

I still didn't know if he was the one who'd sent the men after me at Maeve's flat, and that worried me. The previous twelve hours had been a game of cat and mouse where I didn't know if I was the only one playing. I'd gone to the far side of London and killed time in a fast-food restaurant in White City before zigzagging back to Euston. With a sigh of relief, I'd discovered my jacket, still damp. I left Derwent's in its place. The jacket meant that he had made it to the locker unharmed. There was a note with my jacket, scrawled in a hurry:

Lost them at five. They wasted a lot of time following night buses. Hope you made good use of it.

I left him a note of my own with my thanks, resisting the urge to add a little advice. I was probably the last person who could – or should – tell him what to do about Maeve. It wasn't exactly my dearest wish for them to get together but I wanted her to be happy, above all. I just wasn't sure Josh Derwent was capable of making that happen, even if he was free to try. The physical scars from her last relationship were one thing; the mental damage was another. Not for me to fix, I reminded myself, and missed her.

There was something else to confront. For the first time, I didn't want to work – to lie, to pretend, to face into danger with a calm expression and a dry mouth. When I'd done it before, the thrill had been unbeatable. This time I felt tired to my soul. The reminder of what I'd left behind had given me pause. My old life had been easy – dull, sometimes, and frustrating, but with a clear line separating work from the rest of it. I had fretted at the predictability of it and discounted the happiness, including what Maeve and I had had together. My current job was absorbing and open-ended. It went on until the bad guys were locked up or I was found out. It demanded everything from me, and for the first time I wasn't sure I could fulfil my side of the bargain.

I'd been warned about this during training. I'd been told I could expect to feel burnt out, especially after stressful experiences. I'd have to be literally insane to *want* to put myself in danger again. It would be strange if I didn't mind.

I would do this job, I decided, and then I would see. I would get to the end with Geraint Carter. I would take him down before he could hurt anyone else. And then I would have a proper think about whether I wanted to go on.

I went off and had breakfast in a greasy spoon, not hurrying over it, and then spent another couple of hours wandering aimlessly through London. When I was good and ready, I took a train and taxi back to Haulton House. I spent most of the time hoping that the men hadn't gone back to Maeve's flat. I had no way of knowing. I couldn't contact her again without putting her in danger. Opal would tell me anything I needed to know, until the end of the operation when I would be free again.

And if she didn't, and things had gone wrong for Maeve, Josh Derwent would track me down, undercover or not, to make me regret it.

For all my fears, being back in Geraint Carter's inner circle felt surprisingly natural. I'd slipped back into character with no difficulty as I walked up the drive. Mark would be relieved to have got back safely, and unsettled by his arrest, and wary in case he had done the wrong thing by not returning immediately – all emotions that fitted in nicely with my own feelings.

Now Den was looking amused but not suspicious. 'I hope you had a good excuse.'

I took a mug out of the cupboard. 'I went to see my ex-girlfriend.'

'*The* ex-girlfriend?' Juliet said, her eyes wide, and I nodded.

'How did it go?' Den asked, then laughed. 'Must have been all right if you spent the night.'

Bruno twisted to look at me, the first time he'd shown any sign of knowing I was there. He was sitting at the big table in the kitchen with a coffee in front of him, wrapped in a dressing gown. It was getting on for half past two in the afternoon but he looked rumpled, as if he'd just got out of bed. 'Did you get a shag?'

I didn't say anything, but I grinned to myself as I dropped a teabag into the mug and held it under the boiling-water tap.

'Nice one.' Den punched me in the shoulder. 'Just what I wanted to do when I got back but Cassie wasn't keen. This is why you should never marry them.'

Juliet was sitting bolt upright on her stool on the other side of the breakfast bar. 'Shut up, Den. You're disgusting.' To me, she said, 'Is she still your ex?'

I nodded.

'So fucking her just reminded her why she dumped you?' Bruno sneered and I stirred the tea with great care.

'Not exactly.'

'I can't believe you slept with her,' Juliet blurted out, her face pink. 'I mean – she broke your heart, you said.'

I smiled. 'Yeah, well, we forgave each other.'

'But it's not back on. You're not together anymore.'

I shook my head and she shifted again on her stool, trying to regain her composure as Bruno scowled behind her and Den turned away to hide a smirk.

'What was this mysterious business trip, anyway?' Juliet turned to Bruno. 'You look broken. Den is still wired. Mark disappeared for twenty-four hours. That's not normal.'

'Just business,' Den said, not with any aggression but in a way that didn't invite further questions.

'Were we the only ones there . . . on business?' I asked casually. 'There seemed to be other people there with the same . . . er . . . goal in mind.'

Den shook his head and raised a finger to his lips. Not in front of Juliet, I gathered.

'You three.' Harry leaned into the kitchen. 'The boss wants you. Right now.'

Bruno groaned. 'Is he angry?'

Harry shrugged. He wasn't in trouble, whatever about the rest of us. I abandoned my tea and followed Den, aware that Bruno was behind me. He kept sniffing.

Big night, Bruno?

In the study, Geraint was pacing back and forth, his face tense. 'Sit.'

It was an order. I sat, choosing the opposite end of the sofa from Den. Bruno folded himself into an armchair, crossing his legs casually. His father looked down at him with disfavour.

'Why aren't you dressed?'

'I've only just got up.'

'Why did you stay in bed so late?'

'I was tired.'

Geraint's face darkened; Bruno's replies were perilously close to arrogant. Instead of arguing with him, though, the older man swung around to me.

'And you. Where the fuck have you been? Why couldn't I get through to your phone?'

'I went to see an old girlfriend. I thought it was a better idea than coming straight back here for a debrief, in case anyone was watching. And I switched off my phone once I got out of the police station.'

'That's not what Dad expects from an employee.' Bruno was looking smug.

I leaned back on the sofa. 'I know what he expects. I wanted some space between this family and me in case what I told the cops didn't satisfy them. If anyone checks the phone records, there won't be calls and messages from Geraint to me after the incident on the Underground. No digital connection between us, which is what you'd expect if the situation was the way we presented it to the cops.'

'I didn't think of that,' Den said, and I shrugged.

'Probably unnecessary. But after we got arrested it seemed wiser to disappear for a while instead of hurrying back here.'

'Who's the girlfriend? What does she do?' Geraint's eyes were flint-hard.

'She's a travel agent,' I lied, knowing that it was a job Maeve had pretended to do when she didn't want to talk about being a police officer. It was good cover for coming and going at unpredictable times. 'Works shifts for a little agency in Mayfair that's open twenty-four hours a day. Very high end. They have the kind of clients who don't want to keep their enquiries to London office hours.'

'Why did you want to see her?'

'I needed some way of winding down, after being arrested. I – er – knew she'd be pleased to see me.'

Geraint's face softened. 'It takes you like that, does it?'

'Sometimes. I couldn't believe we'd got away with it when I came out of the police station.' I shook my head, marvelling at our luck. 'No one saw a thing. They didn't have any idea what I'd done. I told them the story you'd given us, and it worked.'

'Me too.' Den was nodding like a toy dog. 'It was easy. They just let me go. They didn't know anything. They had no leads and no ideas. Some CCTV footage that could have been anything. Easy enough to play the innocent.'

'That's what I did too,' I said.

'Can't believe you let yourselves get arrested. No one saw me.' Bruno sounded slightly put out, if anything. 'I just walked off.'

'Did you have two big bald blokes interviewing you?' Den asked me, ignoring his brother-in-law.

'No. A man and a woman. They didn't seem to know what was going on, to be honest with you. They'd been brought in from somewhere else to do the interviews because there were so many of us in custody. It was just a formality in the end – answer the questions, view the CCTV, sign a statement and boom. They let me go. And Bruno, I don't know how you got away because they seemed to have arrested half the people in the station.'

'Short. They couldn't see him on the CCTV,' Den said, unwisely. Bruno jumped to his feet.

163

'Fuck you.'

'Sit down.' Geraint stepped in front of Bruno and shoved him, hard, so he fell back into his seat. 'I've had enough of your bickering.'

'Boss,' I said, 'were there more people involved than just the three of us? At the station, on the platform. I thought . . .'

'Trust you to notice, Mark.' Geraint's eyes flicked over his son and son-in-law, who were looking baffled. 'We weren't on our own, no. I didn't know in advance, for what it's worth. I was informed afterwards that there were other . . . participants, if you like. To ensure that it went smoothly.'

'They didn't trust us to get the job done.' Den scowled. 'Bastards.'

'I'm not sure it was a matter of trust.' Geraint cleared his throat, seeming ill at ease. 'I did point out that our part of the operation worked perfectly. The kind of people they are – they want insurance policies. They want to achieve their goals.'

'Even with their help, it didn't work out exactly the way it was supposed to, did it?' I said slowly. 'No casualties, and a fairly muted reaction in the media. BTP said it was a prank gone wrong. It's all died down by today.'

Geraint grunted. 'Not what we intended.'

'But it was only ever a trial run.' Den leaned forward, elbows on his knees. 'It was just a practice for the big one.'

'That's what I told Max and Ivan.' Geraint paced up and down. 'I haven't been able to get hold of Phil yet. He was the one who supplied the muscle yesterday.'

'How did he manage that?' I asked innocently, and Den gave me a short history of Phil Boxton that more or less matched what Opal's expert had told me.

'Basically, if you want muscle, he's the one you go to,' Den finished up. 'Or if you need people with specific skills.'

'Skills like what?'

'Do I have to spell it out for you? The kind of skills that might get you locked up for a long stretch.'

'He's a good friend,' Geraint said. 'A good man.'

Quite the opposite of that, from what I knew, but I nodded.

'Does it change things?' Den asked his father-in-law. 'The plan? Given that it didn't work out the way we wanted.'

'We might refine our main event. I think we proved our commitment, for what it's worth. You did well,' Geraint added, gesturing vaguely at me and Den and leaving Bruno out. 'But it's more important than ever that we're careful about who we talk to, and who we trust. Any leaks – anything that jeopardises the operation – and heads will roll. And I do mean that, Bruno. It's not up to me now. We're part of a bigger movement. I won't be able to protect you if you fuck up.'

'Why are you saying that to me?'

Geraint bent and grabbed a handful of his son's dressing gown. 'Why do you think? No more drugs. No more booze. No more pissing about. If you step out of line you won't get a second chance. And I won't lift a finger to help you. You've had every chance to get yourself straight and get your act together. If I see you drinking or if I think you've been taking drugs or if you fuck up in any way, no matter how small, you're out. I don't need the hassle.' He straightened up, his face grey. I thought he looked worse than he had since he'd come out of hospital. 'Don't make the mistake of thinking I need you, Bruno. I have other people I can trust. I have another son who can take on the business one day if you aren't able for it, and I have Den in the meantime. You need to prove yourself to me now, and if you don't, I won't think twice about shutting you out.'

I'd expected Bruno to respond with rage but he nodded, his face tight. An unwelcome dose of reality, I diagnosed, and could almost have felt sorry for him.

21

After all that, it was something of an anticlimax to go back to the old routine the following week – running or swimming in the early morning, small domestic duties such as driving Geraint's wife and daughters during the day, a lengthy gym session in the afternoon, and keeping my ears open at family mealtimes to see if anyone said anything of interest. By and large they did not. Naomi was like a ghost, silent, arriving as late as she dared to dinner and leaving at the earliest opportunity. Bruno was silent too, in a different way. It was the brooding silence of someone who has been wronged, looking for a scapegoat to blame. I recognised the smouldering resentment in his eyes when Geraint clapped me on the shoulder or told me a story from his youth, both hallmarks of his favour. To Bruno's mute loathing I returned nothing but bland respect, giving him no opportunity to take offence. The downside of that was my suspicion that if he had no one else to harm it was Naomi who suffered. He was dangerous, I thought, and I made absolutely sure not to catch Naomi's eye, or to be alone with her. There was no way to shield her from her husband, at least for me. I could only be a danger to her, I reminded myself, and hated seeing her hold herself as if her ribs or back or arms hurt.

The other person who was different was Juliet. She was better at hiding her feelings than the others, maintaining her usual cheerful chatter and spending many hours winding her loving father around her little finger. But it was superficial, at best. I noticed her pushing her food around her plate at meal-times, and I thought she was avoiding me. If it was because she was upset with me for sleeping with Maeve, I thought it was a good thing to keep some distance between us – that was a line that I knew not to cross. Other undercover police officers had been less wary, and had had long relationships with suspects – children, even. I would be in serious trouble with Opal if I did anything at all to make Juliet think I was interested in her, and quite rightly.

As it happened, I was correct in thinking Juliet was avoiding me, but wrong about the reasons. One morning, after breakfast, without looking at me, she asked Geraint if I could drive her to Oxford.

'I've got Christmas shopping to do, Daddy, and I don't want anyone else to see what I'm buying.'

'It's only November,' Bruno said through a mouthful of toast. 'Who the fuck needs to do Christmas shopping in November?'

'I do,' Juliet snapped.

'I can spare Mark.' Geraint's face went from indulgent to stern as she skipped out of the kitchen to get dressed. 'Don't leave her on her own, will you? I don't like her being alone somewhere like that.'

Oxford was a sedate little provincial city, and especially in the run-up to Christmas it was as far from mean streets as you could get. I knew that Geraint was haunted by the memory of the two men who'd tried to send him a message through Juliet. I was haunted by them in a different way; I had enabled Geraint to identify them, which led to their deaths. It was a good reminder for me that Geraint was prepared to use lethal force, even if the provocation seemed slight. The danger was real.

It was a bright winter day, the sun low enough to shine between the trees that lined the road. We raced through bars of shadow as I squinted against the stabbing beams of light. Juliet retired behind massive sunglasses. I was driving the new Range Rover that had replaced the one I'd driven at the goons, and it still had a new-car smell. There wasn't too much traffic on the road and I was making good time.

It should have been a pleasant little outing, but the mood in the car was dark.

'Is everything OK?' I asked after the tenth mile had passed without a word spoken.

'Yes.'

'Good.' I allowed myself to sound slightly mystified though, and Juliet sighed.

'Look, it's nothing. Not about you. I'm just . . . busy. And thinking about what I need to get today.' She turned her head and stared out of the window, biting her lip. One glossy fingernail tapped on the door frame and I glanced across to see that she was pointing discreetly at a small black lens mounted on the dashboard. A dashcam, newly fitted, presumably with a wide-angled lens that would take in the whole front of the car. And I could assume it recorded sound as well as images.

I made a big show of shaking my head as if I thought she was being unreasonable. 'Suit yourself. Want the radio on?'

'If you like.'

Bland, forgettable pop filled the car, and we didn't speak again until I'd found a space in one of Oxford's multi-storey car parks and switched the engine off.

'Let's go.' Juliet was out of the car already, a rabbit disappearing down a burrow. I scrambled to follow her, catching up by the lifts.

'So that's new.'

'Yeah.' She kept her face turned away from me. 'He doesn't trust you.'

'He can.'

'I know that.' She hesitated. 'He doesn't trust *anyone*. It's not you specifically.'

When the doors opened the lift contained two middle-aged women who were deeply absorbed in scurrilous gossip. They ignored us. Nonetheless, Juliet waited until we had reached the ground floor and started walking towards the city centre before she picked up the conversation again. Her hands were jammed in her pockets and her head was down, her chin tucked inside her scarf. I had to strain to hear her.

'Look, I don't know what Dad is doing at the moment. I know it's not completely above board. I'm not stupid. I know you and Den got arrested the other week.' She shivered, drawing her coat around herself. 'Don't even bother to lie to me about it. The way the two of you were so cocky when you got back – like you'd got away with something. I didn't think you were like that.'

'I'm not. I mean, there was a bit of a thrill to it,' I admitted. 'But I'm not someone who gets excited by being arrested, believe me.'

'Just excited enough that you had to go and see your ex?' She gave me a look, the false lashes turning her eyes starry. I tried to think about how to answer that but before I could, she flapped a hand at me. 'Don't worry. I don't care about that. The thing is, Mark, you're really not my type. And I wouldn't want to do anything to make Logan jealous.'

'Logan?' He was the personal trainer who Geraint employed

169

full-time in his gym area, a weightlifter with hands the size of hams and a sweet disposition. 'Does your dad know about that?'

'No, and I'm not going to tell him. And neither are you.' She blinked at me angelically. 'Logan fingers me in the weights room when everyone else is getting changed, after we've done our training, when I'm all sweaty. He pulls my leggings down and bends me over the bench and fucks me as hard as he can. Sometimes I sit on his face. You know he's strong enough to hold me in the air while he makes me scream.'

'That's . . . nice.'

She laughed. 'Are you shocked? I'm not Daddy's little girl, Mark. I like sex and I like men who aren't too scared of my dad to make a move.'

I could let her think that I was scared of Geraint, but it seemed more likely to harm her than help. She had enough psychological damage thanks to her upbringing, and it was likely to get worse before it got better. This was one thing I could address with honesty. I stopped walking and turned her to face me. 'Listen, Juliet, you're gorgeous. You're everything any man could want. If I'd met you in the real world, I'd have done my best to make you fall for me, believe me. But this life I've fallen into – it's different. I don't know the rules yet.'

'The rules are that you do whatever my dad says.' She couldn't look at me.

'If the time was right and if you were interested, I would tell your dad to mind his own business.'

That brought her eyes up to mine. 'Really?'

'Seriously. But I'm older than you, and even if I wasn't, I don't exactly have a lot to offer. At the moment, I don't want a relationship with anyone. But if someone wants to be with you, and they're worth your time, they won't wait for your dad's permission.'

170

'He wouldn't like that.'

'You'd be worth the risk.'

'Oh.' She blushed, and pulled her scarf up over her mouth, but I thought she was pleased. She started off again with more energy and I matched her stride.

'Incidentally, Logan is gay.'

That brought her to a halt again. 'What?'

'He's proposing to his boyfriend at Christmas.'

Her face was red again, but this time with anger and embarrassment. 'Fuck you, Mark.'

'It doesn't matter.' I felt sincerely sorry for her, for a number of reasons, and making fun of her for lying didn't seem right.

'Look, it was just . . .' she lifted one shoulder, helpless. 'Everyone sees me the way my dad sees me. His little princess. I'm not that. I'm my own person. There are things that I want and . . . and need . . . and they have nothing to do with my dad and what he wants for me.'

'That's normal.'

'Is it? Is it normal to make up a complete fantasy about being screwed by some random bloke?'

'It's understandable,' I said. 'And not a big deal.'

'Why are you so *nice* all the time?'

'Why do you say that as if it's a bad thing?'

She made a noise of pure frustration and set off again, and that was the end of that. I followed her from shop to shop, watching her choose presents for people with unerring knowledge of what they would like, adding bags to the collection I was carrying without pausing to calculate what she was spending.

In an old-fashioned men's outfitters in Turl Street she pulled out a rainbow of cashmere jumpers in different sizes, ten or twelve of them.

'Extra, extra large. That should fit Harry. His shoulders . . .' She was flipping through the stack of folded jumpers, searching

171

for something. 'Ah.' She turned to me and held a green one up to my shoulders. 'I think that's the right size for you. Not too skimpy.'

'You don't have to—' I began, and she cut me off.

'I know. Do you like the colour?'

A woman leaned in between us to twitch a scarf off the display, jostling me out of her way. I frowned, irritated by the interruption.

'I love it, but I don't deserve it.'

'Yes, you do.'

Shopping wasn't enough to improve her mood, I was surprised to see. If anything, she seemed even more distracted, almost on the verge of tears.

'Meal break?' I suggested as we came out into the narrow street and she followed me into the Covered Market where there was a greasy spoon tucked between the butchers and florists and gift shops, all doing strong pre-Christmas business. It was a proper old-fashioned caff that smelled of cooking bacon and had steamed-up windows, and we were lucky to get a table.

'This isn't the sort of place I usually go,' Juliet observed, pulling her coat around herself.

'More fool you, then. It's great.' I left her peering at the gingham oilcloth that covered the table as if she'd never seen anything quite like it. I went to the counter to order for both of us. When I put my hand in my pocket for my wallet I encountered something unfamiliar: a hard plastic rectangular object. A small mobile phone. Not mine, though; mine was in the inside pocket of my coat. I didn't take it out to look at it, not with Juliet watching, but I remembered the shopper jostling me out of the way earlier and I saw the incident in a new light.

I had said to Opal that I needed some way of contacting her, and Opal had provided.

Back at our table, Juliet was still looking miserable. I set a mug in front of her.

'There you are. Finest builder's tea. That'll cheer you up.'

'Thanks.'

'What's up?' I sat down opposite her, and my knee nudged hers under the small table. She jumped. 'Not still worrying about the Logan thing, are you?'

'No. Not that. Although I'm sorry I lied.' She couldn't look at me. 'Mark, you need to be careful.'

It wasn't what I'd expected her to say. I froze. 'What do you mean?'

'You know about Neil.'

'Neil?' It took me a second. 'The chauffeur?'

'He was nice and kind, like you. He was young. Dad liked him. *I* liked him.'

'And what happened? He left, didn't he?'

'That's what they said.' A fat tear slid down her cheek and she rubbed it away. 'But I don't know if that's true. One day he was there and the next he was gone. I heard something that night. Shouting. Odd noises. I asked Dad about it but he told me not to worry.' A tear slipped down the other cheek. 'He said Neil had stepped out of line and I wasn't to think about him again. And he made me promise not to go near his flat, by the stables, so I didn't.'

The waitress dumped our plates in front of us with a cheery, 'There you go!' and I muttered my thanks automatically. I'd never felt less like eating.

'I don't know what he did, Mark, and I don't know what my father did to him, but I don't want the same thing to happen to you. He's watching you . . . and me . . . and everyone. He's paranoid, now. Whatever he's doing, it must be big . . . and he won't allow anyone to get in the way of what he wants.'

173

22

As warnings went, it was both timely and daunting. The mobile phone in my pocket felt heavier than it should, a physical reminder of the danger I was in. I was sorely tempted to throw it away rather than risk taking it back to Haulton House, but I needed it, I thought; I had to be able to communicate with Opal. It wasn't safe, but the danger of not being able to warn the authorities about another terror attack was far more terrifying.

Once we'd eaten I slipped into the toilets, where behind a locked door I was able to take out the phone and look at it properly. It was switched on, but asked me for a four-digit password that I didn't have. After a moment of blind frustration, I tried 8020, the same number I had been given for the locker in Euston Station, and the phone unlocked for me. The notes app was open on the screen.

Open the email app. Any key stroke you type is downloaded automatically and will be read – do not send any emails. Images taken with the camera on this phone will be downloaded automatically also. Do not save them on the device. Check the deleted items folder for messages; they will only be sent in exceptional circumstances. Delete this.

I deleted it, then went to email and typed a thumbs-up emoji, then deleted that. It felt like shouting into the void but I had to assume it worked. It was a lifeline – or a noose that I was placing around my own neck.

Juliet seemed more cheerful after she'd got the warning off her chest, and after the café we visited some more shops before I ground to a halt.

'My arms are going to give out if you buy anything else.'

'Wimp,' she said lightly. 'Logan wouldn't notice he was carrying anything.'

'Logan would have made you eat salad for lunch, and he certainly wouldn't have let you have that drink.'

She grinned around the straw that she was biting: I'd bought her a strawberry milkshake, as sweet as her nature and bright pink like the tip of her tongue. 'You could carry twice as much as that. Have you finally had enough of shopping?'

'I had enough of shopping about ten minutes after we got here.'

'*Men.*' She sighed in mock irritation. 'All right. But I'm going to need to come back next week. There are a few things I still need to pick up.'

'I'll get Logan to show me some arm exercises between this and then.'

'Anything so you don't look so *weedy*.'

'Oh, I see. Personal insults now.'

We bickered cheerfully all the way back to the car, and if I checked there was no one following us every couple of minutes, Juliet seemed oblivious. I drove back to Haulton House listening to her prattle about Christmas, and the holiday she was planning with her mother for the New Year ('Have you been to Barbados?') that was going to be her father's Christmas present. The headlights behind us changed as vehicles came and went. No one followed us. No one tried to intercept us.

'You do have a passport, don't you?'

'Um . . .' I came back to full attention with a jerk. 'Yes. Yes, I do.' And it was in the right identity, too; Opal had made sure of that.

'I'm surprised. I wouldn't have thought you'd need a passport.' She blushed. 'I mean – I know you were really poor before Dad took you on.'

Yes, why the hell had I spent some of my limited funds on a passport? It was always the small questions that tripped you up, my trainer had told me. Always the things you took for granted, so you hadn't prepared a lie because you never expected to need it.

'I was skint,' I said smoothly. 'I'd decided to emigrate if my luck didn't change.'

'Emigrate? Where were you going to go?'

'Australia.'

'Spiders.'

'Sunshine,' I countered. 'But then my luck did change, didn't it? So I'll stick with the clouds for now.'

Juliet went silent again, but it was a different kind of silence. She waited until I opened the car door for her at the house to speak again, slipping out of her seat and stopping beside me.

'I'm glad you didn't go to Australia.'

'Me too.'

She gazed into my eyes, and she was close enough that I could smell strawberries on her breath.

'I'm pretty sure your dad is watching,' I said softly, and she leaned sideways so she could see over my shoulder.

'Staring out of the study window, right at us. He's on the phone but I don't think it's distracting him.'

'I thought as much.' I took a step back, away from her, and gave her a rueful smile that made her laugh as she sashayed away. I might try not to flirt with Juliet, but Juliet was still

176

going to flirt with me. Thank God for defensive fathers, I thought, as I carried handfuls of bags into the house. Thank God for a cover story that made my reticence understandable instead of insulting. If Juliet started minding about me turning her down, I would find myself out of a job.

Harry stood near the doorway of the study, watching me, his hands in his pockets.

'Do you want to give me a hand?'

'Nope.'

'Thanks very much,' I said, and got a craggy grin in return. Harry knew the score. He'd spent a lifetime around the argumentative, cantankerous Carters. You knew where the invisible boundaries were and you stayed on the right side of them, no matter how hard it was. He didn't have to warn me to stay away from Juliet, and he knew it.

Nevertheless, I stopped next to him on my way out to move the car. 'I take it I did the right thing as far as Geraint was concerned.'

A long, slow nod.

'And I should keep doing that.'

'If you value your skin.'

I did. Not as much as Harry thought I did, but too much to want to risk it for pretty Juliet.

I drove the car around to the garage where I inspected it for damage and trackers and bugs – all part of the daily routine, as prescribed by Geraint – and made a note to wash it the following day to get rid of the flecks of mud we'd acquired on the road. Then, leaving the garage door open, I walked outside and jogged up the steps that led to the chauffeur's apartment above the garage building. I moved with confidence, as if I had a perfect right to be there. Anyone but Geraint would assume I was there on his business, and Geraint was on the phone.

At least, I hoped Geraint was on the phone.

The door to the flat was locked, which shouldn't have surprised me. It was nothing more than a standard Yale lock and I carded the door, resisting the urge to turn around and check for cameras. The cover story, if I needed it, was that Juliet had told me about the chauffeur's accommodation and I'd wondered about moving in there. Space of my own, privacy, the chance to play music and watch television without disturbing anyone – a literal halfway house between independence and being available whenever Geraint decided he needed me.

I hoped like hell I wouldn't need to explain myself to anyone, though. I hadn't forgotten that someone had sent a tail after me when I left Charing Cross police station, or that they'd managed to track me to Maeve's home. I couldn't assume they trusted me and I certainly didn't trust them.

The air inside the flat rushed out with a sigh like a dying breath as the door came open. It was cold and musty; no one had been in there for a long time. I didn't put on the lights. The curtains were open and the floodlighting around Geraint's house was effective enough that I could see everything quite clearly. The space consisted of a decent-sized sitting room with a pitched roof that reduced the usable floor space considerably, a kitchen and bathroom in the middle and a bedroom at the end. Ideal for the single man who lives on his employer's property. Ideal for me, you'd have thought, in my ill-defined position as Geraint's dogsbody.

The first thing that struck me was the sofa, literally. I walked into the end of it as I moved towards the kitchen area. Looking around, I frowned; why would anyone want to put the sofa in the exact centre of the room when it would have fitted under the areas where the ceiling was lower? It didn't make any sense to me – or at least, it didn't until I shoved one end of it out of position and saw the large, wavering stain on the floorboards. The boards themselves were gappy and rough, unfinished, and

I assumed there had once been a carpet laid over them. I looked up at the nearest window. The glass was cracked from side to side with a bullseye ring in the centre, as if something had hit it very hard.

A head?

I left the sofa at an angle and gave the kitchen and bathroom a cursory look. The cupboards were empty, the bathroom clean but with bare towel rails and no toothbrush in the holder. I wasn't expecting to find much in the bedroom, but one corner showed signs of a savage struggle: dents and gouges in the plaster up to about three feet above the floor. I could imagine it all too well: a man crouching, trying to protect himself from an attack with some kind of weapon, maybe breaking free, heading for the door, only to lose the fight in the living room.

They had done what they needed to tidy up, as far as they could without bringing in outside workmen. When enough time had passed from the chauffeur's disappearance, the glass in the window would be replaced. The floorboards would be removed and burned. The plaster would be smoothed over. There would be no trace of Neil ever having lived there, and no sign whatsoever that he'd died there.

I'd been in the flat for a couple of minutes and it felt too long. Moving quickly, I hurried into the bedroom and snapped a couple of pictures of the corner where the plaster was damaged, then the window in the living room, and then, cursing myself for the tremor in my hand, a few pictures of the blood-stains on the floor. I moved the sofa back to exactly where it had been, deleted everything from the phone, closed the door again and ran down the steps to the garage. I started checking the car again, trying to get my breathing under control so my hands would stop shaking. My heart was thudding.

Take it easy.

One more thing to do. I went to the back of the garage, behind the car, where I had scoped out a surveillance blind spot. I tapped out a quick message to say where I was and my very urgent questions, namely: who was Neil? Had he been an undercover officer? Or did he belong to a competitor, like the men Geraint had burned to death for their approach to his daughter? Neither thought was especially comforting.

'Mark?'

I cleared the screen, locked the phone and slid it into my pocket in record time, stepping out from behind the car. Den's face cleared.

'Are you coming to the house?'

'Yeah. I was just checking on the car.'

'I know.' He looked at me oddly. 'That's your job, isn't it?'

Drawing attention to myself wasn't good. I laughed. 'Don't tell the boss but I thought I'd dented it. I was a bit too enthusiastic with my reversing in the car park today.'

'I thought it had rear cameras.'

'It does.' I looked sheepish. 'I was distracted.'

'Juliet?' He chuckled. 'You're a goner, you know that, don't you? Once she's set her sights on you, you might as well give up.'

I closed the garage door and walked across the yard with him. I was barely listening to the jokes he was making at my expense. I was thinking about the man who had lived and died in the building behind me.

23

The cars came back a couple of days later, and I hadn't been expecting them. Three vehicles, black and shiny in the winter sunlight, reassuringly expensive but anonymous. Three drivers, a single passenger in the back of each car, all arriving on time, for a meeting I'd known nothing about. I stood on the front steps beside Geraint, part of a welcoming committee that otherwise consisted of his son, his son-in-law and Harry, and I wished someone had trusted me enough to tip me off about the meeting in advance. A sidelong glance told me little: Geraint was smiling faintly, his expression hard to read. Harry was glowering but that was the default for him. Bruno looked bored and Den was rocking back and forth on his heels, a giveaway that he was feeling tense. None of them looked as if they felt completely unprepared for a confrontation with Max Burniford, Phil Boxton and Ivan Manners. I assumed my face wasn't betraying my own feelings of uncertainty, frustration and fear. If I wasn't to be included in this meeting I'd have to find some way of listening in, and it was high risk.

'Gentlemen.' Geraint moved forward and shook hands with each of them in turn. 'It's a fine day. I thought we'd talk in the summerhouse.'

It seemed Geraint – or someone else – didn't want this meeting in the house, which was a worry. I didn't want Geraint to be suspicious, of me or anyone else.

Burniford grunted, obviously displeased. He was leaning heavily on his stick and his face was already red from exertion after covering the short distance from his car. 'How far is it?'

'Just over there.' Geraint pointed at the summerhouse, which was one of the more ornate features in the grounds. It stood beside a carefully planted and maintained stream that looked convincing but was artificial, fed by a small river that ran inside the less picturesque boundaries of the estate. The stream had a water pump to feed it, some distance away, behind the pool house. Typical Geraint to decide that the beautiful gardens lacked something, and to realise his dream with maximum cost. Juliet had told me the summerhouse was the centrepiece for elaborate parties in the summer, with the bar and a string quartet inside. In the winter it was shuttered, the door locked. Today the shutters were open.

Without further complaint, Burniford set off, breathing loudly enough that I could hear him from some distance away. I followed the others as they walked across the grass at a pace that matched Burniford's effortful progress. Until someone told me I wasn't welcome, I would behave as if I was allowed to be there.

Boxton and Manners walked together, one with a springy stride that hinted at his past as a successful featherweight, the other more awkwardly. Their heads were bent, both of them staring at the ground, and I thought they were talking to one another but at too low a volume for me to hear them. Harry was closest to them and he wasn't the sort of person you could casually engage in conversation afterwards to find out what he'd overheard. I swallowed my frustration and caught up with Den, so that it was natural for me to go into the summerhouse with him.

I didn't know how the space was usually arranged, but one of the housekeepers had been busy that morning. Four wicker armchairs were set up in the centre of the space, under a tinkling chandelier. A low table in the middle was set with china teacups, milk, sugar, and a couple of plates of delicate biscuits. The house-keeper – Malee – appeared in the doorway, a shade out of breath, with a tray containing a teapot and a thermos.

'Hot water,' she said shyly to Geraint as she set it down on a side table, indicating the thermos. 'I pour?'

He barely acknowledged her. 'No. Not now.'

Malee withdrew, and I waited for Geraint to issue an order to one of us to pour the tea instead, but the atmosphere had the kind of chill that the summerhouse's underfloor heating couldn't dispel. Four armchairs: we were not invited to sit at the table. Geraint threw a glance at his son-in-law and gestured to his left. Obediently, Den pulled a couple of upright chairs off a stack in the corner and set them out where Geraint had indicated they should go. Without saying thank you, Bruno sprawled on one, an arm hooked over the back, his legs spread wide. Den sat beside him, legs crossed, arms folded. Did they know, I wondered, how they gave away what they were thinking through their body language? Did they care? Harry's never changed: he was standing by the door with his hands by his sides, the scowl still fixed on his face. I found an unobtrusive place to stand where I could see almost everyone, missing out only on Ivan Manners.

'So,' Burniford said heavily. 'Here again.'

'And you're all very welcome.' Geraint, in full lord-of-the-manor mode.

'Cut the bullshit.' Phil Boxton's voice was harsh. 'We don't need tea and biscuits, you stupid prick. We need to talk about what went wrong on our little outing the other week.'

'Nothing went wrong. It was executed as it should have been.

There were certain . . . unexpected developments, but as a trial run it was effective.'

'Was it?' Manners leaned forward, his elbows on his knees. 'What we talked about was panic. Chaos. What we got was the opposite. You said it would be front-page news. It was dismissed as a *prank*.'

'As I said, it was a trial. A learning experience. You can't just expect these things to work first time. Even the IRA fucked up half the time and they had plenty of practice.'

Burniford jerked in his chair. 'I don't happen to like that comparison, Geraint.'

'I'm not saying we're them. Of course not.'

'We've got a very different set of goals.'

Geraint came as close to looking flustered as I'd ever seen. 'No – look, I misspoke. What I'm saying is that we planned it, we executed it and the elements of the plan that didn't work can be controlled in future attempts.'

'Controlled how?' Manners snapped. 'You said that you'd thought it through. You said that it couldn't fail. You said you were only using people you trusted.'

'And I did. But there were some things we couldn't control, and that's helpful. It makes it easier to make a good choice about what sort of place we need to target. We need to think about somewhere that has fewer exits and entrances. We went for maximum impact by choosing the Underground, but they were too good at sorting out the evacuation. They've had more practice at it than we have, being realistic. They train for it. For our next practice we want somewhere that you're not going to have highly trained staff, and you're going to have a limited number of entrances and exits.'

'The more we "practise",' Ivan Manners said coldly, 'the better our chances of being caught. I'm beginning to wonder if that's what you actually want, Geraint.'

'Of course not.'

'You wanted to play with the big boys. Well, we have big plans. They don't include losing half of my lot to a police sweep after each attempt.' Boxton threw himself back in his chair, rubbing one hand over his mouth again and again, as if he was self-conscious about the white flecks that had gathered at the corners of his lips.

'They got arrested?' Geraint pulled a face. 'Maybe you need to find less recognisable muscle.'

'I used guys that the police didn't know about. Brothers of people who owed me a favour, that kind of thing. They should have blended into the crowd.' Boxton jabbed a finger at Geraint. 'Someone who was there tipped off the cops to look for my guys. You need to see if you've got a leak. We've been careful, all along, and it's only since we involved you that anything has gone wrong.'

'It's also the first time you've actually done anything.' Geraint leaned back in his chair and steepled his fingers, calm again. 'You talked a lot, and you planned a lot, and you put the foundations in place but when it came to actually going out there and making shit happen, you came to me.'

'You're expendable.' Burniford growled it, and Geraint laughed, not remotely intimidated.

'I know too much for you three to drop me in it. Now, I know you can trust me, but you don't know that. You have to stay on the right side of me, and I'll stay on the right side of you. That means that you don't second-guess me. You don't add people to operations without asking me. You don't get surprised when that doesn't work out. I sent four people out to do that operation, and they're all in this room. They all made it back. If you'd left it up to us on our own, who's to say that it wouldn't have gone better?'

'No one should have noticed my men,' Boxton said, but with less heat.

185

'Mark did.' Geraint nodded at me. 'He saw them straightaway.'

Shit. I did not want to be the focus of anyone's attention. 'They stood out,' I said. 'People were wary of them. I think the passengers did the opposite to what they suggested, if anything.'

'He's right.' It was Bruno who backed me up, which came as a shock. 'I'm not surprised the police worked out who they were, to be honest with you. They weren't subtle.'

'I told them—' Boxton cut himself off. 'I obviously didn't brief them so they understood what was expected of them. That's on me.'

'Small groups. As small as we can manage.' Geraint stretched. 'I can help with a bit of training, if you like, for the next one.'

'What is the next one?' Ivan Manners asked, and I could have kissed him.

'I was thinking a cinema. We pick something popular on its opening weekend. Pitch dark. Quiet. Everyone's attention on the screen. Then a flash and a bang. We set off a stun grenade. Nine out of ten people won't have noticed where the emergency exits are. They'll be disorientated. They won't know where to go or what to do. We'll see broken bones, hospitalisations, panic, fear, a bit of economic fallout . . .' Geraint trailed off, noticing that Burniford was shaking his head. 'No?'

'Not big enough, not exciting enough, and too risky. If you're going to use these four again, they'll get arrested and identified as having been at the previous incident, so you'll lose them. You'll come under suspicion. We'll come under suspicion. We need to move on.' He rapped his stick on the wooden floor, so loudly and unexpectedly that I jumped. 'We need to go for the big prize.'

'Agreed.' Manners leaned in. 'My boys are ready. The work has been done.'

'We all know what we want. We've got to go for it,' Boxton said. 'No more fannying around. Nothing small scale.'

186

'But the first attempt didn't work as well as we wanted.' Geraint looked from one face to another, almost pleading. 'We will get one shot at the big event. One. If we haven't got ourselves right by that time, all of this will have been for nothing.'

'I don't like that half of my guys are now on the radar for the Old Bill. It's too close to me,' Phil Boxton said. 'We need a distraction, not another opportunity for them to work out what's happening. Go big, focus the country's attention on the threat from the P****, take it from there.'

Burniford got to his feet, slowly and with Den supporting one elbow. He glared down at Geraint. 'You may know about us, but we know about you too, and you're the only one who's actually done anything that could end up in court. The rest of it is just talk. We know who you sent, and we know what they did, and if you want to look after your family you'd better wind your neck in, son. Now we've discussed it, the three of us, and we're happy for you to go on being a part of this, but you need to listen to what you're told instead of trying to act like the big man. This is a collaboration, not the Geraint Carter show. You need us and we don't really need you, as I said. I could find someone else to take your place. You're not bringing as much to the table as you think you are.'

'Max,' Geraint said. 'There's no need.'

'We all need to pull together. The three of us think it needs to be the spectacular next. You're the one who makes things happen – well, make it happen. But keep an eye on who knows what.' He turned his massive head to look around the room, and I almost flinched when his eye fell on me. He didn't linger on me, glowering at Harry and Den before he went on. 'I'll say this for you, Ger. You're right about one thing. We only get one chance at this, and we've got to get it right.'

24

That afternoon, before it got dark, I went for a run. The clear morning had dulled into grey cloud and there was a sting of sleet on the wind. It was entirely not the kind of day where you would go out running if you had a choice about it, but I didn't have a choice; I wanted to send Opal a message as soon as I could, to tell her to focus on communications between the three conspirators, and to fill her in on Geraint's role as subordinate. I thought he was being set up to take the fall if it all went wrong, and couldn't bring myself to care except insofar as I didn't want the others to get away with it.

Geraint paused in the hall as I prepared to set off, which did my heart rate no good.

'What the fuck would make you want to go outside on a day like this when there's a gym on the property and a heated sodding pool?'

'Can't beat a bit of fresh air.' I grinned at the expression on his face. 'You know how it is. Sometimes you just need to run it off outside.'

He hesitated and I felt myself start to sweat. A suspicious

Geraint might ask me to turn out my pockets, and the secret phone was zipped into my running jacket. But he wasn't thinking about me at all. 'That meeting this morning – I don't want you to think they don't value us.'

I translated that in my head. *I don't want you to think they don't value* me.

'They're worried. They're under pressure. It's natural that they want to make sure nothing else is going to go wrong. I was glad you were there to stand up for us though.'

'Course I did.' He clapped me on the arm. 'You three didn't do anything wrong.'

'Neither did Harry.'

'Harry? Oh, he's dependable. No one needs to worry about Harry. But you three – I wasn't sure how you'd all cope. You did well. They know you did well. They're just pissed off that it didn't work out better.'

'As you said, we learned a lot.' My turn to waver: ask him now or wait and never get the chance again? 'This big spectacular you were talking about – what is it?'

'I can't tell you yet.' Geraint tapped his temple. 'It's all up here. Nothing in writing. Nothing shared with anyone else, not yet. I need to get it straight in my mind. Then I run it past Max, Phil and Ivan. Then we move to operational planning. That's when you come in.'

'OK.'

'I want you involved, Mark. I want you to set it up. You have that kind of mind. You can look at the big picture. That's what I've always noticed about you.' He smiled wolfishly. 'And this is a very big picture indeed.'

I headed out of the back door and jogged past the garage with a heavy heart. Whatever Geraint had in mind, there was no clue to it in his study or his private library of evil on the top floor. I had to wait for him to feel like talking.

189

And if he changed his mind about me, or if one of the other three men convinced him I was too risky to trust, I'd be cut out. Geraint would never go against their wishes on something so important. If I'd learned nothing else that day, it was that Geraint was the very bottom of the pile.

My route took me across the estate and out the other side, into a wooded area that belonged to the National Trust. It was crisscrossed with tracks and bridleways, and provided the kind of dense cover where you could risk sending a clandestine message or two. I wouldn't stop for long, I'd decided, in case someone checked my Strava profile and saw that I'd taken a few minutes to rest. I wanted to be traceable and accountable so they could check up on me. When I reached a particularly dense copse of trees I stopped and went through a little pantomime of wincing and limping, afflicted with an imaginary cramp in my calf. I leaned against a thick tree trunk as if I was stretching and took out the secret phone. It took a minute or two to type my update for Opal and I tucked the phone away with a sense of relief: duty done, unobserved. I remembered to go slowly as I set off again, favouring my right leg. Ridiculous precautions, except that I was all too aware of the consequences if I made a mistake.

I had gone about ten metres when I heard something that made me stop: a rustle and crack in the bushes that could only be someone moving through them with purpose. To intercept me, I assumed with a sinking feeling, but I was wrong.

Naomi stepped out onto the track in front of me, brushing twigs and leaves from her clothes, and it was only when I cleared my throat that her head snapped up. Her face paled, immediately, and she put one hand behind her back: a giveaway, if I'd needed it, that she was hiding something. She was thinner than ever and the skin around her eyes looked bruised. Her delicate prettiness had faded, even in the time I'd known her.

'What's up?' I aimed for casual but because of who I was, and because I worked for Geraint, it sounded all too threatening.

'N-nothing.' She swallowed, her face blank with fear. 'Please. It's nothing.'

Let it go. I didn't need to borrow any trouble. What she wanted was for me to forget I'd seen her, which was exactly what I should do. All I had to do was say something bland and keep running.

But I'd been watching her from a distance for weeks, and I hadn't had a chance to speak to her. This was an opportunity I couldn't pass up.

'It's all right. I'm not going to tell him.'

She flinched. No need for me to specify who I meant.

'Is that a phone you've got there?'

'P-please. He'll k-kill me.'

'He will if he finds you with a phone, yes.' I took her by the elbow and steered her into the cover of the trees, looking around to make sure we were still unobserved. Her arm was shaking under my fingers but she went with me, biddable as ever. She was wearing pale pink, a colour that was far too visible against the grey of the winter woods and I felt the hairs stand up on the back of my neck. If Bruno saw me having a tête-à-tête with his wife, he'd kill me, no questions asked.

'I can't offer you anything to keep quiet, but please if you have any kindness in you, don't give me away. If I get away I'll give you money. I don't have anything at the moment, but as soon as I'm safe, I will. I promise.' She was gabbling, the words tumbling over one another.

'What are you doing, Naomi?' I took the phone out of her hand, but gently. 'What's this?'

'You don't need to know.'

'No, but I'm concerned for your safety.' I hesitated. 'You

191

have no reason to trust me, I know that, but I don't want to see you get hurt.'

'It's fine. I won't get hurt. I won't get hurt.' She was muttering it like a mantra, her eyes fixed on the ground.

I gave her a little shake to get her attention. 'Look, Naomi, I'm on your side. I won't say anything to Bruno or Geraint.'

That got through to her. 'Really?'

'Really. Your husband treats you like dirt, and his father isn't much better.' I weighed the phone in my hand. It was a small, cheap phone, a throwaway, not a million miles away from the one I had in my pocket. 'Is this an escape plan?'

She nodded.

'You should ditch it. This' — I held it up – 'is evidence that you're planning something.'

'There's a charity – they help women like me. They gave me the phone.'

'It's risky if you're involving other people. You only need one person to decide to give you away. Geraint would make it worth their while.'

'Would you? For the money?'

'No, obviously not. Look, can't you just walk out? The more complicated you make it the more likely it is that you'll get found out.' *Especially because you're really bad at lying.*

'I can't. I don't have any money, or any friends. I don't have anywhere to go or anyone I can trust. I've only got my mum and he'd find me straightaway.' She wasn't crying but the lifeless tone of her voice was almost worse than tears.

Opal would kill me for getting involved, but I couldn't ignore the danger she was in. I thought about what I'd said to Maeve about wanting to stop bad things from happening instead of dealing with the consequences. What was the point of being a police officer if you couldn't help someone in Naomi's position?

'I can get you some money. Not a lot, but enough to give you a head start. A car. I can leave the keys in one of Geraint's vehicles. Your best plan is just to drive away and keep going. Dump the car as soon as you can. Don't go anywhere you know anyone. Pick somewhere and keep your head down.'

'I couldn't.'

'He'll kill you either way.' It was brutal, but I had to get through to her. I'd seen this before, from the other end – standing over a dead woman, arresting her husband when it was all far too late.

'I know.' She took the phone back and slid it into the waist-band of her jeans. 'I can't leave unless I have somewhere to go. Somewhere to hide. They'll come after me.'

'Maybe not. Geraint has other things on his mind. He might be able to persuade Bruno to let you go.'

She shook her head. 'He'll want me back. I'm not leaving my daughter behind.'

'No. Of course not.'

'You know that Geraint will never forgive me for taking Tessa. He'll go to the ends of the earth to find her and punish me.' She shrugged. 'There's no future for me here. Bruno will kill me if I stay. I need to go, but I can't leave Tessa, and once I take her, I'm dead. These people said they can help me. I know I shouldn't trust them, but I have no choice.'

The beginnings of an idea began to form in the back of my mind. I couldn't decide if it was ethical, or even sensible.

'What if you could get them locked up instead? Bruno and Geraint?'

'How?'

I wasn't a gambler – quite the opposite – but there were times when it was the only appropriate course of action. I put it all on red and hoped for the best. 'I'm only telling you this because I want to help you and I can't see another way to do it. I've heard the police are interested in what they're doing. They're trying to recruit someone to find out what they can about Geraint's businesses and plans for the future. They would pay for information.'

Her face remained blank. 'That's nothing to do with me.'

'No, me neither. I heard about it, that's all.' Back-pedalling furiously. It only dawned on me a moment later that she wasn't interested because she simply didn't have room in her head for anything other than her own worries, not because she was loyal to Geraint. 'Naomi, if you can help the police, they can help you, that's all. If you hang on for a week, or a month, your problems might go away instead of you having to run away from them. And as I said, if you can find out anything useful, you might be in line for a pay-out from the police that would give you enough to start a new life somewhere else while Bruno is in prison. You could get away from him for good.'

'I don't think I can wait any longer.' It was a whisper. I was about to argue with her, to persuade her that staying was less of a risk than going, when she turned back the sleeve of her jumper so I could see a row of inflamed marks all the way up her arm: cigarette burns. 'He's getting worse and worse.'

'I'm sorry.'

'You're kind.' She tried to smile and her lower lip split, a thin line of dark red blood running down it. She seemed oblivious. 'The thing is, I need to do this my way. I only get one chance at this. And like you said, I'm dead anyway.'

25

Naomi and her problems occupied my thoughts, in the absence of anything else specific to worry about. I watched her covertly, noticing how she flinched when Bruno walked into the room. I watched Bruno too, looking for signs that he was getting more unstable, more overt in his manipulation of her. I'd been trained to spot different stages and risk factors in domestic violence, but that had been years earlier. I could have done with a refresher course. What I half-remembered was that a period of violence could be followed by a calmer phase, but that was no less dangerous for the victim. Bruno on drugs was unpredictable and uncontrolled; Bruno sober was more likely to notice that his wife was edging towards leaving him.

I still thought that I could make use of Naomi, if she was prepared to spy for me, and that it would be far safer for her than trying to run away, but she had avoided me ever since the meeting in the woods. At least she hadn't given me away, I thought, as I tried to sleep. It was hard not to strain to hear raised voices coming from the family's wing of the house. It was hard not to scan Naomi for the physical signs of Bruno's violence.

A couple of days after I'd met Naomi in the woods I ran into Juliet by the garage, where I was washing the unused Mercedes for want of anything better to do. She was wearing a clinging polo-necked jumper, skin-tight black jodhpurs and riding boots polished to a high shine, and she was carrying a riding crop.

'Let me guess,' I said. 'Ballet.'

'How did you know?' She was playing with the end of the riding crop, as if it was the only thing that interested her. 'It was actually my dressage lesson. You should have come to watch.'

'I was busy.'

'You're always busy.' She pouted but I had the sense it was automatic; her attention was elsewhere. Her eyes were focused on something behind me. I looked back, casually, and realised she was staring at the chauffeur's apartment. When she spoke again, her voice was low. 'Can we talk for a minute? Somewhere private?'

'Sure.' I threw the sponge into the steaming bucket of soapy water at my feet and walked into the garage. When I turned around, she was right behind me. She put a hand on my arm and pulled me close to her.

'Make it look as if we're flirting.' Her face was strained, her expression a million miles away from seduction.

I leaned an elbow on the roof of the nearest car – the Aston Martin – and traced the curve of her cheek with my thumb, slowly. Her face was tight with tension.

'Naomi talked to me.' It was a murmur, nothing more, and I had to strain to hear the words.

'Did she?' *Shit*. I'd taken a chance with Naomi, even though I hadn't said that I was connected with the police myself. I began to think of ways to talk myself out of it before Juliet took her concerns to her father. An approach by a stranger – of course I hadn't wasted any time on it. And I hadn't mentioned it to Geraint because . . . because . . .

'She said you offered to help her get away.' Juliet's eyes were wide, beseeching. 'She said she turned you down.'

'I'm worried about her.'

'Me too.' Juliet swallowed. 'Bruno was always mean, you know. I avoided him, even when I was tiny. He would break my toys just to see me cry. He punishes anyone who's weaker than him. Anyone who Dad loves is fair game.'

'I've noticed that.' I switched to stroking her hair and she shook her head as if I was an irritating fly. I should have guessed that her hair was off limits. I ran my other hand down her arm instead, and she shivered, but not from pleasure.

'You notice everything. I told her she should have taken you up on your offer – if you meant it.'

'My offer.'

'The car. The money.'

So Naomi hadn't given me away by mentioning the police informant role I'd had in mind. It was a shame that I couldn't recruit Juliet, I thought, because she would be the ideal person to find out what was going on, but she was too loyal to Geraint for me to take that risk.

'I did mean it, but it's dangerous for her.'

'And you.'

'I don't care about that. But . . . couldn't your dad help?'

'He won't do anything.' She shut her eyes for a moment. 'Family comes first, you see. She's an outsider. Bruno is Dad's priority, even though he's a piece of shit.'

'I can understand that.'

'Can you? I can't.' She sighed. 'Last night, Bruno choked her so hard she blacked out. She wet herself.'

I winced. It was a bad sign that he felt confident enough to choke her until that point. 'It's involuntary when you lose consciousness like that.'

'That didn't stop him from punishing her for it.' Juliet

moistened her lips. 'I've got some money. Some cash. I was saving it in case . . . in case I ever needed it.' In case the door of the gilded cage was ever open. I felt very sorry for Juliet. 'I want Naomi to have it. If I give it to you, can you make the other arrangements, like you were saying?'

'If she'll go.'

'She has to.'

'What's going on here?' Den was standing outside the garage, peering in. I stepped back, my hands up.

'Nothing.'

'Nothing? So I'm nothing? Charming.' Juliet glared at me and sashayed out to Den, who was grinning. 'Forget you saw anything, Den, all right?'

'Yes, please.' I came out of the shadows, looking rueful.

'Bit of advice, Mark, speaking from experience. You've got to watch the Carter women. They're a lot of work. Worth it though,' Den added hastily, as Juliet's eyes widened.

'As if he'd get the chance. As if—' Juliet broke off. A loud yell, full of rage, filled the air.

'Den? Mark? Get in here.'

Geraint, in a towering rage. I set off at a run; there was a time and place for being casual and this was not it. Harry met us at the back door, his face troubled.

'I was just coming to find you.'

'What's up?'

'Study.' Harry jerked his thumb in that direction. 'He's waiting for you. Don't hang about.'

'And I suppose I'm not allowed to know about it. Fantastic.' Juliet pushed past me and disappeared into the kitchen, her boots loud on the floor.

Den went into the room ahead of me. 'What's up, Geraint?'

'They've been arrested.' Geraint's voice was already raw with anger and fear. He had come straight from the golf course and his outfit was incongruously jaunty: patterned trousers and a pale blue jumper. It clashed with his face, which was dark red, a stroke or a heart attack waiting to happen.

'Who have?'

'Boxton, Manners and Burniford,' Harry said. 'Last night. We just heard.'

Looking shocked was no effort. I assumed that Opal had found out something alarming enough to make her pull the trigger on arresting them, but I wished I'd had some warning.

'Oh shit,' Bruno drawled from where he was half-lying on a sofa, looking unmoved. He was wearing gym shorts and a T-shirt but I guessed he'd thrown them on to come downstairs; his hair was all over the place and his face was puffy from sleep. 'That doesn't sound like good news for us, does it?'

'No, it doesn't.' Geraint swung around, staring, wild-eyed. 'I don't think they would give me away deliberately, but we have to assume the police will come here next. We have to make sure there isn't anything here that could get us in trouble.'

'But the plans are all in your head, aren't they?' I said.

'You've been upstairs. You know what's up there.' His breathing was rapid. 'I wouldn't be able to explain it away.'

I held up a hand, genuinely worried that he was going to collapse. 'Calm down. Your collection is of historical interest. It's got nothing to do with whatever Boxton and Burniford and Manners were planning, which you knew nothing about. If the cops turn up here and search the place, we don't want them finding any guns, so I'd move them, but everything else? You're a keen student of history. That's it.'

'What about the computers?' Den asked, and I could have killed him. 'We should wipe them.'

Geraint grimaced. 'I don't like that idea either. Getting rid of all the information seems risky. I'd want to go through it – see what I want to keep. And I don't have time for that.'

'We can hide them too.' I snapped my fingers. 'There's a storage place I used in Swindon. The guy who runs it doesn't ask any questions. If we box up the computers and the guns and anything else that you don't want to see the light of day, I can take it over to him. He has fuck-all in the way of CCTV or records – it's all cash in hand. The best way to make them disappear.' Disappear right into Opal's hands, did Geraint but know it.

He nodded. 'Right. All the computers. All the guns.'

'How did they find out about the others? Do we have a leak?' Den looked around at the rest of us, wary. I felt my stomach clench.

'It's going to be that stupid fucker Boxton's guys who got arrested.' Bruno yawned. 'Bet the other three wish they hadn't been so chummy with one another. All those meetings without us, laying a trail for the cops to follow.'

'Why do you think I didn't mind staying on the outside?' Geraint folded his arms, looking happier. 'I never pushed to be one of the big boys. They thought I was intimidated, and I let them think that. But now I have deniability and they have connections they can't explain away.'

'What's the plan?' I asked.

'Harry, get hold of some boxes. Den and Mark, you start putting everything together. Bruno, get dressed for fuck's sake. When all the stuff is packed up, Mark, take it to your guy in Swindon, then come back here.' Geraint sighed. 'And I'd better call my lawyer.'

I was convinced that something would go wrong – that someone would reconsider handing over all of the most incriminating material in Geraint's house to me, a virtual stranger, to be deposited with someone they didn't know in a place they couldn't locate – but Den and a reluctant Bruno helped me to clear the estate's van of miscellaneous tools and equipment, and then loaded it up neatly with everything I could possibly have wanted to hand over to Opal. The hard part, as they saw it, was driving a load of contraband goods to Swindon without getting stopped by the police. Geraint gave me to understand that, if that happened, I was on my own, and I agreed that I would take the blame for the guns and the really quite impressive array of weaponry he owned: swords, daggers, shuriken and katanas, as well as a handful of grenades that seemed all too viable. I drove to Swindon carefully, and went to the lock-up, and unloaded the boxes, and told the bristle-faced and yawning man in charge to send the bill to Opal.

'Right you are.' Not a hint of excitement, but he was already lifting the phone when I left.

I headed back to Haulton House with the radio turned up, singing along to classic rock, euphoric. It couldn't have worked out better – a dream result. I went in the back gate and parked the van out of sight behind a barn, to be cleaned later, then made my way to the house to give Geraint the good news.

They were all in the kitchen when I let myself in, which wasn't in itself unusual: the whole family and Harry, standing around the table. What was unusual was the atmosphere in the room, which was practically solid with tension. The cheery greeting died on my lips as I took in grim faces, Cassie holding hands with her mother, Juliet and Naomi in floods of tears with their arms around each other. Juliet stared straight at me, desperately trying to convey some sort of message, but I couldn't interpret it quickly enough.

'What's going on?'

Geraint turned. 'Ah, Mark. Glad you're back.'

He didn't look glad.

I had an instant physical reaction – pure knee-trembling, gut-clenching fear – as he stepped aside to show me what lay in the middle of the table.

A mobile phone.

Geraint folded his arms. 'So what do you have to say about that?'

26

'A phone?'

I came forward to look at it as if I'd never seen it before. It took a moment for me to convince myself that it wasn't mine, to confirm that I was safe. But if it wasn't mine . . .

'Whose is it?' I asked, and my voice sounded normal to me even though my thoughts were running at a hundred miles an hour.

'That's what we want to know.' Geraint looked around the room. 'We're just waiting for someone to *remember* it belongs to them.'

'Where did you find it?'

'In the mud room, at the back of one of the shelves.' Den was looking unhappy. 'While you were out, Ger decided we should search the whole house in case there were any listening devices or signs that someone was watching us.'

I thought of the secret phone that was in my bedroom, tucked behind a skirting board I'd loosened for the purpose, and thanked my guardian angel that it had been a quick and shoddy hunt through the house. No POLSA team that I'd ever worked with would have missed it.

'I wanted to know if someone was spying on us. I never thought it might be a member of the family passing information to the police.' Geraint's voice was granite-rough.

'Big leap to think this is anything to do with the police, isn't it?'

'Is it?' he snapped, and I held my hands up.

'OK. It could be that. Can I have a look at it?'

'Help yourself.'

The phone was switched on but not unlocked, the screen asking for a password. I weighed it in my hand. 'This could belong to anyone who was in the house and came in through the mud room, which is everyone except your guests and the family. A plumber or an electrician. The florist. One of the personal trainers. A housekeeper.' I dropped my voice, addressing Geraint. 'Look, we know that the other three were compromised because of Boxton's men being arrested. You haven't been contacted yet. That means the trail stops with them. Boxton's guys don't know about you, so you're all right. This phone is nothing. A red herring.'

'It was fully charged. We haven't had anyone outside the family here to work in the last week. The battery would have run down if anyone had left it then.' Den, ever-helpful.

'What I'd like to know,' Bruno drawled, 'is why my wife is shaking.'

My heart dropped as I looked at Naomi, like everyone else around the table, to discover she was trembling. Her fear was written all over her face.

'Maybe because she's terrified of you,' Juliet snapped. 'Maybe because she knows you'll turn this into a bullshit reason to hurt her.'

'Bullshit?' There was a light in Bruno's eyes that I'd never seen before and I realised that he was enjoying himself. 'I don't think it's bullshit if *my wife* has been hiding a phone from me. Who have you been calling, Naomi?'

Deny it, I thought. *Just deny it. He can't make you admit it's yours.*

'Tell me now or it will be worse when I find out the truth. If you're honest with me, I'll respect that.' He paused. 'I'll be surprised that you're capable of honesty, but I'll respect it and treat you accordingly. The only catch is that you have to start right now. Ten minutes from now is too late.'

The room was hushed, apart from Naomi sobbing. Juliet was holding on to her so tightly her knuckles were white.

'You know there will be consequences, don't you? But it's up to you how serious they are.' He moved around the table to stand next to her and picked up her hand gently. 'Don't make this hard for me, Naomi. If you love me, tell me the truth, right now.'

And Naomi nodded.

'What's that? What does that mean?' He was stroking her hand. His voice was quiet, tender. 'Is that yes, it is my phone?'

She nodded again.

'Why do you have a phone, my darling? Why do you need one?'

'I – I wanted to be able to call my mum. She – she's not well. I tried to tell you.' Naomi looked around at the rest of us, woebegone. 'She has cancer. She had it before but now it's come back. I wanted to check that her treatment was going OK.'

'Why can't you do that from a house phone?' Geraint asked. 'There's a landline in your room.'

'I'm not allowed to use it.' Bruno's hand tightened on hers for an instant so brief I might have imagined it, and Naomi caught her breath.

'Not allowed?' Geraint looked at his son, his expression faintly nauseated. 'What have you done, Bruno?'

'What a monster I am.' He leaned over and picked up the phone. 'What's the password, pet? So we can call your mother and find out how she's doing.'

'No.'

'Tell me.'

She shook her head, her eyes screwed shut.

'Tell me right now, or I will make you regret it. Don't make me ask again.'

Don't say it, I thought. *Just keep stalling.*

I suppose Naomi knew Bruno better than I did. He had trained her to expect the worst, and it was coming either way.

'Three. Five. Five. Three.'

He tapped it into the phone and held it up to show everyone the unlocked screen. 'Let's just see how honest and trustworthy poor Naomi is, shall we? Mean old Bruno, not letting her call her poor sick mother. Let's have a look at the last calls. Oh, it's the same number every time – well, that fits with the story.'

'Just leave it,' Juliet said. 'Dad, make him stop.'

Bruno was pressing buttons. He held the phone up again and we could all hear the sound of a phone ringing, once, twice, three times.

'Kevin speaking.'

A man's voice, gentle and quiet. Bruno raised his eyebrows and held the phone out to Cassie.

'Hi,' she said.

'Is that you, Naomi? What's wrong? Is everything OK?'

Bruno ended the call and threw the phone into the middle of the table. 'Who the fuck is Kevin, Naomi? And don't tell me it's your long-lost brother because I know that's not true.'

'I—'

'Is he police?' Geraint was pale now. He was leaning on the table as if he needed the support.

'No. *No.* I would never do that.'

'Who, then?'

'No one.'

'Are you fucking him?' Bruno asked.

'No, of course not.'

'Then why do you need a secret phone to talk to him?' He put his hand on the back of her head and tugged her towards him, so Juliet had to let go of her. He looked down into Naomi's face and again it seemed more like tenderness than anything, as if he loved her most when she was most scared by him. 'You must think I'm stupid.'

'No . . .'

'You lied to us all about your mother to make me look bad. I think you're still lying.'

'I'm not. I—'

'I think I can persuade you to be honest, though.' He took her by the shoulders and shook her so her head snapped back and forth and she cried out. 'I think I can make you tell us the truth.'

'Bruno,' I said. 'Let her go. You're hurting her.'

'Fuck off. This is none of your business.'

'Daddy, make him stop.' Juliet was weeping now. She might as well have stayed silent for all the reaction she provoked from her father or his son.

'Fucking *Kevin* on the phone, asking for you by name, and you expect me to think you're not up to something behind my back? You really are thick, Naomi.' Without warning he backhanded her across the face, so hard that she fell to the ground, and I took a step towards him before Geraint put his hand out to stop me. Bruno hauled her back up and began dragging her out of the room. She was limp, unresisting, barely able to walk.

I went after him, of course, but Den caught hold of me.

'Leave it. I know it's tough, but it's not up to you to interfere.'

'He'll kill her.' I looked past Den to Geraint, and the others who were ringed around the table. 'You all know it. We have to stop him.'

'Why did you help him?' Juliet was staring at Cassie. 'Why did you do what he wanted you to do?'

'What if she had been talking to the police? What if this Kevin is a cop?'

'He didn't sound like one,' Harry said, which saved me the trouble.

Cassie shrugged. 'Well, she's not one of us and Bruno is. He wanted me to help him and I did. And I don't see what's wrong with that.'

A scream cut through the air.

'He's *killing* her.' Juliet looked around wildly. 'Aren't any of you going to help her? Mark, don't listen to Den. You have to do something.'

I pulled away from Den and ran for the door, and this time no one stopped me. I was in the hall, listening for a sound that would tell me where Bruno had gone when I found Harry by my side. I tensed, ready for a fight, but he grimaced.

'This isn't right. Hitting a woman. There's something wrong with that little shit.'

A thud came from the drawing room on the other side of the hall and I ran to try the door. It was closed and locked. The drawing room was in the old part of the house where the doors were enormous, made of solid wood, with brass handles and locks. I swore, stepping back.

'I'll try to kick it in.'

'Let me have a go.' Harry slammed into it, shoulder first. Any ordinary door would have broken immediately, but the old wood was stubborn. As the seconds crawled past, we took turns at it, and all the time Bruno was taking his temper out on poor, fragile Naomi. The rest of the family had come into the hall, standing in an awkward huddle behind us. None of them offered to help. They had chosen their side, I thought bitterly. It was too slow; we were going to be too late.

Harry had obviously reached the same conclusion. He leaned into the next attempt, hitting the door at just the right angle, with pent-up force and frustration. The wood splintered around the lock and it swung open. Harry staggered forward, off balance, and I shot past him to where Bruno was kneeling astride his wife. He was breathing hard, punching her with the kind of monotonous regularity that you can only manage when the resistance you're dealing with is zero. A glance told me that Naomi was unrecognisable, blood-soaked and not moving, and I felt my heart plummet. I had to concentrate on Bruno who was trying to bite me as I dragged him away from his wife. I cuffed the back of his head and stepped on his leg, hard, working through my repertoire of painful distraction blows until I could get him under control. He screamed and twisted in my grasp but he didn't really try to fight back; I was bigger and stronger than him and he knew it, and he was a coward when all was said and done. I got him on the floor with one hand up between his shoulder blades and kneeled on him while he screamed.

'You're breaking my arm! Stop. Get off! My *arm*.'

I let him move it down a few inches to take the pressure off his shoulder joint as the room filled up behind us; I didn't want Geraint to spot that I was restraining him like a police officer would. I kept my hand on his arm, though, and with the other hand I leaned on his back, forcing him to lie flat on the carpet. As he stopped struggling and accepted the inevitable, I became aware that Harry was crouching over Naomi, not touching her. I looked a question at him and he shook his head, his face grim.

Dead, I thought, or dying.

'She's OK, isn't she?' Geraint's voice was weak, uncharacteristically.

'Sorry, boss.' Harry stood between her body and the others, blocking her from their view. 'The others need to go.'

'Let me see her.' Juliet ran towards her and Harry caught her, turning her around.

'No, Juliet. No one needs to be in here except the boss and me. And Mark,' he added as an afterthought. 'You can make yourself useful, can't you?'

I nodded, incapable of speech. My hands had gone numb with shock.

'You heard him,' Geraint said. 'All of you. Out.'

I surrendered Bruno to his brother-in-law. He was glazed in sweat and glassy-eyed. He had started to tremble. His hands were badly grazed where he'd knocked the skin off them.

I wanted to kill him, and knew it was because I was angry with myself.

If only I'd done something sooner. If I'd reacted faster. If I'd actually saved her instead of holding back for my own selfish reasons.

When the shattered door closed behind the other members of his family, Geraint sat down abruptly.

'Check her.' That was a command thrown at me. Harry turned away as I went to the body and checked Naomi's throat for a pulse. My fingers slipped in her blood and I swallowed, fighting for composure.

'She's dead.'

'What a fucking mess.' Geraint looked up at Harry. 'What do we do?'

'You don't need to know anything about it,' Harry said heavily. 'The less you know the better. We'll sort it out.'

'What about Bruno?'

'What about him?' Geraint glared at me. 'We're going to look after him, that's what. Get him cleaned up. Clear this up. What else would we do?'

Call the police, I wanted to say. *Get your very dangerous son locked away so he can't do this to another woman.* The words stuck in my throat.

'We sort this out and we forget it happened.' Geraint stood up, stiff. 'Christ, I need a drink.'

I watched him leave the room and I had felt many things for him over the months I'd been working on his case – disapproval, reluctant fondness, horror, bewilderment at the attitude that let him risk hundreds of strangers' lives for his own sick beliefs. At that moment, I felt the purest kind of hatred, the red mist I'd heard of before and never experienced. I wanted to kill him, to wipe him off the face of the earth. If I'd had the opportunity, I would have done it, without question, without reference to a judge and jury.

Harry touched my shoulder, bringing me back to myself. His face was sombre. 'Come on, mate. You and I need to make a plan.'

27

I drove sedately down a deserted motorway in the middle of the night, one car behind me matching my careful speed. I was driving a car with fake plates, an old car that would be scrapped as soon as the business of the night was finished, and the engine had a worryingly throaty sound. I hoped it wouldn't break down. We were heading north and west, into Wales, to a spot that was remote enough for our needs. As the miles disappeared under my wheels, I wished I had further to go. I needed more time. The car in my rear-view mirror seemed tethered to me; there was no escaping it, and I needed to escape it, somehow.

We need a plan, Harry had said, but one plan wasn't enough. There was Harry's, which involved wrapping Naomi's body in plastic sheeting and placing it in the boot of the car and driving through the night until we reached the place where he'd suggested disposing of it. And there was mine, which involved getting hold of Opal and telling her what was going on.

I had wrapped Naomi up myself, taking the opportunity to snap a couple of pictures on my secret phone. A huge risk – an insane one – but I couldn't see a way out of it. Bruising had bloated her features, the blood on her skin blurring away anything that was left that might have made her recognisable. I made sure to photograph her hands, which were bloodied and pale but still elegantly manicured with pale pink varnish, her rings loose on narrow fingers. I needed a record of what they had done, and I needed Opal to have it in case I was found out or killed myself. There was nothing the Carters wouldn't do to protect their interests, I knew. The family came first.

'You done?' Harry leaned into the room just after I'd put the phone away – a near miss that made me sweat.

'Yeah.'

'Cassie's going to clean up in here.'

I looked around the room, at the blood that had soaked into the carpet and the tiny flecks of it on cushions and couches and the marble fireplace. 'Good luck to her.'

'I didn't know she could tell one end of a mop from the other, to be honest with you.'

I almost laughed and Harry favoured me with one of his rare grim smiles. It faded as he looked past me. 'Is she ready?'

'Yeah.'

'Want a hand?'

'No need.' I got up and lifted the plastic-wrapped body, cradling her against my chest. She was painfully slight in my arms. I carried her out to the car, Harry walking slowly behind me. I pulled the plastic sheeting back from her face once I'd laid her in the boot, staring down at her and the harm Bruno had done to her. It wasn't that I'd needed another reason to bring the Carters to justice, but Naomi made it personal.

'Can I see her?'

Juliet was standing close behind me when I turned. I slammed the boot shut. 'Not a good idea.'

'I want to say goodbye.'

'Think of her as you knew her,' I said coldly, and she sobbed once, heartbreakingly.

'How can you be so horrible? You shouldn't help them.'

'It's my job.' I walked away from her to wash the blood off my hands and change my clothes, leaving Harry standing guard over the car so no one was tempted to inspect what remained of Bruno's poor wife. I felt like a shit, and Juliet certainly thought I was that, but I had no choice.

We left at one in the morning, frost glinting in the headlights and clear skies overhead as the cars processed down the driveway. I was following Harry's plan exactly, as far as anyone could tell. I had no phone with me, at least officially, and no satnav; the car didn't have any of Geraint's listening devices or video. There would be no electronic link between what I was doing and Geraint himself. What they had given me was a map with a cross on it marking our destination, and a torch so I could check the map on unlit roads. I had the body and a couple of spades in the boot. If I was stopped by the police, Harry would drive on without so much as a sideways glance. If I wasn't stopped, we would go together to bury Naomi's body in remote woodland, and dump the car I was driving, and then Harry would drive us both home.

I'd thought up a few ways that I could deal with Harry's presence, but just as we were about to leave the situation got a little bit more complicated. Geraint shoved Den towards Harry's car.

'Go on. Go with him.'

'I don't need him,' Harry had snapped, and got a glare from his boss.

'Three of you will get it done quicker.'

I hadn't been able to argue with Geraint but it was a disaster. With two of them watching me, there would always be someone hanging around. I'd been counting on Harry needing a break at some point on our long journey. Now I couldn't count on anything.

I would need to ditch the secret phone before I went back to Geraint's paranoid supervision so there was no need to keep it pristine anymore. Knowing that the car wasn't under his surveillance was a staggering relief; for as long as I was in it on my own, I was able to be myself. I phoned Opal's number as I left Haulton House, thumbing in the digits as I drove and putting it on speaker. It was essential that I didn't look as if I was talking. I popped some gum into my mouth in case Harry and Den noticed my jaw moving.

'Yes.' She sounded alert even though it was the middle of the night.

'Did you get the pictures?' No time for polite conversation. 'Who was it?'

'Naomi, Bruno's wife.'

I heard the air go out of her lungs. 'What happened?'

I told her. When I'd finished, she said, 'You didn't stop him.'

'I couldn't get into the room.' I would never forget it, I thought. I'd never get over it.

'Rob—'

'It wouldn't have happened,' I said tightly, 'if it wasn't for the arrests.'

'We had to do it.'

'That's what I assumed you'd say.'

'I couldn't have known.'

'No,' I said, matching her tone, which was studiously neutral. She minded. I minded. Both of us understood that.

'So where are you going? We can see you're on the move.'

I filled her in on Harry's plan, and on how mine deviated from the official version, my eyes on the rear-view mirror where the headlights were steady on my tail.

'I'm going to need some time to sort this out,' she said at last.

'How long?'

'I don't know yet. We're working that out right now.'

I imagined a room full of people at her end listening, planning, making arrangements with speed and skill, and I felt very slightly comforted. At least I wasn't on my own.

'I can't drive too slowly. And it needs to happen soon.'

'I know.' A pause. 'Sorry, I'm not taking it out on you.'

'Not like you to apologise.'

'Don't get used to it.' I heard a voice mumbling in the background, though I couldn't make out the words. After what seemed like an eternity, Opal said, 'Are you listening?'

'Of course.'

'We've found a suitable place for what you have in mind. It's about forty-five minutes from your destination. That gives us as much time as possible, but it should be feasible for you to stop there without arousing any suspicion.'

'Give me the details.'

She read them out and I memorised them.

'I'm signing off now.'

'Be careful.' The urgency in her voice came through very clearly.

'I always am.'

After the call ended I slid the phone into the gap between the back and the base of my seat, retrievable if I really needed it but invisible. Now that the car was silent I felt alone, travelling through the night with my terrible burden. I kept thinking about the kitchen, and the phone, and whether I should have claimed it as my own to save Naomi. I could have come up with a story on the spot to explain it. I had training for that, and the nerve to make it convincing. Naomi hadn't stood a chance.

Opal would have said no, that it was too much of a risk.

She hadn't even hinted that she thought I could have handled the situation better, or that I should have taken the blame.

I wished I'd done it anyway.

I almost missed the sign for the services, even though I was looking out for it. The buildings glowed on both sides of the motorway, which made it perfect for me: twenty-four-hour shopping and petrol and food, whether you were travelling into Wales or out of it. I indicated and came off the motorway, Harry following faithfully. We hadn't discussed a stop and as his car came up behind mine I could see he was frowning.

I pulled into the car park (mainly deserted, at that time in the morning) and found a dark corner where the floodlights had gone out. Harry stopped nearby, his engine still running. I jumped out and crossed to his door.

'Why are we here?'

'I need a break.' I was shivering; the night air was cold and I was genuinely tired. 'I'm falling asleep.'

'How can you?' Den swallowed. 'I'd have thought the stress would keep you awake.'

'Yeah, well, it's not working.' I yawned widely. 'If I crash it'll be awkward.'

'All right.' Harry turned off his engine and lights. 'We might as well have a break too.'

'Not here. We can't be seen together. If we're seen in the same place ignoring each other it'll raise as many questions as if we're together.' I nodded in the direction of the other services. 'If you go there for your coffee and petrol, I'll meet you back on the road. Set off in an hour exactly?'

'Fine.' Harry started the car again and Den put his hand out to stop him.

'Hold on. We can't just leave his car.'

'Why not?' I was jumping from foot to foot, trying to stay warm.

'You know why.'

'She's not going to run away,' I said flippantly.

'Christ.' Den's face was blank with shock. 'You really are cold, aren't you?'

'Freezing,' I agreed.

'That's not what I meant.'

'I know.' I sniffed. 'Look, it's not what I wanted to happen but there's no point in getting wound up about it. Her troubles are over.'

Den gave me a sick look as Harry slid his window up, effectively ending the conversation. This version of me was ruining my reputation as a nice guy, but it would probably impress Geraint's family, I reflected, jogging towards the buildings without risking a look back at Harry's car or my own.

The best I could say about the next sixty minutes was that they passed. I drank coffee and tried to look as if I had nothing on my mind except the remainder of the journey, when in fact all of my thoughts were focused on what might be happening outside.

When I went back, the car was still sitting where I had left it. No one moved in the car park; there was no sign anyone had come or gone. I had a strong compulsion to open the boot and check inside but it was far too risky, even if I thought there was no one around.

I took my time about getting back onto the motorway, but when I came down the slip road headlights from behind dazzled me in the rear-view mirror: Harry and Den, right on time.

Opal had been wrong; it didn't take us as long as she'd expected to get to our destination. We made good time on the motorway, and then a main road, and then a series of smaller roads that cut through the dark, sleeping countryside. I went wrong once, accidentally, and got a toot from Harry's horn to call me back to the right route. Left to my own devices I'd never have found the woods, let alone the narrow, rutted track Harry had indicated. I stopped the car when it could go no further, the wheels losing their grip on icy mud so the vehicle slewed sideways. I got out and stretched cramped limbs as the other car stopped, a little way back. The air stung my skin and the forest pressed in around me, dense and threatening, like something from a fairy tale – or a nightmare. On the purely primitive level, it was an unsettling place to be, but that wasn't why my heart was thumping.

Nothing was more frightening to me than the men who had followed me all of that way.

I had no illusions. If Geraint had decided it was safer for me to be dead, given what I knew about him and his son, this would be the end of the road.

28

'It's harder than you'd think, isn't it?'

Den was crouching at the side of the trench Harry and I had dug during a miserable, sweating hour. He was holding a powerful torch so we could see what we were doing, but he kept forgetting and pointing the beam away from where we were digging, illuminating distant tree trunks and, once, the bright eyes of an animal that disappeared the next second. The place we had chosen was on a slight slope under some sparse pine trees, well away from the road, where the disturbed ground wouldn't be particularly noticeable but there wasn't too much undergrowth for us to battle.

I straightened up and leaned on my spade, easing my back. I had stripped down to a T-shirt despite the cold, and sweat was gluing it to my body. 'I hadn't thought it would be easy.'

'Ever done this before?'

I shook my head. 'You?'

'No.' He was barely doing it now, if it came to that. Den had dug for about ten minutes early on and then handed the spade back to me. Gravedigging was an occupation for the staff, not for Geraint's son-in-law. He nodded at the other end of the trench. 'Harry has.'

Geraint's minder had been ignoring us, his spade biting into the ground with efficient regularity. He turned at that, fixing Den with a reproving eye. 'Less of that.'

'What?' Den spread his hands. 'I thought – Mark's one of us, isn't he?'

Is that it? I wondered. *Or is it that you don't mind talking frankly in front of me because you know I won't have the chance to pass it on?* I grinned to hide the dark direction of my thoughts, and said, 'Digging a grave fits with your overall image, Harry, for what it's worth. I'm not shocked.'

He gave a short, bitter bark of amusement. 'Nothing shocks you.'

'Not much,' I agreed, and started digging again, the air heavy with the old-wine smell of turned earth, and the sweet scent of the pines.

'That was a while before you came,' Den said. He wedged the torch between his knees and rubbed his hands together to keep warm. He was a compulsive talker when he was nervous, I had noticed.

'Is that what happened to the chauffeur? Neil, wasn't it?' I looked up to see the other two had stopped what they were doing to stare at me. 'Look, I'm not stupid. There was a vacancy for me to fill. I don't know what happened to him, but I guessed it might have been a messy departure. Juliet told me he didn't get to say goodbye.'

'You can say that again.' Harry's voice was pure gravel.

'What happened?'

'Geraint shot him,' Den said. 'It happened in the flat above the garage.'

I blinked. 'He shot him himself?'

'There are some things he outsources and other things he

likes to do personally.' Den smiled, a shade uneasily. 'It was a message.'

'Who was the message for?'

'Neil was one of Evan Verdi's lot. We roughed him up and he admitted it. He must have thought Ger would let him go if he told the truth, but that was never going to happen.'

I looked blank, even though I had been at a briefing that meant I was familiar with every detail of Evan Verdi's criminal history. He was a Welsh thug with Italian ancestry, a small-time operator who had got big all of a sudden, a few years earlier. One lucky deal involving a vast shipment of cocaine was what had changed his fortunes. We'd heard about it too late to intercept the shipment, and the money was hidden away before we could trace it. He had settled into a life of criminal activity that was increasingly ambitious and concerning. He would see Geraint as competition, I thought, and he would want to make a name for himself by bringing down the older, more successful man. No wonder Geraint had been stressed enough to have a heart attack, with someone like that snapping at his heels.

'Who's Evan Verdi?'

Harry scratched his head, leaving a streak of mud. 'Remember the goons who tried to get hold of Juliet?'

'Yeah.'

'His men.'

'Right.' It was falling into place now – why they would want to frighten Juliet, why Geraint was so upset about them bothering her, and why he had reacted with such unfathomable violence. *You spy on me, I'll kill your spy. You come after my family for revenge, I'll kill the people you send. Keep trying and you'll be a dead man too.* 'So the chauffeur disappeared. Where did he end up – somewhere like this?'

'Somewhere like this.' Harry pointed towards the road where

we had left the cars. 'About a hundred yards that way, on the other side of the forest.'

'I wondered how you knew about this place.'

'It's a useful spot.'

'Used it before that?' I hoped it came across as making conversation rather than questioning him, but he just smiled and shook his head. Harry was too wily to offer me any information he didn't have to share.

'I thought it was just that Neil had had a falling out with the boss,' I said, getting back to digging. 'And you wondered why I've been working so hard.'

'The boss likes you,' Harry said.

'I'd still watch your step with Juliet if I were you.' Den gave me a wry smile. 'He's a hard man to please and even more so if you're the reason his daughter is happy. Or unhappy, if it comes to that.'

'No shit.'

We dug in silence for another thirty minutes, until the trench was thigh-deep and Harry declared himself satisfied with it.

'I'll get it.' Harry made heavy work of scrambling out of the grave.

It.

Her.

'I'll come with you,' I said. 'They're harder to handle when they've stiffened up.'

Den made a gagging sound that seemed involuntary, but it more or less expressed how I was feeling.

I levered myself out of the hole and made my way through the woods, not hurrying, with Harry breathing heavily behind me. This was the most dangerous moment, I thought, of the many I'd survived so far. I would be allowed to carry the body to the grave, because there was no point in killing me near the car and having to drag my big, heavy body all that way.

If the plan was to kill me, Harry would wait until Naomi had slid into her final resting place and then he would put a bullet in the back of my skull. The grave was deep enough for two, if you were prepared to do a shoddy job of it. Out here, in the middle of nowhere, there was no need to go as deep as we had dug, I thought. No one would pass by for a long time, if ever. The land we stood on was private, according to the sign I'd driven past on my way in, and I was willing to make a guess about who owned it.

I managed a tuneless little whistle as I opened the boot of the car and looked down at the plastic-shrouded figure. I'd seen her when I took out the spades and had taken the opportunity to cover her face with a flap of plastic sheeting so the brutal injuries weren't visible. There was enough of a suggestion of ruined features and clotted blood to make Harry catch his breath.

'Is she definitely dead?'

'Definitely.' I reached in and jabbed a finger into the unyielding flesh, which made Harry hiss in disapproval. 'Sorry. I thought you wanted to check.'

'I did. But I always liked Naomi.'

'Me too.'

'He shouldn't have done it.'

'No.'

'This is part of looking after her. Burying her properly, I mean.' He rubbed his eyes with the back of his hand. 'God love her.'

Yes, you should cry for her. I bent and picked up the body with a grunt of effort, slinging her stiff form over my shoulder. 'She feels heavier.'

'Dead weight.' Harry sniffed a couple of times. 'Can you manage?'

'Yeah.' I carried the body back towards Den's torchlight, and Harry followed after shutting the boot.

'Drop her in,' Den commanded, taking charge. He wanted to take over from Geraint, I thought, because Bruno was never going to be capable of running any kind of empire. Den was a businessman at heart, not a killer, but needs must. He was as dangerous as Bruno, and I wanted to lock him up.

I let the body slip down off my shoulder and lowered it into the grave as gently as I could. She was curled up with her hands to her chest inside the plastic wrapping, and the body looked pitifully small at the bottom of the trench. The tape had a pearlescent sheen in the torchlight, zigzagging up her body.

I picked up a spade. 'Better get on with this.'

'Wait.' At the sound of Den's voice, my heart stopped. This was the moment when I would learn my fate, if my death had been planned before we ever left Haulton House. Or this was the moment when my plan would unravel in front of me, if something had made him suspicious. Either way, I had a profound sense that I had reached the end of the line. This clearing, this dark and secret forest, was a place for endings. But I wasn't ready yet. The spade trembled in my hands as I considered what I could do: swing it to hit Harry hard enough to knock him out, and then tackle Den? It was a matter of guessing which one had the gun. A fifty-fifty chance.

Now or never . . .

Den jumped down into the grave, one foot on either side of her. 'I want to get her rings.'

'Fucking hell,' I began, and Harry grabbed my arm to warn me to stop.

'They're too identifiable.' Den pulled out a folding knife and slit the plastic, rummaging inside it. 'Shine the torch down here.'

Pale pink varnish gleamed in the torchlight. I watched him slip the rings off: wedding ring, engagement ring, a weighty eternity ring from her slender right hand.

'At least they came off easily.' He straightened. 'Was she wearing earrings, can you remember?'

'No. And no watch.'

'Good.' He tucked the poor little hands back inside the sheeting and clambered out. 'That was hideous. She was cold.'

'As you'd expect,' Harry commented.

Den looked at us both, defensive. 'Geraint would have asked about the rings. They're worth a lot of money.'

Neither of us said anything and after a moment, Den shrugged. 'Fill it in now. Make it look as if we were never here. I'm going back to the car.'

He disappeared between the trees, and we stood there, waiting until we heard the clunk of the car door. Then Harry moved, stiffly, to pick up the second spade. I tried to work some saliva into my mouth. I still wasn't sure that I was safe, but if Harry was filling in the grave, he was unlikely to be planning to put me in it.

'What's that saying?' Harry said, shovelling earth. '"He knows the price of everything and the value of nothing." That's Geraint.'

'You know him better than I do,' I said, refusing to be drawn.

'I know him too well not to see his flaws. I love him, but he gets things wrong.' Harry stood for a moment, looking down at the body. 'This is wrong. And I'll tell him that myself.'

29

I wasn't naive enough to think the Carters would change their ways after Naomi's murder, but it still shocked me how completely she was forgotten once the dark earth of the Welsh woodland hid her from view. Bruno might have mourned or wallowed in guilt but he was out of sight, at a phenomenally expensive rehab facility in France. His every physical and emotional need would be met, the brochure promised, with complete discretion. Money would smother what he had done, just as it blurred away the gap Naomi had left. No one spoke about her; no one cried over her. Juliet went around in a daze but when I tried to talk to her she slid away from me. What had Geraint said to them when I was driving his daughter-in-law's body to her secret grave? Enough of a warning to make Naomi's name unspeakable.

Little Tessa was too young to ask awkward questions about where her parents had gone but I heard her crying, shushed by one of two nannies that Geraint had hired. They were from a most prestigious agency and were far too professional to ask questions, but their presence in the house changed things as they moved smoothly through their shifts, caring and tending and cooking. Tessa stayed with Cassie the rest of the time and Cassie was competent enough with her, but clearly resented the extra work. Most of the time it was the nannies who cared for the little girl, at least when they were in the big house. I cursed them internally as all discussion about Geraint's businesses – and any plotting for the spectacular he was planning – was conducted behind closed doors. It shouldn't have mattered, except that somehow I'd lost my position of trust. I was being left out.

Geraint was the problem. He was paranoid at the best of times; now he was guarded to the point of avoiding me.

I knew the three conspirators had been released without charge; I also noticed that there was no talk about them anymore. They were out of the game, if I had to guess – too worried about being implicated to play an active part in the planning. But that didn't mean the game was over. Knowing Geraint as I did, he would be even more determined to make it happen. If he succeeded where they had failed, it would be all the sweeter. It would give him status and respect he could otherwise only dream about.

At last, in desperation, I lay in wait for Geraint early one morning as he swam joyless lengths up and down the swimming pool. I had hoped he would be in a good mood once he'd finished his exercise for the day, but he climbed out of the water and took the towel I offered him without a smile. I watched him rub his head.

'Sir . . . if it's something I've done . . .'

'What?'

I swallowed. I didn't have to pretend to be on edge. 'I feel as if I've got it wrong and I can't work out what I did.'

Geraint shrugged, not meeting my eyes. 'Can't help you, I'm afraid. You're reading too much into it.'

'No, with respect, I'm not. I'm loyal to you, sir. I've proved it over and over again. I'll do whatever you need me to do.'

'So it seems. And not a word of complaint.'

'Are you angry with me because I've done what you wanted?'

'I'm suspicious.' He wrapped the towel around his waist, water racing down his skin in droplets. 'You make it too easy for us. You should have kicked off about Naomi, and you didn't. You've got integrity and you're acting as if you don't. That bothers me.'

I shoved my hands into my pockets. 'I was down on my luck and you picked me up. I've given up everything for you, at your request, so everything I have now is because of you and only you. I've changed my life to work for you. And I'm not in a position to be morally outraged about anything. You don't know the things I've done in my past. I've got plenty of memories I'm not proud of.'

'Things you don't talk about.'

'Things I've left behind. I'm good at that.' I stared him out, not backing down. 'I tried to stop Bruno beating Naomi to death, and I wish I'd been in time to do it, but once she was dead it was too late. You needed me, and I came through for you. That's it.'

'Very loyal.'

'You gave me my confidence back,' I said, almost convincing myself with the sincerity in my voice. 'You gave me opportunities I'd never dreamed of.' That at least was true. 'You brought me into your world and you left it up to me to prove that you were right. I did everything I could to live up to your expectations and I don't know why that makes you doubt me.'

The next words Geraint spoke chilled my blood. 'Max Burniford was asking about you. Where you'd come from. What I knew about you. He reckons all of our problems started when you turned up.'

'You had a heart attack and I saved your life,' I said slowly. 'Everything after that was up to you. You asked me to your party.

229

You offered me a job. The reason our problems started after that was because you tried to set off explosives on the Underground and that got you noticed. If Boxton hadn't put his men on the platform, they'd never have got picked up and questioned. You know that. Don't let Max Burniford get into your head just because they blew it.'

Geraint looked away from me, but he was thinking about it. 'How loyal are you, Mark?'

'I think I've shown that I'm very loyal.'

'Would you die for me?'

'I'd try not to,' I said, honestly, and Geraint smiled in spite of himself. 'But if you needed me to do something that risked my life – yeah, I'd do it.'

'It's cold. I'm going into the sauna.'

'Sorry for holding you up.'

He grunted and set off towards the door to the sauna. As he reached it, he turned. 'It's not that I don't trust you, Mark. It's that you know a lot about us. The family.'

It made sense to me, all of a sudden: how he could be dubious about me but keep me around, in case I went to the police and told them about Bruno and what he had done. Keep me close and he could control me. Get rid of me, and I was my own man – unless he got rid of me in a way that was final.

'You literally know where the bodies are buried, and I don't know anything about you. That makes me nervous.'

I stood very still. 'Right.'

'But you're not wrong about the timing. And I know it was pure chance that we met, even if I don't remember it.' He flapped a hand at me, dismissing me. 'Don't worry about being shut out. I have plans for you. When the time comes, you'll know about it.'

Plans were what I was afraid of: specifically, not knowing them in advance. I hadn't forgotten what it was like to be swept up in one of Geraint's plans with no opportunity to head it off. My phone, my lifeline to Opal, had been scrapped with the car I'd driven to Wales. I felt cut off from everyone on both sides, and I was deeply frustrated.

It was frustration that made me take a chance when I'd have done better to be patient, and I wasn't sure I was going to do it until the last possible moment. I stood leaning against the wall of Juliet's bedroom, listening to the sounds in the house to identify which footsteps were hers, one quiet afternoon when everyone was busy elsewhere.

The biggest risk I was taking was that Adele or Geraint would come into Juliet's room. Geraint was unlikely, but Adele frequently popped in to borrow cosmetics or retrieve accessories that Juliet had taken from her walk-in wardrobe. The second biggest risk was that the housekeepers would arrive, singly or together, to change the sheets and clean the bathroom. I was fairly confident I could talk my way out of the second situation. The best excuse I could offer Geraint or Adele – the very best – was that I was trying to get Juliet on her own so I could seduce her, and that would get me sacked. Anything else would get me killed. Everything was relative, I thought, staring at myself in Juliet's dressing-table mirror. I looked strained, the pressure of the last few months telling on me in the shadows under my eyes and the tightness of my mouth. When I didn't have to have an insouciant game face on, every moment of stress showed. I couldn't do this again, I thought, and was shocked that the idea even crossed my mind. What was the alternative? Giving up? I'd only just settled on this as the area of policing I wanted to work in.

The price is too high.

Not the mindset I needed to be encouraging. I straightened my slouching shoulders and gave myself a narrow-eyed glare. *Pull yourself the fuck together.*

The rattle of the doorknob took me by complete surprise. She was halfway across the room before I had a chance to react. It was Juliet, at least, and she was focused on taking out her earbuds. She had been out for a run; mud flecked her leggings and her expensive waterproof jacket. She unzipped it and let it fall to the carpet, and I reached to catch it before it landed. The movement made her spin round and I put my finger on her lips quickly.

If your dad bugged the car, could he have bugged this room?

She wasn't stupid, thankfully, and she had plenty of courage, and she knew why I needed her to be quiet. She jerked her head towards the bathroom. I followed her in, matching her stride so it sounded like one person moving. A couple of twists of the tap sent a rushing stream of water in the bath and she automatically tipped in a slug of bath oil.

'We don't have long,' she whispered. 'The bath fills up quickly.'

'I don't need long.' I took her hands. 'Juliet . . . I know you're upset about Naomi. You have to trust me. I did everything I could for her.'

'I know.' She wouldn't look at me. 'But you helped them.'

'I did. For a reason.' I bit my lip. 'Look, I need to know what your dad is planning. The thing that got us arrested – it was a trial run. I need to know what the main event is going to be.'

'What do you mean, you need to know?'

'People will die if I don't find out.'

'Are you a cop?' Absolute, stark horror on her face.

'No,' I said, without hesitation. 'Of course not. That's not what this is about. You know what your dad is like – he gets obsessed with things and it's impossible to talk him out of it. I know enough about what he wants to do to know that it's risky, and that it will hurt a lot of people, and he'll get locked up for it, for life. You won't see him again, except during

232

visiting hours now and then. I can't persuade him that whatever he's doing is a bad idea – he doesn't trust me enough for that – and I doubt you can either even though he adores you. Our best hope is to tip off the cops that someone is planning something so it's too difficult for him to do whatever he has in mind. But we can't do that if we don't know what it is.'

We. You and I are in this together.

I was still holding her hands; she hadn't withdrawn from me. I pushed a little further. 'For his sake – because we love him – we need to stop him.'

'OK,' she whispered, her eyes fixed on mine. 'I'll try.'

30

'I found out something.'

It was a couple of days since I'd recruited Juliet, and the first chance I'd had to speak to her alone. I was walking her to a specialist ski shop in Gloucester where she was getting fitted for new boots. In the car there had been no sign of any news, Juliet chattering away so the bug that Geraint had planted there picked up nothing of note. The Caribbean trip was off but they were still planning the annual family skiing trip to Verbier in February. Juliet was bored and it was something to look forward to. They stayed in a five-star hotel rather than a chalet because Geraint liked to network while he was there, and no matter how luxurious a chalet might be it meant nothing if people didn't know you were enjoying it. At one stage it had been mooted that I might travel with them, but that was before Naomi's death. Now, I wasn't sure if I would be going, or if I would be allowed to stay at Haulton House while the family were away. It would be an unparalleled opportunity to investigate Geraint, if I was left behind, always assuming events didn't run ahead of me.

'It's a football match.' There was a tremor in Juliet's voice as she spoke.

'How do you know?' I said it calmly, my eyes scanning the street around us as they had been ever since we left the car park, and my heart rate spiralled.

'I managed to get a look at some of Den's papers. There's a floorplan of a stadium with all the exits marked and a star with circles around it drawn in the middle of one of the stands.'

She was a good actor, I reflected: I'd been prepared to accept that she didn't know anything new. Currently her face was unreadable because of giant sunglasses and a goose-down jacket that was zipped up above her chin.

'Which stadium?'

'Something bridge?'

'Stamford Bridge? Where Chelsea play?'

'That's the one. I couldn't remember the name.'

'Are you sure it was Stamford Bridge?'

'No.' Behind the sunglasses she was blushing. 'I mean, I think it was. But I don't know much about football. It was definitely a stadium.'

'It's OK.' I smiled to reassure her. 'It's a good start.'

It was terrible news. A Premier League football match – high profile, huge attendance, televised worldwide. You couldn't get much more of an impact. I thought of the disasters of the 1980s – the overcrowding at Hillsborough that killed ninety-six fans, the fire in Bradford that killed fifty-six people, and the Heysel stadium where thirty-nine fans were crushed to death. I'd been taught about those catastrophes on first-aid courses that pointed out how many of the victims might have survived if the first responders had been prepared; I'd seen the pictures. It was likely that Geraint remembered watching those events live, and the idea had burrowed into that dark part of his brain where he pondered how to cause maximum distress and as many casualties as he could. The authorities had introduced countless safety measures since those incidents – the death toll would be lower unless we were very unlucky – but an explosion could set off a panicked reaction that would hurt very many people in the most public way possible.

In the meantime, we were almost at the shop.

'Did you see anything that referred to a date?'

She shook her head. 'That's all I can tell you. It's not much, is it?'

'A lot better than nothing. I'll see if I can get him talking about it. You've given me something to go on.' I nudged her elbow gently rather than making a bigger gesture. 'Thank you.'

'I hope it helps.' She looked through the door of the shop. 'Ugh. A queue. I'll probably be about half an hour. Maybe longer.'

'I'll be back here in half an hour. Wait for me inside the shop.' The last thing I wanted was for Juliet to get mugged again, on my watch, leaving me having to explain what I'd been doing instead of looking after her.

Opal was not pleased to hear from me, when I found a working pay phone a few streets away from the ski shop. Partly it was because it was too dangerous for me to make contact with her, and partly because the team were busy.

'You've given us plenty to work on already. We're still processing the material they put in storage.'

'This plan won't be in there. It's something Geraint has come up with on his own, and I don't have many details.'

She sighed. 'Go on.'

'He's planning to target a football stadium – I think possibly Chelsea but I'm not sure. And I think with an incendiary device designed to cause a panic, but I would anticipate a bigger one than the smoke grenades on the Underground since it's not an enclosed space and he wants to create a memorable image. I don't know when.'

'Soon?'

'I'd assume so.'

'What else?'

'Nothing.'

There was a pause that I resisted the urge to fill.

'Try to find out more. We'll let the Premier League know they need to be more vigilant about security at matches and they should try to catch anyone doing reconnaissance. Anything else?'

'No.'

Opal's voice changed to her softer tone. 'I know you feel you're close to getting him, but be careful. You're going to be tempted to take risks, like this call. It's not worth it for the level of information you've just given me. We're working, I promise you. Leave it to us to pin him down so he can be arrested and charged – and that should be any day now. You won't need to worry about the football plan. You don't need to do any more heroics. If I need you, I'll find you.'

I went back to retrieve Juliet, who had acquired two large bags of shopping and lost her air of tension: a successful day out on all fronts. I drove back to Haulton House feeling that I'd played my part and if I was going to be sidelined from now on, it was probably for the best, but I didn't really believe it. I wanted to be in at the kill, I acknowledged to myself. Geraint was my target and I was going to be the one who brought him down.

At the house, I was carrying Juliet's bags through the hall when the study door opened.

'Juliet? Can you come in here, please? And you, Mark.'

Geraint's manner was quite calm; I had no sense of foreboding as I dumped the shopping and followed Juliet into the study. It seemed full of people aside from Geraint: Harry, and Den, and Cassie. I looked around, trying to gauge the mood and failing. Harry looked grim, as did Den. Cassie had been crying. What the—

'What is it, Daddy?' Juliet put her hand on my arm, a possessive gesture which wasn't lost on her father. 'I got such a nice outfit for skiing, and new boots, and I bought the cutest hat.'

'I need to talk to you, sweetheart.' Geraint looked past her to me, and the warmth faded out of his eyes. 'Both of you. Cassie came to me and told me a story that worried me greatly.'

'What was it?' Juliet looked at Cassie, faltering.

'You can't be surprised,' Cassie snapped. 'You should never have asked me to spy for you.'

'You didn't – you wouldn't—'

I felt as if time was slowing, a catastrophe unfolding. I'd believed Juliet when she said she'd seen the plans, but Juliet had wanted to please me, and she hadn't wanted to give up when she was thwarted. She had gone to someone who had access to the paperwork, and thought it was just as good as doing it herself.

'I don't know what you expected.' Cassie's face was hard. I wondered if the tears had been for herself, if she had been in trouble before we came back. Her arms were folded and her legs crossed, defensive. She picked at a cuticle. 'You asked me to find out more about what Dad was telling Den. I had to tell Den that I'd been snooping around among his papers. He's my husband. I wouldn't lie to him, even for you. And he made me tell Dad.'

'I can explain,' Juliet began, and I put my hand on her arm to stop her.

'She only did it because I asked her to.'

Geraint grunted, surprised that I had said anything at all. 'Why did you want to know?'

'I was worried about it. About you. I thought you might be taking risks. I didn't want to see you get in trouble.'

'I see. Very laudable.' Geraint didn't look in the least impressed. 'And now the truth, if you'd be so kind.'

'That is the truth.' I sounded convincing, even to myself.

'Maybe this will help.' He took a phone out of his pocket and flicked through screens until he reached a video. 'This came in ten minutes ago.'

'What is it?' Juliet angled her head, trying to see. I stared at the screen.

The technical definition of an explosion is a rapid expansion in volume with a vigorous outward release of energy. It happens over a measurable but brief period of time, in scientific terms, but to the onlooker, there's no warning. One second, everything is fine. The next, devastation. I was standing in Geraint's study, but it felt as if he'd blown my entire life apart.

The video was taken from inside a car, from the passenger seat. Two occupants, at minimum, I thought, trying to concentrate. The view was a residential street, and all too familiar.

'Where is that?' Juliet leaned in further. 'Who's she?'

The camera turned, following the woman who was walking along the pavement towards her flat, oblivious. She was carrying a bag of shopping, and she was muffled up in a coat, a big scarf and a woolly hat, but I knew her immediately. She stopped on her doorstep in the shelter of the porch and pulled the hat off, letting her hair tumble down around her shoulders. A glance around, out of habit, her eyes not resting on the car or its occupants. She had no idea she was being watched. She pushed her key into the door, let herself in and closed it behind her, thinking she was safe.

Geraint was watching my face, and whatever he saw on it made him nod, grimly satisfied.

'This has nothing to do with her.' My throat was tight with tension: I could barely get the words out.

'We'll see.'

'No.' I gave the phone back to him. 'Tell them to leave her alone.'

'Who is that?' Juliet asked, still bewildered.

'His girlfriend,' Den said, from the sofa. 'Hey, you never said she was beautiful, Mark.'

'She is,' Juliet said in a small voice. 'But I don't understand why you've got a video of her, Dad.'

'Mark does.' He patted her arm. 'Don't you worry about it.'

It wasn't nice watching Juliet realise the truth about her father from one minute to the next. She stared at him, the pieces falling into place to make a new and horrifying pattern. Then she turned to me.

'I couldn't think of any other way to find out what you wanted to know. I had to ask Cassie. Did I – did I do something wrong?'

'Not a thing,' I said, and smiled at her, or tried to. 'It's all right.'

'Are you cross with me?'

'No, of course not.'

She threw herself against me, wrapping her arms around me, and I felt her shuddering as I held her lightly. Geraint sagged into his desk chair, running his thumb over his chin.

'That's enough, Juliet,' he said eventually, and she sniffed and gulped as she turned away from me, like a little girl.

'You won't hurt him, will you? Promise me, Daddy.'

'I won't hurt him.'

Not personally.

Cassie got up and put her arm around Juliet's shoulders. 'Come on. Let's get you cleaned up.'

'What about Mark?'

'You can leave him to Daddy. It'll be all right.' She wouldn't look at me as she guided her sister past me, and I thought Cassie knew exactly what was going to happen next.

240

31

As the door closed behind the two women, I turned to Geraint. 'I'll talk. I'll tell you whatever you want to know. Just leave Maeve out of this. She doesn't know about you. I'll do whatever it takes to keep her safe.'

He nodded slowly, his eyes on me. 'I thought you might.'

'Call off your men.'

'Not yet.'

I was a long way from the cool composure I usually managed. 'Why not? I told you I'd talk and I meant it.'

'We might need to encourage you.'

'If you go near her—'

'What?' Den demanded, getting up and crossing the room to stand in front of me. 'What's your plan? It doesn't look to me as if you're in any position to demand anything.'

'Sit down,' Geraint snapped, and Den stepped back, folding himself on to the sofa, his hands braced on his knees. His ears were red.

The interruption gave me time to collect myself. *Get a grip*, I thought. *Geraint respects toughness, not desperation.*

'Look, she's not even my girlfriend anymore. The last time

I saw her, I fucked her and left. She probably hates me. But I don't want to see her hurt. This isn't her fight, is it? This is mine. And I've lost.'

Geraint turned away from me and stared at the wall of the study. When he spoke again, his voice was dead. 'The thing is, Mark, I liked you. We all did.'

Past tense.

The end of the line; I'd known I might reach it. I'd wanted to be in at the kill, I thought with a wild urge to laugh.

There was no point in begging, or coming up with excuses now. I still had a tiny scrap of hope. Either he knew who I really was or he was just suspicious of me. There was a chance I'd talk my way out of it the way I'd talked Juliet into it. *I was worried you'd get in trouble . . . I know you want to make something happen but it doesn't make sense to rush into it and get arrested . . .*

The next thing Geraint said knocked me sideways.

'Who's Opal?'

'Another ex,' I said, without hesitation. The extent of the disaster was becoming clear; wherever he'd got hold of her name it was bad news for me.

'That's a lie, isn't it?' Geraint looked down at the phone in his hand and pressed a button. We all listened to the sound of the call connecting, the phone at the other end ringing.

'Yeah,' said a man's voice.

'Pick her up.'

'No.' My mouth had gone dry. If they attacked her – if they hurt her, or worse . . . 'Opal is my boss.'

'Hold on,' Geraint said into the phone, his eyes on me. 'Don't do anything yet.'

'OK.' The man ended the call, business-like. They knew what they were doing. They knew why they were watching instead of steaming in and grabbing her. She was tough, Maeve – she

242

might even put up a fight. That would be just about the worst thing she could do. The anxiety made me want to be sick, but I swallowed, and tried to hide it.

'Are you working for Evan Verdi?' Den asked, still trying to catch up.

I shook my head.

'Who, then?'

'He's a police officer,' Geraint said heavily. 'He's been spying on us. For months. He knows enough to get us locked up for life.'

'Depends on the judge.'

Geraint's face darkened. 'Is that a joke?'

'Not really. How did you know about Opal?'

'You called her when you were arrested. She got you some very special treatment, didn't she? You didn't have the same cops interviewing you as everyone else.'

I thought back. 'The custody sergeant. The blonde.'

Geraint showed his canine teeth in what was perilously close to a snarl but intended for a smile. 'She owed me a favour. I looked after her brother once. Nice girl. Shame she's one of your lot, but it comes in handy now and then.'

'And I thought she fancied me,' I said. That made him laugh.

'Maybe she did. I only got in touch with her the other day, to confirm the details – you know how it is. Trust no one.'

'I know.'

'You went off to see this ex-girlfriend. Phil Boxton had already decided to have you followed when you came out of the police station and you almost lost them on the way to her flat, but that we put down to natural caution on your part which was fair enough in the circumstances. Then you did lose them when you left, which annoyed them because they're good at their job. After that we couldn't find out anything about the girl. It made us suspicious. Not very suspicious, but a little.

There was a question mark there. But I didn't want to believe you were wrong, Mark.' He winced. 'That's not even your real name, is it?'

'It'll do.' He didn't need to know my real name: even now, something in me resisted saying it. 'Is that why you shut me out?'

'I wanted to see what you'd do. And you went through Juliet.' He shook his head slowly. 'You shouldn't have done that.'

'I didn't tell her what you are.'

There was a flicker in his eyes that might have been shame. 'I should thank you for that. And not making a fool of her when she threw herself at you.'

'She wouldn't have deserved it. She's a good person. Just . . . don't punish her for what she did. She didn't understand. She thought she was helping you.'

Geraint sat down again. He put a hand to his chest. 'It hurts me, Mark. It hurts me here. What you did.'

I knew he wanted me to apologise, so he could have the pleasure of refusing to forgive me.

Instead, I shrugged. 'There's nothing I can do, here, is there? I am a police officer. I've been watching you. You know that. I'm not going to lie to you again. I'm not going to take the risk in case you harm Maeve.'

'You must love her very much.'

Yes.

'No. It's just not right for her to be involved. We split up a long time ago. She was a good girl but she's in my past. And the other thing that's in my past is being a copper. I was going to quit anyway.'

'Oh yes? Lost your taste for it?'

I nodded, my eyes locked on his. 'I haven't told my boss half of what I know. I've been struggling to keep her happy without dropping you in it. I haven't told her about Bruno. Not a word.'

'I don't believe you.'

'I can't help that.' I folded my arms, leaning against the wall as if I was relaxed. 'Look, when I got into this, it was by chance. You know that. You *died* and I had to intervene. I wasn't expecting to become a part of the family – because that's how you made me feel.'

'You'd rather be one of us than one of them, is that it?'

'Easy decision to make in the circumstances,' Den chipped in unhelpfully. I ignored him.

'I stopped caring about the job a long time ago. It just took me a while to come to terms with it. Now – yes, I asked Juliet to find out what you were planning. But it wasn't to pass information to my boss. It was to stop you so you didn't do something that would get you in real trouble. They're just waiting for you to put a foot wrong – you know that, don't you? I was working for you, not them.'

'Playing both sides,' Geraint said, his tone icy.

'I've put myself on the line for you, over and over again. I've helped your kids. I've done whatever you asked me to do, and I've been glad to do it.' I hadn't taken my eyes off him. Everything depended on convincing him one more time that he'd been right to trust me. 'I don't want you to blow up a football stadium because I don't want to see you go to prison for the rest of your life. That's it. Believe me or don't.'

He looked away from me, considering it. 'The trouble is,' he said, almost to himself, 'if I let you play me for a mug, anyone will think they can get away with lying to me. And that won't do. So thanks for the help. But you're still fucked.'

A short silence. Then, I said, 'I understand.' I did, too, and in some ways it was easier now. I'd abandoned any hope for myself; I'd gone somewhere beyond fear. I had one goal in mind, and only one. 'The thing is, you still owe me something for saving your life. Call those guys off. I know what will happen to Maeve if they pick her up. She won't make it out alive.'

'You won't be around to worry about it.'

'I took the risk. I knew what might happen. She didn't.' I swallowed, hard. 'I saved your life. Give me hers.'

'I've had enough of this,' Geraint said heavily, turning away, and I felt absolute and total despair. 'Harry, you know what to do. Get him out of my sight.'

32

Harry bounced me off a few hard surfaces on the way out of the house to discourage me from fighting. It left me with a seeping cut on my head that sent blood trickling down the side of my face, a rapidly swelling eye, and an ache in my side that I guessed was a cracked rib. None of it mattered in comparison with the sick feeling I had about Maeve, and what Geraint might be planning to do. Killing me was one thing. Killing my girlfriend sent a message: even the people you love aren't safe if you come after me. And it wouldn't matter that she was my ex, or that she was innocent. They'd kill her anyway. They'd take their time over it if they knew she was a cop.

Harry put me in the back of the big, battered estate Land Rover, behind the passenger seat, and Den got in beside me. If I'd had any thoughts of trying to escape, the handgun Den was jamming into my side would have changed my mind. At that range, he couldn't miss, and he was just waiting for an opportunity to use it.

'The only thing you can do is make it worse for yourself,' Harry said, so close that I could smell the sourness of tension on his breath as he tied my wrists together. 'You can't escape.

I can make it quick at the end or I can spin it out. Annoy me and I won't make it quick.'

'All right.'

'Where are we going?' Den was showing a lot of the whites of his eyes: panicked and not able to hide it.

'Somewhere close.'

So I wouldn't have the pleasure of the drive to Wales while hoping that someone would send up a distress flare Opal might see. I ran through the options available to me. Fight. Try to run. Die. Leave Maeve to her fate.

I tried not to think about the last bit.

'You should have kept the boss talking.' Harry tied the last knot with a particularly vicious twist. 'Spun it out a bit longer.'

'It wouldn't have changed anything. I'd have ended up here.'

'Why are you being so nice to him?' Den hissed.

'He was doing his job. Just like you are.' Harry straightened. 'But you wouldn't have the balls to do what he did.'

'I wouldn't be that stupid.'

'You should be pleased,' I said. 'No Bruno, no me – you're the only person Geraint can trust now. He'll leave you the lot.'

Harry laughed. 'Can't imagine it will last long after that.'

'Fuck you.' Den glowered at him. 'Don't think there'll be a job for you.'

'I'd beg on the streets before I'd work for you.' Harry looked back at me and nodded. 'You'll do.'

I understood that I'd earned some kind of respect from the hard man, and not to read too much into that. He had his job to do, as I'd done mine. I sat in the back seat and ran through the options again, uselessly. Harry got into the driver's seat, and we left Haulton House, the windows blank, no one waving goodbye. Instead of heading out to the main road, Harry drove up towards the back end of the estate.

'Where are we going?' Den seemed to be trying to drill a hole in my ribcage with the barrel of his gun.

'We need somewhere private. Can't do this anywhere we might be seen.'

Opal would scour the grounds, I knew, looking for anything that might be evidence – a speck of blood, a bullet in a tree trunk. Harry would know that too. If it had been me, I'd have gone up to the part of the estate near the woods, where the sound of a gunshot might not be all that remarkable, and I'd do it somewhere near water where blood would just wash away. As I'd expected, he took the track that led that way, and I started thinking about whether there was any advantage to being near the back gate, whether I might make a run for it when the car stopped, even with my hands tied. I was fairly sure I could outpace Harry.

I couldn't move faster than a bullet, though.

'Harry,' I said, hoping against hope that I'd built up enough credit with him for one single favour, 'if I give you her number, could you call her? Just tell her to be careful.'

A headshake.

'Worried about her?' Den laughed, unpleasantly. 'Bit late now. You should have stayed away from her, shouldn't you?'

I looked out of the window, clenching my jaw so I didn't say anything that would get me shot then and there. The worst part of it – the absolute misery of it – was that he was right.

All too soon, the Land Rover drew up in a secluded area, about five minutes from the back gate.

'Get out.' Den jabbed me and I fumbled to open the door, clumsy with my hands tied together. The latch gave with a soft click and Den spat, 'Hurry up.'

I was waiting to hear Harry's door close. It slammed shut and in that instant I was gone, running for my life, knowing that I had a couple of vital seconds while Harry came round the car and Den scrambled to follow me. He'd have to stop to shoot too or he wouldn't have a hope of—

The bark of a tree splintered, near my head. I ducked and dived sideways, zigzagging so I didn't make an easy target, flinching away from branches that reached out to grab me and hurdling fallen logs. The earth underfoot was soft and muddy, but I made some ground. If I could get away . . . if I could warn Maeve . . . all I needed was a phone, but if I was too late already . . . I had gone about half a mile, following the river, trying to find a way out of the estate. The water was running high, too fast for me to risk crossing it. The pursuers were nowhere within sight when I lost my balance on a particularly slick bit of ground that sloped down at a sharp angle. With my hands tied together it was impossible to recover; I went all the way down, landing on my side, hitting the exact spot where my rib was already complaining. The world went white for a second and a wave of nausea swept over me, leaving me chilled and sweating and *hurt*. I rolled, trying to get control of myself, and splashed into the edge of the river. Icy brown water seeped into my clothes instantly, which didn't matter, but I floundered for an eternity trying to fight the current and get to my feet again, the pain from my rib limiting how much I could move.

There were two problems with falling in the river: I lost time and I made too much noise. The sound of my floundering was a beacon for the other two men, and as I waded out onto the bank I heard a shout, terrifyingly close. Desperate, I struck away from the water and headed into the thickest cover I could find. It would have to be winter, I thought, when the trees were all bare and there was no useful undergrowth to limit sightlines. I ran as fast as I could, careless of the direction: distance from danger first, and then I could work out where I was going.

I miscalculated badly. I ran into a clearing and found myself face to face with Den. He was as surprised as I was, his jaw slack, his gun down by his side. My luck was all the way out that day, I thought, and swung my hands at him, clubbing him with them before he could remember what he was supposed to be doing. He fired wildly, the bullet aimed low and to one side, and I hit him again, grabbing for his arm. It was a battle of wills as much as strength; which of us wanted to win more? I was strongly motivated not to die, but Den wasn't going to make it easy for me, and I was already injured, and my hands were still tied together, so everything I did was awkward. We fought for control of the gun for a minute, and he was making smaller and smaller movements as he tired, his breath coming in ragged gasps. I was going to beat him, I thought, and a voice came from behind me.

'That's enough.' For a big man, Harry's approach was silent. 'Get away from one another.' He was breathing heavily.

I took a step back, and another, obedient because I had no choice. I was exhausted from the fight, and the fall, and running, and Harry's rough handling of me. I couldn't see Harry but it was safe to assume he was armed. I could practically feel his breath on the back of my neck, he was so close, but if I tried to tackle him, Den would shoot me in the back. Something in me rebelled at the thought of it; I wanted to look death in the eye, if I had to. Den's chest was heaving, his face pained. He lifted the gun and pointed it at my chest with a wavering arm, but the range was so short that he literally couldn't miss. I closed my eyes and listened to a bird somewhere, far away, and a dog barking, and the wind in the trees.

'Any last words?' Den panted, unable to resist a final taunt, and I opened my eyes to see the two of them, side by side. Den was triumphant, Harry's face troubled enough for one last attempt at appealing to his better side.

'Harry – please. Just a call.'

251

'I can't.'

This was it. The end. I stood and waited, defeated and alone.

And a red circle blinked into life in the centre of Den's chest. A second joined it, and a third swung across to Harry's. He glanced down, saw it, and grabbed Den's arm, pushing it down.

'Den . . .'

'What?'

The world exploded into a chaos of shouted orders.

Armed police.

Drop your weapons.

Hands in the air.

Kneel on the ground, on the ground.

Get down and stay down.

Hands on the back of your head, now.

Don't look at me. Keep looking down.

I dropped to my knees as well, because standing was suddenly impossible, and uniformed, heavily armed officers filled the clearing, gathering the guns, cuffing Den and Harry, a blur of efficient motion. A dog handler had his German Shepherd on a short lead, but she was dancing on her hind legs, desperate to get at the two men in custody. The dog I had heard, I thought vaguely. They had been on their way to save me.

I was alive, and all I could think about was Maeve.

33

I sat on the steps at Haulton House, my head in my hands, and ached.

Someone came down the steps beside me, and I heard the grating sound of a mug set down on the granite.

'Cup of tea?' Opal suggested.

'It's traditional in the circumstances,' I said, and picked it up in a hand that barely trembled at all.

'After that, maybe you could get your head looked at. And the rest. The paramedics are desperate to get their hands on you.'

'It's fine.'

'Doesn't look it.'

'I'll look better once I've had a shower.'

'You should do that then.'

'I will. It's just—'

'I know.' She tilted her head to one side. 'You haven't said much.'

'No.'

'You'll need to talk to someone. Officially, I mean.'

'Yeah. I will.'

'Don't just go through the motions. You need it. I've been worried about you.'

I winced as the hot tea stung my mouth: an injury I hadn't even noticed yet. 'Can't imagine why.'

A car was nudging up the drive which was full of vehicles. Opal's team and the local police had been in and out of the house ever since I got back. The family were in custody. I'd seen Geraint, stumbling, stiff-legged with shock, and met his uncomprehending gaze, and that was enough for me; I didn't want to see the rest of them. I'd sat in the back of another police car and dozed for a while, the shock as effective as any sleeping pill. Now I was fogged with exhaustion too great for me to even think of going to find the paramedics, a sign that I really needed to.

'From what I've heard, we were just in time.' Opal looped her hands around her knee, watching the car as the driver attempted to park it in a very small space. 'No chance he's fitting in there.'

'Probably not.'

'How do you feel about that?'

'The car?'

'The fact that you nearly got shot.'

I shrugged. 'Nearly's the important word there – oh, he's done it.'

The car, a standard job Skoda, had a matter of inches to spare between it and the van in front, but it was parked. I shaded my eyes, trying to see the occupants. There was a reflection across the windscreen.

'I hear you were more worried about the other officer than anything else. Your ex.' Opal sipped her tea. 'And she was worried about you.'

'She was?' That got my attention. I turned to focus on Opal, trying to ignore the ache behind my eyes.

254

'That's how we knew you were in need of urgent assistance. She spotted the car outside the house. Called it in. Someone had the brains to get in touch with me. We got the locals to swing by and they found you. Easy.'

'I didn't think she'd notice the car.'

'You underestimated her.'

'I should apologise.'

'You can start now.' Opal nodded in the direction of the Skoda, and I turned to see two people walking across the gravel towards us, one with a long stride that was just on the edge of running, the other hanging back, his hands in his pockets. I got to my feet and then stopped, too exhausted to do anything more than wait for Maeve to reach me. Her expression was horrified.

'Rob. You look—'

'I'm all right,' I said, and had to steady myself by grabbing her shoulders, which was an effective way of proving I was lying. She steered me over to the left side of the steps where I sat down on the edge of a plinth. I looked up at her for a long moment, taking it in that she was unharmed. Then I put my hands on her hips and leaned my head slowly against her stomach. She put her arms around me and I closed my eyes, ignoring Opal's wry expression, and the thunderous disapproval emanating from Josh Derwent. All that mattered was that she was safe and sound.

In the end, I went to hospital because Maeve dragged me to see a paramedic herself, and the paramedic diagnosed concussion on the spot. I put up with the simply extraordinary levels of fuss from the nurses and the doctors and varying degrees of sympathy from Opal and Maeve. When I had finally persuaded them to go to the hospital café for something to eat, I snatched another nap. I opened my eyes to see the dark, suited figure of Josh Derwent standing beside the bed.

'Christ, you scared me.'

'Good.' He had been uncharacteristically silent up to now, but the look on his face promised trouble. Anger, pure and hot. 'I warned you, didn't I? I said I'd make you regret it if you put her in harm's way.'

'Do your worst,' I said, resigned. 'I deserve it. I've learned my lesson, if it helps. I won't do it again.'

'You fucking idiot.' He sat down, though, in the chair beside the bed, and stretched out his legs with a wince. 'There are two reasons why I haven't punched you to oblivion.'

'Go on.'

'One, you're too pathetic. I was ready to lay hands on you but when I saw you at the house, I didn't have the heart.'

'That's . . . kind.'

'Yeah. Well. Two reasons, like I said.'

'I bet I know the second.'

He raised his eyebrows, inviting me to guess.

'You'd have done the same as me.' I wished the nurses would come back with some more painkillers; I was aching all over. 'You wouldn't have been able to stay away either.'

'I don't know if I would or not.' He leaned his head back against the wall, staring into the distance. 'I don't blame you, that's all.'

'I love her.'

'Yeah.'

'You know what that's like.'

He lifted his head, wary. 'What do you mean?'

'You know.' I tried to find a comfortable way to sit. 'It's obvious.'

'Not to her.'

'I won't tell her,' I said. 'And you shouldn't either.'

He flinched at that. 'You think it would be a bad idea.'

'I know it would be a bad idea.' I weighed it up: what did I owe him? Then again, how much was I prepared to sacrifice

256

to make Maeve happy? 'Just because if you tell her, she'll run a mile. You'll never get close to her again even if she's standing right next to you. Give her time. If it's meant to happen, it'll happen. But she's got a long way to go to get over whatever happened to her.'

'And you.' He grimaced. 'It's taking her a long time to get over you.'

I shook my head. 'She doesn't feel that way about me anymore. I wish she did.'

'You never deserved her.'

'Neither do you,' I snapped, and the two of us glared at one another, locked in mutual jealousy and loathing, before the situation struck both of us, at the same moment, as completely ridiculous.

Maeve stepped through the curtains. 'What's going on? Why are you laughing?'

'No reason,' Derwent said, still grinning.

Maeve looked from him to me, and I blinked, all innocence. 'No reason at all.'

34

The safe house was a 1950s bungalow on the edge of a seaside town I'd never visited before. It was unremarkable in every way, which was its job. A small hatchback was parked on the drive and a children's swing set stood in the garden.

'What kind of security have you got?' I asked Opal as we walked up to the front door.

'A decent alarm system, panic buttons in every room and a couple of armed officers to stand guard.'

'That should do it.'

She nodded, but I could tell she was worried about it, and why not? This was a key witness in one of the biggest terrorism trials of the year, if not the decade. Only the strictest safety measures would do.

'Have you been here before?'

'A few times.' She knocked on the door and nodded to the officer who answered it. He eyed me in a way that suggested he'd know me again. He looked tough, as if he had come to the police via the Special Forces. *Not taking any chances*, I thought.

'It's only us,' Opal called.

'We're in the kitchen.'

I followed my boss down the hall to the kitchen where two women were sitting. One was pale and had an arm in plaster, but she was smiling.

'Mark!' The exclamation came from the other one – Juliet, who was curled up on a chair by the radiator. She looked stunned. 'Except you're not Mark, are you?'

'Technically, no, but Mark will do.' I smiled at her. 'I heard you'd be here.'

'Whereas I didn't know you were coming.' She sat up straight, tweaking the neckline of her top. 'It would have been nice if someone had mentioned it.'

'I forgot,' Naomi said, biting her lip.

'Where's the little one?' I asked.

'Nap time. She's been on the go all morning. She was so excited to see her auntie again. Gosh, where are my manners?' She got up to fill the kettle, calling over her shoulder to the cop in the hall, 'Tony, will you have a cuppa?'

'Two sugars, thanks.'

She hummed as she set out an array of mismatched, chipped mugs. The kettle was a cheap white plastic affair with a discoloured spout and it juddered as it came to the boil. The kitchen was tiny, the cheapest IKEA had to offer, but spotlessly clean. I thought Naomi looked far happier than she had been in the marble and chrome perfection of Haulton House.

'Doesn't she look well?' Juliet was watching her fondly.

'Better than the last time I saw her.'

Naomi chuckled, and it struck me that was the first time I'd ever heard her laugh. 'I'm told I have you to thank for saving me.'

'You don't have to thank me. I was just doing my job.'

Naomi looked at Opal. 'You said that was what he'd say.'

'Predictable.'

'Well, it's true,' I protested. 'And really Harry is the one who deserves to be thanked. He was the one who backed me up when I told them you were dead.'

Harry. Harry who had been working as a confidential informant for one of Opal's colleagues for some years, without Opal knowing, and certainly unsuspected by me. He had done his best for me, he said when we had a debrief in a blank room in an unremarkable office building outside Reading. He had been preparing to tackle Den for the gun when the police came crashing through the bushes. Harry had been living a double life for an unimaginable length of time. He was better at it than me, I'd told him, still amazed that I hadn't spotted him for what he was, and he'd agreed.

'You looked dead, Naomi.' Juliet shuddered. 'And then no one was allowed near you. Mark wouldn't even let me say goodbye.'

'I didn't want you to give the game away,' I said. 'It was her only chance.'

'And they'd have killed you too if they found out you lied.' Naomi said it calmly, but I saw Juliet wince. She'd learned a lot about her family in the last month, and none of it was good.

'It was a long shot.' I looked at Naomi. 'You were unconscious. I thought you might die, but I knew I could give you a chance. And Opal ran with it.'

'Naomi said you found a body that matched hers and swapped them at the motorway services.' Juliet looked up at me, shaking her head. 'I can't believe you came up with that plan. Totally insane. Vile, too.'

Opal's eyes were shadowed with the memory of it. 'Not my favourite moment in all of this. She had died of a drug overdose. No next of kin. Some of our technicians gave her a makeover to match the pictures we had of Naomi. They covered her in stage make-up – fake blood, contusions, the lot. They even painted her nails. When we got to the services we brought a medical team for Naomi. We transferred her into our secret ambulance, which was in the back of an unmarked lorry, changed over their clothes and swapped the rings. Then we put the poor woman into the boot in her place.'

'Which was lucky, because Den went looking for the rings,' I put in. 'And there they were. Proof that the body we were burying was yours.'

'I'm glad I didn't know any of this,' Naomi said frankly. 'I'd have hated to pretend to be dead.'

She had spent two weeks in hospital, I knew, with bleeding on her brain and an array of other injuries. If it had taken me longer to hand her over to the doctors, she would have had a very different outcome. We had put the plan together quickly, but it had very nearly been too slow for Naomi.

'I was sure we'd forget something.' Opal shivered.

'So was I. But you didn't.' I grinned at her and she pulled a face at me.

'What happened to the rings?' Naomi asked.

'We recovered them from Den's house. He'd given them to Cassie.'

'I don't know how she could take them!' Juliet exclaimed, colour rising in her cheeks again. This was her family we were discussing, I recalled. It wasn't all that pleasant for her to hear about what they had done and what they had intended to do.

'She was just being pragmatic. I suppose she knew I wasn't coming back. I don't mind.' Naomi tried to lift the tray with one hand and I took it from her.

'I mind.' Juliet looked up at me as she took a mug. 'What about Harry? Is he going to get in trouble even though he helped you?'

'Harry will be fine,' I said firmly, and Opal caught my eye again. They didn't know about his double life and they didn't need to know. They'd dealt with enough revelations.

I carried on to the hallway, where Tony was waiting stolidly for his tea. When I came back, I leaned against the kitchen counter.

'It's good to see you both. But we're here for a very specific reason.'

Juliet was instantly wary. 'I knew you wouldn't have let me visit Naomi unless you had an ulterior motive.'

'Naomi wanted to see you,' I said gently. 'That's why you're here. But since you are here, will you give evidence about what happened to you, Naomi? Both of you? It's a very small part of a very large case but I don't want Bruno to get away with anything.'

'We can protect you,' Opal said. 'You can give evidence by video-link, or behind a curtain. You don't have to see them.'

'I will.' Naomi was already nodding. 'I want to.'

'I'm not sure.' Juliet looked down at her hands. 'It's hard.'

'Think about it,' I said, and got a glower from Opal, but I frowned back. I knew Juliet better than Opal did – better than Juliet knew herself. It would take her a while to come to terms with it, but she would do the right thing in the end.

'Have you made any plans for after the trial? Where you and Tessa might go?'

'Yes,' Naomi said with decision. 'My mum died a couple of weeks ago. I got to see her before she went, so that was something. She was the only person I had left here. She's left me enough money to leave this country and start somewhere else. We'll go somewhere we can have a good life.'

'Nowhere you know,' I said.

'No. Somewhere completely different from here.' Naomi's face softened as she looked at Juliet. 'I'll miss you, though.'

'I understand. Completely.' Juliet gave a long, heartfelt sigh. 'I wish I could do the same.'

'What's stopping you?' Opal asked.

'I need to stay and see this through. I need to look after Mum and Carl. I need to face up to what happened and help put the good bits of the family back together.'

'You'll do it, too.' I smiled at her with genuine affection and she blushed, and shrugged.

'I don't really know how.'

'You'll work it out. You're capable of anything. It was a very big, shiny cage you were in, but it was a cage all the same. Now all you have to do is fly free.'

'It makes me feel bad for running away instead of staying to help,' Naomi said, but Juliet shook her head firmly.

'You have different priorities. You're not running away. Everyone knows you need to go.'

'And speaking of which . . .' Opal checked her watch. 'We should make a move.'

I hugged Naomi. She was still so fragile I felt I might break her if I squeezed her too hard. She smiled up at me. 'I'll never forget what you did for me. You were so brave.'

'Whatever I did was nothing compared to leaving an abusive husband. I knew Opal had my back. You had no one, except Juliet.'

'And I was no use.'

'You did what you could.'

As a reply, Juliet stepped forward and buried her face in my neck. I held her gently, not rushing her. Eventually she leaned back to look at me.

'Will I see you again? At the trial?'

Opal answered her. 'No. We need to keep him out of the spotlight. He's no use to me if everyone knows who he is and what he looks like.'

Juliet looked appalled. 'You're not going to do this again.'

'I don't know yet.'

'You could have died.'

'Yes . . . but I didn't.'

On the way to the car, Opal narrowed her eyes at me. 'You let them think you weren't scared. Why was that?'

'Because I wanted to be a hero.'

'Not buying it,' she said briskly. 'Try again. I got Harry's version of what happened when Geraint found you out and he said you played it cool. He said it was as if nothing unusual was going on. He said it drove Geraint mad that he couldn't break you. The only thing you wanted was for him to leave Maeve alone. He said you didn't seem to care about your own safety.'

'I was scared,' I said. 'All the time. And the only thing I could do was not show it. So . . . I kept not showing it.'

'Until you knew you were safe.'

'Basically.'

'Interesting.' She paused for a beat. 'Will you do it again?' The casual tone didn't fool me; she really wanted to know.

I looked at her across the top of the car. 'Risk my life? Lie? Pretend to be someone I'm not? I'd have to be insane.'

Opal grinned. 'I'll take that as a yes.'

Keep Reading . . .

Read on for a sneak peek of *A Stranger in the Family*, the incredible new thriller in the Maeve Kerrigan and Josh Derwent series from Jane Casey, out now!

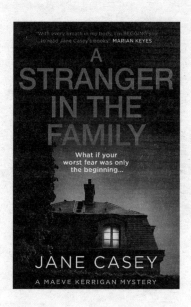

1

Did you notice anything
out of the ordinary?

Afterwards, when the whole horror of it had been laid out, and their innocence – or rather, the degree to which they should feel guilty – had been debated by people who knew them, and many more who didn't, it was the small, uneasy details that lingered in the mind.

What went missing with her, and what did not.

What happened during the holiday a month earlier.

The argument two days before.

The car with a broken number plate, and how many times it was seen near the house.

The tiny, bare bedroom with blood on the floor.

The visitors to the house that week.

The letters before.

The phone call after.

The open door.

The river.

The bruises and scrapes.

The way her brothers reacted, or did not; the things they said, or did not.

The way her father cried.

Her mother. Her mother. Her mother.

But most of all, how long it was before anyone realised she was gone.

2

For some time now, Helena Marshall had been waking up every morning in a panic. It was instant, a punch of fear that struck before she was even aware that the day had begun. Today was no different.

She peeled off her eye mask and blinked at the ceiling, at the lightshade that probably needed dusting, and a smudge that had once been a mosquito in the corner, and the crack that wandered across the plaster, and a cobweb. The house was full of spiders because August was when they started preparing for cold weather, and it was an old house, with sash windows that were loose in their frames and gaps in the floorboards and fireplaces in bedrooms, and the chimneys needed sweeping now that she came to think about it but the sweep had been so *rude* the last time he came.

There was a notebook by her bed, with a pen, and she could start a list of jobs to do – *dust shade, remove cobweb, find new sweep* – but it was so *boring*. And no one else noticed these things, or did anything about them. It was always her job to sort out the house, and the children, and remember to buy school shoes (school shoes! that needed to go on the list that she wasn't making) and actually, she had better ways to spend her time. Work that needed to be done.

Beside her, her husband gave a long, quavering snore. If she was a man, no one would expect her to bother about the chimneys being swept and the gutters cleared (which they would need to be; there were thriving miniature rain forests in three or four places and August had been so wet and the brickwork would take any excuse to soak up damp and present it to her in bouquets of dull grey blooms on the wallpaper).

It was (she checked, peering in the half-light) ten minutes past six. The sun had risen, in theory, but it was a dull day and the forecast was for rain again and *that* didn't help her mood.

Her age, Dr Fuller said. Her age seemed to be the answer to every question she asked the doctor these days. The aches in her joints. The skittish unreliability of her memory. The way her skin looked in the morning, and the evening, and after a glass of wine. The sense of impending doom. There was no other reason for it. Her life was busy and fulfilling. She didn't like seeing the changes that time was making to her famously lovely face but that was what happened.

Count your blessings.

Lying there, Helena tried. She was *getting things done* when it came to her work, and that was good, even if it meant unpleasantness from ignorant people.

Her husband was rich, reasonably nice, supportive of her and *present*, unlike several of her friends' husbands who had slid away to new lives where they could pretend to be young again. Bruce was thirteen years older than her, which made him fifty-nine (and she would have to plan a party for his sixtieth; that was another job that would take up time she didn't have). They had met later than their contemporaries, married within six months, and he had already been fading into comfortable middle age. She had been a minor star, famous enough to have her picture in the paper, often, coming out of nightclubs or at the races. A sort of celebrity, on the guest list for parties and launches even if no one quite knew why. She had thought he was wonderful and he had thought she was beautiful and that had seemed like enough.

Then marriage, and motherhood, which was another life.

Helena was not the sort of person to run away from things, but she sometimes dreamed of packing a bag and going away for a week or a month, meeting a stranger, having a wild affair, and only coming back to the cobwebs and the draughts and the homework and muddy sports kit and maddening questions when she was good and ready. And *that* was why she hadn't overreacted on holidays.

That was why Bruce still snored beside her.

Helena wriggled her shoulder blades flat against the mattress to try to relieve the ache at the base of her neck. The boys should have come first on her list of blessings, probably. Ivo was fourteen and, overnight, had gone from sweet-natured compliance to frowning silence. He only seemed happy when he was playing some sort of sport (which, at least, he was good at). Magnus was twelve and (a squirm of genuine anxiety at this) insufficiently focused on his school-work. He was lazy, and not bright enough to get away with it. His school report had made it impossible to ignore the issue, along with the phone call from his headteacher suggesting that if things didn't improve he might be happier at a different school. So they were paying, at vast expense, for a tutor to come all summer.

And Rosalie, of course. They had Rosalie, who was nine. Rosalie's room was the smallest and it needed a new carpet thanks to her experiments with making perfume out of pilfered cosmetics and household cleaning products. Helena had been thin-lipped about it and Bruce had laughed. Rosalie was a wilful child, demanding in a way that the boys had never been. Girls were different, she'd been warned.

Helena kept her preferences strictly to herself but if she had to choose – in a fire, say – she would rescue her boys first (and of them, Magnus had her heart, but that was something she thought no one else knew. Ivo was a good boy but Magnus had charm). And then she would go back for Rosalie – assuming she hadn't *started* the fire in the first place. What Helena often asked herself was whether Rosalie was *disturbed* or just too bright for her own good. She was intelligent. Interested in everything. A sponge for facts. Prone to awkward questions, and doggedly focused about them. She had never been playful. Helena had thought it would come in time, and had been wrong.

She took several deep, slow breaths, focusing on the positives: they were as happy as most people could expect to be.

Enough wallowing.

She levered herself out of bed, braved the bathroom (chilly) and the bathroom mirror (unflattering), and pulled on a dressing gown. Now that she was upright, her anxiety had translated itself into energy. It was Friday but they were at the tail end of the summer holidays; it would be hours before anyone else woke.

On a whim, Helena went upstairs instead of down. The ceilings were lower up here but there were two large bedrooms and a bathroom that made their Bulgarian cleaning lady shake her head. The important thing was that the boys occasionally showered in it. She missed the soapy-clean smell that they'd had throughout their childhoods. Now a waft of sweat and muskiness and socks greeted her when she opened Ivo's door, like the men's locker room in a gym.

He was face down, his head turned to one side, his arms and legs trailing off the bed. A spasm of tenderness made Helena tweak the duvet into place to cover his (enormous! calloused!)

feet so he didn't get cold. His room was neat – Ivo was an organised child and always had been.

Magnus's room next. It was wildly untidy. No chance of reaching the bed here, Helena registered, eyeing the floor. It was covered in clothes and miscellaneous crap that she wasn't allowed to throw out. Her favourite child was rolled up in the duvet like a sleeping gerbil. A tuft of his silky fair hair was just visible.

Was he breathing? Could he have died in the night? Was that the reason for the feeling of doom that had been shadowing her since she woke up?

Helena stared at the ball of duvet, which didn't move. She was a new mother again, terrified of cot death. Surely it should rise and fall; surely—

Magnus shifted and a low fart vibrated through the mattress. The porcelain-delicate newborn was long gone. She retreated, closing his door. It was a long time since she had checked on the boys while they slept and she wondered if it would ever happen again, which was depressing. What was it they said? *Long days, short years.*

She shivered as she hobbled down the stairs, trying to be quiet, thinking about the opinion piece she was writing for the *Telegraph* and whether it was too angry and might put people off. Tone was so important.

Not for a moment did she hesitate on the first floor. Not for a second did she consider going to check on Rosalie. Afterwards, she would struggle to explain that, but the last thing Helena wanted was company while she was writing, and specifically Rosalie, who would want to know what she was doing and why. No matter what Helena said, she would linger in the room like a black-eyed ghost.

Helena wandered into her study and turned her computer on, shuffling through her notes, already half absorbed. Back out of the study, into the sitting room, her nose wrinkling at the mess

273

of squashed cushions on the sofa and a stale smell. She tidied the room briskly, shuffling papers, plumping cushions, mouthing good lines to herself as she went.

The supreme act of love, as a mother, is to give up a child to someone who can offer them more. Love isn't about blood, but care, kindness and guidance . . .

Too early for post, which was something of a relief given the sort of messages she'd been getting since the last time she was on *Woman's Hour*. But she couldn't allow herself to be intimidated into silence. She went down the steps to the kitchen at the back of the house and filled the kettle. All of this mattered, that was the problem. Life and death, literally. Wishing things were different wouldn't help, and in the meantime children were suffering. The best place for a child to be, Helena thought, was with a loving family. Producing a child didn't make you a mother, and—

A thin line of pale light ran down the edge of the back door. It wasn't properly closed. Helena had gone to bed before the boys and her husband, so one of them must have left it open, she thought, and strode across the kitchen, her slippers scuffing the floor in a way that would have the forensics officers shaking their heads a few hours later. The handle felt sticky as she shut the door. She sighed and went to the sink for bleach cleaner and a cloth. There was dirt on the paintwork – something dark – so she wiped it vigorously until it was spotless. The key wasn't in the lock, or hanging on the hook where it lived, and Helena sighed again, and went to make her tea.

And she never, for one minute, thought that there was anything to worry about, because she had been in practically every room of the house and nothing was missing.

3

The Toyota Land Cruiser bumped up the track, the four-wheel drive barely coping with the heavy rutted mud and large stones on the only access road to Windholt House. Heavy gates topped with barbed wire blocked the track every mile or so, with signs warning that this was private property. The fields on either side of the road were muddy and straggled with unkempt grass, since the sheep no longer cropped it. Their absence had left the land without a purpose, without life.

The rain had been constant for days. The third gate sat in a giant puddle that made the driver swear as he splashed through it, dragged the gate open, drove through, stopped, got out again and swung the gate closed. Easier with a passenger, he thought, and winced at that thought too. This wasn't a journey he made often.

Today was different. Today was an emergency.

Tearing anxiety tightened his hands on the wheel and turned his stomach into a sea of acid. The letter was where he had flung it on the passenger seat. It had been waiting in the PO box he visited once a week, an innocent-looking white envelope with his name in familiar handwriting.

I don't know when you will read this but you will be too late.

He stopped at the last gate. The rain seemed to gather force as he got out of the car, drumming on his head and shoulders. Now that he was nearly at the house he was afraid of what he would find, and more afraid of what he might not find.

At first glance, everything at the house looked as it should: the Land Rover was parked near the front door. A light in the hall made the windows glow softly. He hurried around the side of the house, the wind catching the breath from his body as he faced into it.

In the yard the kennel was empty, but that meant nothing. The dog, a sheepdog, had died before Christmas. He hurried forward, stepping on something that gave under his foot with unpleasant softness. It was saturated with mud, but he held it up and shook it out. A jumper, hand-knitted, the colour impossible to guess. Pearl-pink buttons at the neck.

He gave a low moan and looked ahead, to the back door. It was standing open.

He hurried through to the hall, leaving a trail of prints from his boots, careless now as he flung open doors. Empty rooms. He ran up the stairs, praying under his breath.

How could he have left her here?

How could he have done anything else?

The brass doorknob chilled his palm as he turned it, and he swung the door open on a nightmare.

Order your copy of A Stranger in the Family *now*

And, catch up with other recent books
in Jane Casey's Maeve Kerrigan series

A murder without a body

Eighteen-year-old Chloe Emery returns to her West London
home one day to find the house covered in blood and Kate,
her mother, gone. All the signs point to murder.

A girl too scared to talk

Maeve Kerrigan is determined to prove she's up to her new
role as detective sergeant. She suspects Chloe is hiding
something, but getting her to open up is impossible.

A detective with everything to prove

No one on the street is above suspicion. All Maeve
needs is one person to talk, but that's not going to happen.
Because even in a case of murder, some secrets
are too terrible to share . . .

THE *SUNDAY TIMES* BESTSELLER

an post
IRISH
BOOK
AWARDS

They said he was
a serial killer...

But now they've
set him free

CRUEL
ACTS

'Clever, classy crime fiction. I couldn't put it down'
ERIN KELLY

JANE CASEY

Guilty?

A year ago, Leo Stone was convicted of murdering two
women and sentenced to life in prison. Now he's been freed
on a technicality, and he's protesting his innocence.

Not guilty?

DS Maeve Kerrigan and DI Josh Derwent are determined to
put Stone back behind bars where he belongs, but the more
Maeve digs, the less convinced she is that he did it.

The wrong decision could be deadly . . .

Then another woman disappears in similar circumstances.
Is there a copycat killer, or have they been wrong about
Stone from the start?

Rumours . . .

Everyone's heard the rumours about elite gentlemen's clubs, where the champagne flows freely, the parties are outrageous . . . and what goes on behind closed doors is darker than you could possibly imagine.

Scandals . . .

Paige Hargreaves was a young journalist working on a story about a club for the most privileged men in London. She was on the brink of exposing a shocking scandal. Then she disappeared.

Secrets . . .

DS Maeve Kerrigan must immerse herself in the club's world of wealth, luxury and ruthless behaviour to find out what happened. But Maeve is keeping secrets of her own. Will she uncover the truth? Or will time run out for Maeve first?

Suburban bliss

The new neighbours seem just right for Jellicoe Close, a pretty street filled with perfect houses and happy families.

Sinister secrets

But one neat front door hides a ruthless criminal – and the new neighbours aren't what they seem to be either. DS Maeve Kerrigan and DI Josh Derwent are undercover, posing as a couple to investigate a deadly conspiracy.

Murderous deception

As they try to gather the evidence they need, they have no idea of the true threat they face – because someone in Jellicoe Close has murder on their mind . . .